About the Author

Karen Rymarz lives in the Midlands with her husband, two teenage children, a crazy cockapoo and a groovy little schnoodle. She spends her free time studying sign language, playing the piano, ignoring the housework, and eating chocolate biscuits.

There All Along

Karen Rymarz

There All Along

Olympia Publishers
London

www.olympiapublishers.com
OLYMPIA PAPERBACK EDITION

A CIP catalogue record for this title is
available from the British Library.

ISBN: 978-1-80074-587-2

This is a work of fiction.
Names, characters, places and incidents originate from the writer's
imagination. Any resemblance to actual persons, living or dead, is
purely coincidental.

First Published in 2022

Olympia Publishers
Tallis House
2 Tallis Street
London
EC4Y 0AB

Printed in Great Britain

Dedication

I dedicate this book to Mike, Sullivan and Zoe.

Acknowledgements

Thank you to my husband, Mike, for his constant encouragement, support and supply of hot drinks and snacks during lengthy writing sessions.

Thank you to my son and daughter for their never-ending patience on hearing me say, for the umpteenth time, 'Just a sec — let me jot this sentence down before it falls out of my head.'

Thank you to my mom and dad who gave me the best childhood and who have always believed that I can achieve whatever I set my mind to.

Thank you to my sister, firstly, for all the belly laughs, and secondly, for sharing her books with me when we were young, inspiring me from an early age to put pen to paper and create my own story.

Thank you to my in-laws for their unquestioning acceptance of the role of proof-reading guinea pigs, and subsequent excellent red penmanship.

Thank you to all the staff at Olympia Publishers for seeing value in my writing and for helping me to fulfil a lifelong dream.

Chapter One

"Oh my God, Vic, you have the best job ever!" I gasp breathlessly as I jump down from a wonky wooden stile onto a well-trodden patch of dewy grass and dried mud. I am trying desperately to keep up with my ultra-fit, long-legged best friend Vicky, who is striding effortlessly across the field whilst a bouncy springer spaniel called Bobby circles her legs excitedly.

Vicky, undeterred by the stile, sailing over it gracefully without so much as a hint of slowing down, is by now several metres ahead of me. She stops briefly to pick up a drool-covered, fluff torn, balding tennis ball that Bobby has dropped at her feet and throws it far into the middle of the field for him to chase.

Seeing this and realising it's my chance to catch up with her, I summon up the necessary energy and burst into a run. I reach her side, panting and wheezing most unattractively. Then, leaning forward with one hand on my hip and the other grabbing hold of her arm, both for support and so that she can't charge off again, I spend the next few moments concentrating on refilling my poor, stunned lungs with air. A minute later, with fresh oxygen in my system, I find I can once again stand upright. Brushing my mousy brown, naturally wavy and by now undoubtedly wild-looking hair out of my face, I look around and take in the view.

The weather is glorious! It's one of those bright, sunny, crisp October mornings with a beautiful, cloudless blue sky and the surrounding scenery is truly breath-taking! The trees are in that splendid stage of turning from green to orange and red, and the meadow floor is lush and healthy after a mainly sunny and showery summer.

We're high up on a hill, looking down below at the village of Butterford, where both Vicky and I grew up, and I can see the familiar sights of my happy childhood. Albeit small, the primary school where nervous little four-year-old Vicky and I met for the first time all those years ago is easy to spot with its multi-coloured gates and bright red frontage. Its modest playing fields, which felt so big when we were little, spread out to the side and overlook the church with its humble spire and pretty graveyard.

Behind the church, further into the distance, the farmer's hay barn, farmhouse, and stables are clearly visible, and I can see his sheep grazing lazily in one of his many sprawling fields. A little way back into the village is the post office, nestled in amongst a cluster of former farmworker cottages, which have since been turned into a farm shop, hairdressers, convenience store and a sweet little bakery-cum-cake shop. This specific establishment I am particularly well acquainted with.

Opposite, on the village green, a small war memorial stands proudly next to an iron bench and is enclosed by a dainty little white wooden fence. Further down the lane sits the family-friendly village pub, The Golden Barrel, with its charming beer garden complete with brown picnic tables and cream parasols and a rickety old wooden bridge spanning the village brook. I can even hear the gentle tinkling of the water from all the way up here as it babbles past the bottom of the field and meanders its way through the village.

I've lived in Butterford practically all my life; however, the sheer natural beauty of the village and the surrounding countryside never fails to impress me. I know how easy it is to take these sights for granted though when living amongst them every day, and I make a mental note to take more time to venture out and appreciate them more often, although maybe on my own in future, without having to keep up with my super energetic, champion speed-walker of a friend. That way, I can set a much more reasonable pace for a not-so-fit and loves-cake-a-bit-too-much, healthily proportioned woman in her early thirties, who really should exercise way more than she does, which at the moment is a big fat zero.

My current embarrassing state of total lack of fitness reminds me that I still need to actually arrange my new starter induction session for the gym that I joined a while back in a moment of sheer 'what was I thinking?' madness. If I'm brutally honest with myself though, I know exactly the thought process behind signing up for a gym membership. Try as I do to ignore my reflection in any mirror at all times, I can't help but notice, as a busy professional with a stressful full-time job and a penchant for sweet treats and the odd glass of wine of an evening, I haven't exactly escaped the extra pounds creeping on over the years. My once naturally slim-*ish* body of my younger years has pretty much done a hike and presents itself now as rather more of a relaxed and cuddly, some might say 'squidgy', version of me.

It's not even that I'm anti-exercise. It's just that, like most people, by the time I've finished work each day and run any errands or made dinner, the last thing I feel like doing is a hard-core workout session at the gym. However, I have realised that the older I become and with no specific regular exercise regime, those extra pounds are here to stay, and if I want them gone, I've got to get off said squidgy arse and do something about it.

I make yet another mental note to check my diary at home later and make an appointment for the induction first thing tomorrow morning. As ever, this mental to-do list of mine, is getting worryingly long, but who knows, if I commit to this exercise malarkey properly, maybe this time next year I'll be as fit as Vicky, and it'll be *me* striding across fields and elegantly launching myself over fences like some ultra-energetic, supercharged gazelle.

I gaze at my friend enviously, standing there seemingly totally unaffected by the exercise, her lovely, fine blonde flyaway hair resting just below her shoulders and wafting gently in the breeze. Slim, strong, and tall and standing with her back straight, chin up and hands on her hips as she surveys her surroundings, she looks just like Supergirl. I'd probably hate her gorgeous guts if she wasn't my friend and one of the nicest, most inspiring people I know.

"I still can't quite believe this is your actual day job!" I say to her once I've got my breath back.

"It's not always this blissful," she replies. "You should try tagging along on a blustery winter's day, soaked through to the skin, the wind whipping up round your ears, covered from head to toe in dog hair, mud and drool and lugging around several bags of stinky dog poo. And don't get me started on some of the owners!" she says with widened eyes. "I do get some odd requests at times you know, especially from the more, shall we say, doting of doggy parents. Do you know, only last week, Timmy's owner, old Mrs Simpson, asked if I could actually *carry* Timmy around in my arms for the full hour's walk, stopping every few yards and holding him near trees and lampposts for him have a good sniff. She said he was looking a bit too tired to manage the walk himself, but she didn't want him to miss out on the fun of the outing. I totally adore dogs, as you know, Sam, and of course I was happy to do as she requested but I wouldn't have minded so much if Timmy was a tiny dog like a chihuahua or a yorkie but he's a rather overweight, over indulged — weighs a bloody ton — English Bulldog!"

Laughing, we set off again, heading across the field to catch up with Bobby, who has now found the ball and is excitedly charging back to Vicky at full speed, pleased as punch with his find and ready to deposit it at her feet for her to throw again.

"Okay, so granted, not every day is like today, but it must be amazing when it is and you love it though really, don't you?"

"Oh yes, I really do. Gosh, nothing beats it, Sam!" she replies with real genuine passion in her voice. "The fresh air, the scenery, and the clients who are always pleased to see me and lick me all over my face."

The shock of that last statement momentarily stops me dead in my tracks, and I stare at her in horror before realising she means the actual dogs this time and not the owners.

"No restrictive suits," she continues, "no feet-crippling heels, no exhausting travelling into the city on a packed and hot commuter train day after day. Not to mention I'm my own boss now and don't have to answer to any unrealistic, out of touch managers or sit in countless stuffy meetings for hours on end. And I just *adore* spending time outdoors with the dogs and walking for hours each day. I'm basically being paid to play with dogs and exercise!" she exclaims, astonished almost, as if still not quite believing it herself.

"I'm pleased for you, Vic, I really am!" I say, smiling.

And I mean it. Vicky had endured a tough, few years in her previous role as a bookkeeper for a leading accountancy firm in the city. It was a difficult job keeping demanding clients happy, and she had found herself more and more put upon by her managers to hit impossible targets and produce unattainable results. A few years later, finally fed up and almost totally burnt out, Vicky recognised she needed a big change.

What started off as an ordinary Tuesday morning two years ago became a pivotal moment in Vicky's life when, fed up with the mounting piles of work and ever-increasing deadlines, she found herself doing the unthinkable and jacking it all in. In an intense moment of bravery, and let's be honest, desperation after a particularly dull meeting involving endless presentations and PowerPoint slides, she threw down her pen, stood up and declared that she was simply, 'Done with it all!' and marched straight out of the building onto the street.

Of course, as brilliant and rousing as the moment must have been for the rest of the staff to see in the open-plan office they all shared, she hadn't quite thought it through properly enough and realised later on that day that she hadn't actually formally resigned or even spoken to her boss about her decision to leave.

So, the next morning, she swallowed her pride and headed back into the office to tie up loose ends and formally hand in her resignation. After a difficult conversation with her manager and the HR department, it was agreed that, with the overtime and holiday accrual she had built up over the years, she could work till the end of the week and then leave for good.

She did just that, and after a further three, rather calmer and more subdued days, she finally cleared her desk, packed up her personal belongings, hugged her colleagues goodbye, and in somewhat of a more anti-climactic manner compared to Tuesday's drama, she took her leave and headed out of the offices for the last time.

After a few days of frantic, 'What have I done?' texting to both me and our close friend Emma, and some deep contemplative soul searching involving long countryside walks with her beloved little westie, Dougal, Vicky had a miraculous revelation and realised exactly what she wanted to do with the rest of her life. The very next week, she set about starting up her own self-employed business as a dog walker.

I was in awe of her courage and so happy that she had found a new focus in life. It had all worked out so well, and the cherry on top was that only six weeks later, at an animal first aid course, she had met and fallen in love with Will, another professional dog walker, and soon after, the love of her life!

With a mutual passion for everything to do with dogs and the outdoors, a whirlwind romance and a wedding only three months later, Vicky and Will joined forces and opened their new canine care company, *Wondrous Woofs,* providing all manner of services to people and their cherished pooches from daily walks to home boarding and day care. In fact, their doggy creche is where Will is at this very moment, manning the morning drop-offs for the day care side of the business whilst Vicky, with me in tow, is completing an early morning dog walk for one of her regulars.

"Honestly, Sam," Vicky continues to explain, "I know I've said it before, but that day I upped and left my job was like one of those genuine, bona fide lightbulb moments, a calling, if you will. I just thought, I can't do this any more. I don't want to be here, cooped up inside this suffocating office surrounded by spreadsheets and databases. Life's too short to be miserable day after day! You should really think about getting out too, Sam," she advises, suddenly all serious and big sisterly, keen to help me escape the daily grind just as she did. "Although not this exact same thing, obviously. You'd need at least a modicum of fitness to cover the kind of miles I do each day, plus a shred of some sort of sense of direction."

Tad rude, I think to myself, and her comment does smart a

little, but I forgive my tactless friend for her insult pretty much instantly, knowing full well she doesn't really mean any hurt by it, and I don't want to burst her bubble seeing how happy she is when talking about her new way of life. I also silently acknowledge that she is one hundred per cent spot on in her estimation of my walking capabilities.

"Get out of the rat race," she continues. "Leave the office world behind. I know you've been stressed in your job lately and it isn't healthy."

She makes a good point. Vicky had recognised she was unhappy, taken a leap of faith, and choreographed her life into the one she wanted. Now why couldn't I just do the same? As opposed to Vicky's fun and enjoyable job, mine, on the other hand, is currently a humongous stress in my life and the reason I am out here at ridiculous o'clock in the morning pacing through the countryside at breakneck speed so I can, in my dear friend's words, 'get away from it all for a bit and clear my head'.

"I get it, Vic, I really do," I reply. "But I love my job, you know that! I'm happy at the hospice normally. It's just that lately this threat of potential closure hanging over us all is a giant headache and I'm struggling to see a way out. Besides, I couldn't leave them, not when they need me in this time of uncertainty and worry. I owe them so much, and if I'm brutally honest, I need them too. They're like family to me, you know that."

As the fundraising manager in Green Meadow Hospice, a residential palliative care hospice in the nearby town of Sandlefirth, my work is regularly testing and upsetting, but on the other hand, at times, it can be so very rewarding. It's the place I'd visited as a child weekend after weekend during my beloved Nanna Rose's stay there as she lived out her final days in the care of the wonderful doctors and nurses.

It is my own personal experience of the hospice that encouraged me to join the on-site fundraising team several years ago. One day, having randomly seen a job advertised in a newsletter posted through my door, I bit the bullet and applied. My previous work experience in the field of fundraising wasn't particularly abundant, and it was a daunting task to try and convince the retiring manager that I could fill his shoes. But, as I explained to him in the interview, I couldn't think of anything else I'd rather do than spend my days trying to make a difference, working hard to raise both awareness and the necessary funds for the hospice to continue providing vital services to individuals like Nanna Rose and their families. My passion was clear, and I was subsequently given the job, and along with it, the chance to prove that I could be good for the hospice. And I did just that, very successfully, for many years.

Unfortunately, recent economic hardship for many has meant fewer donations, which in turn has meant the charity's income taking a big hit. My team and I have been finding it increasingly more difficult to raise funds and reach the yearly million-pound target needed to keep the place open and the services running. It's highly pressurised at times, but there's no way I would bail out now and leave the rest of the staff coping alone after the love and help they've given my family and countless others over the years. I will continue to strive towards finding a solution even if it kills me, and I will never give up on them!

"Besides, you know I couldn't possibly up and leave my future husband before he's had a chance to ask me out!" I add, keeping the mood light but also being deadly serious.

"Oh, not that again," sighs Vicky, shaking her head.

I ignore my friend's gentle mocking tone and carry on.

"One day, Vic, it's like I keep saying, he's going to have that lightning bolt moment and realise there I am, that I've been there all along. He'll reach for my hand, look me in the eyes and simply say, 'Samantha, let's go for coffee'. Nothing fancy or false, none of these silly unrealistic and flamboyant dates like trips away and hot air balloon rides. Just fuss-free, pure and real, let's go for coffee," I sigh day-dreamily, repeating it to reinforce my point.

Vicky laughs and scrunches up her face in dismay.

"Yes, I know, I know. You've been going on about him for months now and saying how one day he'll realise you're the woman he's meant to be with and simply can't live without! Have you actually considered the chance that he's just not ever going to see you that way?" she asks softly. "I mean, he's been involved with the hospice for a little while now hasn't he, and he doesn't seem to have noticed you so far, has he?"

"In my defence, he just hasn't had the opportunity to get to know me properly yet," I reply indignantly. "Whenever he's in the building, it's always so busy. There's always something else going on, someone else needing his or my attention and we never get a moment's peace to have a conversation by ourselves," I explain.

The man in question and the object of my affection is Ross Carrington, a successful property developer and the son of one of the trustees on the board of the charity, Charles Carrington, a retired solicitor at a local law firm. Comfortably well off but with a heart of gold, Charles has dedicated many years of his working life helping out on the board of trustees. A lovely, kind elderly man and a true gentleman who also spends a lot of his time, when not on the golf course, providing free advice to patients helping them to sort their wills and personal affairs.

Ross joined the hospice not too long ago as a newbie

volunteer, drafted in by his father with the idea of utilising his position as a prominent businessman in the local community to network with other local businesses and arrange additional financial support. Ross — or, as I like to say, 'future Mr Sam' — is that kind of textbook, old fashioned handsome. Broad-shouldered, tall and dark, and I whole-heartedly, gut-wrenchingly fell, ding-dong, out of my mind in love with him from the very first knee-wobbling, yet humiliating moment I laid eyes on him!

Chapter Two

I remember the moment like it was yesterday, in all its mortifying splendour, most likely along with several other members of the local population, and more regrettably, Ross Carrington himself. It was the day of the Green Meadow Hospice Easter Fete six months earlier.

Held in Springtime every year in Sandlefirth Community Centre, the Easter Fete Fundraiser is always a bustling event, well attended by the local residents along with the families of the patients, who are often either roped into manning the stalls or, if they're lucky, allowed to happily wander around, browsing the eclectic mix of products on offer.

Like most charity fetes and bazaars, items such as home-made knitted dolls, jams and chutneys, garden plants, greetings cards and all sorts of diverse bric-a-brac are available to buy. Both kids and adults alike can be seen enjoying themselves spending pocket money and small change on cute little knick-knacks and easter chocolates, plus there are always plenty of chances to win prizes on the raffles and tombola. The food stall never fails to do a roaring trade offering mouth-watering lunches from the reliable favourites of the sausage and bacon butties to the more exotic paninis and quesadillas along with much needed liquid refreshments in the form of teas, coffees, or cartons of juice or squash.

Much to my delight, and thanks to what can only be described as the divinely blessed, culinarily gifted hands of a small group of miracle-working hospice volunteers, the fete's pièce de résistance comes in the form of an exquisite cake stall selling all manner of home-made heavenly treats. There are delicate, little, perfectly-sculpted cupcakes, scrumptious muffins, indulgent, rich tray bakes, wonderfully soft and spongy doughnuts, and my personal favourite, delicious, light and fluffy, large-as-your-fist, jam and butter scones.

It takes pretty much all my willpower and then some to stay clear of the cake stall while working this event. In the past, mistakes have been made, and I have been known to spend a disturbing amount of time lingering at the stall, lusting after the delicious array of baked goods. This has inevitably led to me buying a portion of just about every single delicacy there is on offer — it's only right after all the volunteers' hard work — and then happily stuffing several paper bags filled with goodies into my bag, only to take them home and gorge myself at the end of the day, leaving me feeling full to bursting and somewhat ashamed of myself afterwards.

It is a well-known fact amongst everyone involved with the hospice that cakes and pastries are a weakness of mine, my Achilles' heel if you like, and on my full instruction, the volunteers manning the cake stall are all forewarned and ready to hold back the goods and deny me sales if they think I have visited the stall too often and am getting out of control. I liken it to a drunkard in a bar but without the shouting and cursing, as I like to think I have more class than that and will gracefully accept their kind and gentle refusals when they think I've had too much. I thank them for it afterwards, but it is torture at the time, especially once I've set my sights on the stall that is always decorated so enticingly with pretty pastel bunting and light pink gingham tablecloths. Delightful fancies pile high up on cake stands, tier after tier, positively oozing 'come eat me' vibes.

With this affliction of mine, I've found that the safest course of action is just to visit it once, take one portion, and then steer clear for the rest of the day. However, I do like to pride myself on not having many vices, and if overindulging on sweet treats is to be one of mine, then it's really not the worst trait in the world. On the other hand, I'm sure my hips and thighs would, quite rightly, struggle to agree!

In addition to all the stalls at the fete, there are also usually several forms of entertainment on offer throughout the day, along the lines of children's dance groups, magicians and local amateur teenage rock and pop bands, and we always do try to put on some sort of activity to pull the punters in, keep the donations flowing, and everybody amused and happy to stay for hours on end.

As the hospice fundraising manager, it's my job to organise these events from initial conception right through to completion. The team is only small, made up of me and one other paid member of staff, and then the rest of our help comes in the form of the highly appreciated and valued volunteers.

The aforementioned other member of staff is my wonderfully fun friend Emma. The same age as me and Vicky and also a resident of Butterford, Emma grew up only a few streets away, and the three of us were pretty much inseparable during our teenage years and saw each other as the sisters we each never had.

Vicky and I are only children, and Emma's only sibling is her brother Adam. Being a few years older than us, he and his mates seemed so cool and interesting to us three younger girls, and we'd often follow them around like lost sheep wanting to be included in their games and to be accepted into their group. They were kind boys though and didn't mind us tagging along, often letting us join in with whatever their latest game or scheme was. Of course, being typical lads, they'd still enjoy teasing gullible, trusting younger sisters and their equally naïve friends, and we'd often find ourselves the butt of their jokes or as guinea pigs for their crazy madcap stunts, such as skateboarding blindfolded down steep slopes or swinging from tree ropes with our hands tied behind our backs.

It was always mainly light-hearted fun though, never anything too mean, and no real harm came to any of us aside from the usual bumps and knocks, and we all became really good friends. I have so many happy memories of endlessly sunny summer days filled with fun activities, like riding our bikes around the village, climbing trees, building dens, or simply lying about in the daisy-covered meadows, chatting, laughing, and dreaming up silly dares and forfeits for each other whilst sharing packets of sweets and giant bottles of brightly coloured fizzy pop. Our parents despaired as we filled our evenings and weekends avoiding homework and family chores and getting ourselves into various minor scrapes and fixes with other village residents. Nothing ever too serious or naughty, but we weren't exactly beautifully behaved kids either and sometimes had a tendency to be a bad influence on each other.

Out of all of us, Emma definitely developed the wildest streak as she grew, and it was frequently due to her inventive ideas and daredevil nature that we would find ourselves in a neighbour's bad books whose garden ornaments we had damaged or the village hall caretaker whose flower displays we had trampled.

After leaving school, we each went our separate ways for a while, but us girls remained close throughout our respective university years, speaking on the phone and visiting each other often. At the end of Emma's particular studies, all grown up and now an adult version of the playful scamp she was as a child — slim and very pretty in a tomboyish way, with a short, dark brown bouncy bob and bright, adventurous green eyes — she came back this way and moved in with Adam to share his flat with him in Sandlefirth.

With no specific set career path, she found herself drifting a little, not knowing what to do for a job. I was already settled at Green Meadow by this point, and with her brother also working there as the groundskeeper, it seemed an obvious place for her to start. I encouraged her to come and volunteer in the fundraising team temporarily to gain some work experience while she figured out what she wanted to do.

However, it soon became apparent that, as long as it was properly channelled, her wonderful natural energy and creative imagination, which, as children, had got us friends into trouble on more occasions than we could count, now enabled her to be rather inventive when it came to dreaming up fantastic fundraising opportunities. This, along with her friendly, approachable, bubbly personality, meant she was the perfect fit for the hospice, and after as little as three months, she was offered a permanent position as a member of the team.

Part of Emma's role as a fundraiser is to assist me in organising all the events, and over the years, her input has helped create some exciting events that have appealed to the masses and drawn in the crowds, helping to raise both the awareness of the hospice and much needed funds. She is indispensable, and I couldn't cope without her help, and it was on this basis that I decided to give her a bit more freedom on this year's fete activity.

A decision that, in hindsight, was perhaps not one of my better ideas and one that I would later come to regret. I should have known that my wonderful, devil-may-care, uninhibited best friend would bring her own crazy vibe and that I would somehow get mixed up in it all. It was during this latest idea of hers and my somewhat calamitous involvement that I encountered Ross Carrington for the very first time.

The activity Emma had organised was donkey rides for the children around the community centre car park. I was sceptical at first; however, she assured me that it was perfectly safe and would help to keep the children entertained outside whilst the parents, grateful for the break, shopped in peace inside. More importantly, it would be so popular that it would make an absolute packet for the hospice. I couldn't help but agree. It's common knowledge that most children adore spending time with animals, and after reassuring me the company she was hiring was above board, and there were no issues with the welfare of the donkeys, I could find no reason to object.

Knowing very little about donkeys, not being an especially massive animal lover myself, and if truth be told, also a bit of a wuss when it came to any animal bigger than me and of the hoofed variety, I was initially against the idea but after listening to Emma's reasoning, and with the need to make as much money as possible for the hospice, I hesitantly conceded and gave the go-ahead. However, naively assuming this activity would involve cute furry angelic donkeys, lazily idling around with happy little smiling children on their backs, little did I know *our* donkeys would turn out to be satanic little havoc-wreaking beasts!

It was about halfway through the day, and I was in the middle of doing the rounds, checking everything was running smoothly with the fete and that all the stallholders were happy. Having practically starved myself all morning with the intention of a brief visit to the cake stall and the purchase of the one and only treat I was allowing myself, I was, by then, extremely hungry and starting to feel a little lightheaded. Like many women, having a digestive system and blood sugar levels that demand regular eating and grazing throughout the day, I have often found dieting difficult, as fasting and skipping meals is just never an option for me. An additional problem is, of course, that for me, *little and often* regularly turns into *a lot and often*.

I selected a portion, my agreed, solitary slice — albeit a big fat whopping delectable-looking wedge of Victoria Sponge with a lovely juicy jam centre, which I had spied earlier as the stall was being set up — wrapped it neatly in a napkin and gently placed it in my trusty event bum bag, careful not to mark my notebook and recently printed batch of shiny business cards, safely tucking it away ready to be savoured later. After a manic morning of setting up stalls, dealing with any last-minute problems, and welcoming visitors, I was starting to flake and eagerly awaiting a break where I could sit and enjoy five minutes alone to devour my cake. My plan was to quickly peek outside to check the progress of the donkey rides before nipping up to the privacy of the first-floor offices of the community centre.

Pretty proud of myself for indeed only buying the one piece of cake and not needing to be manhandled away from the stall on this occasion, I mentally patted myself on the back and ventured out into the car park. I was instantly pleasantly surprised as, from what I could see, it all seemed to be going extremely well. Lots of happy-looking children were taking it in turns to ride a small herd of about four or five smartly groomed and well-cared for donkeys, all of which appeared to be very tame and docile.

Or so I thought. It's quite a large car park at the community centre, and Emma was standing on one side in a little corner of hay nets, straw bales and flexi tubs of water and was holding onto four donkeys whilst the owner was on the other side, having stopped the tours momentarily as he fiddled with some stirrups and a beaming child wriggled excitedly in the saddle. Catching me spying, Emma waved her free arm in the air beckoning me over. Cursing my curiosity and now unable to slink away for my much-needed cake time, I tentatively walked over to her and the four donkeys.

"Thank God!" she cried as I reached her. "I'm absolutely bursting for a pee and Donkey Dude said the resting donkeys get fidgety and anxious if left on their own, so I haven't been able to go. Can you just hold them for a few minutes while I nip to the loo?"

Not wanting to appear a coward but reluctant to accept, I tried to quickly conjure up a very important reason why I couldn't possibly take over the reins, so to speak; however, before I could come up with one, Emma had thrust four lead ropes, each with a stinky little donkey attached, into my hands and dashed off across the car park back towards the building.

A little uneasy, I took a deep breath and reminded myself that there was no need to worry and the best thing to do would be to just stand still, avoid eye contact and pray that Emma wouldn't be too long. I remembered hearing once, that horses can sense fear and have now come to realise that fact must also be true for their donkey counterparts as only seconds after Emma had left me alone with them, they must have picked up on my nerves and discomfort, and they began to become a little agitated. Snorting and bobbing their heads, the donkeys clearly weren't happy about having been left with me either, and the longer we waited, the more they seemed to want to show their discontent by pawing at the ground and irritably braying and swaying.

Now you'd be easily fooled into thinking a little donkey, the supposedly sweet carrier of the blessed Mary, would be easy to control, but as I very quickly discovered, they are powerful little creatures, and when you have four of them barging against you and pulling in all different directions, there's not really a lot you can do about it. Plus, one of the naughty beggars seemed to have taken rather a strong dislike to me and was also deriving great pleasure in trying to rip chunks out of my arms and legs with his teeth.

More minutes passed, and the pesky little beasts were becoming increasingly more restless, and I, in turn, was getting pretty panicked myself but trying my best to remain calm and ignore the rapid pounding in my chest and the beads of sweat I could feel popping up on the back of my neck. Conscious of the queue of children waiting for their turn on the darling fluffies, I tried in earnest to get Donkey Dude's attention, but without a free hand, and by this point, a rather trembly voice, he was totally oblivious to the situation.

"Hurry up, Emma, pleeeease hurry up!" I begged shakily under my breath, wondering why on earth it was taking her this long to do a pee! "You can do this, Samantha." I told myself determinedly, not believing it for one second though and instantly being proved wrong when one of the donkeys, the biggest one and quite evidently the evil ringleader of the pack, decided to up the ante, and with an incredibly accurate aim, spat right in my face!

Spitting donkeys! I mean, I'd heard of llamas spitting when in a grump but not donkeys! Taken completely by surprise and temporarily blinded by disgusting donkey goo, my hands flew instantly to my eyes, and at the same time, I let go of all four lead ropes. The donkeys, sensing the slack as the ropes fell to the ground, and realising that this was their chance for freedom from their tense and incompetent minder, decided to make a run for it and bolted across the car park. Something by this point I was actually quite happy to allow, the only problem being that, while the donkeys had been dramatically thrashing their heads back and forth displaying their obvious dissatisfaction and hatred towards me, one of the head collars had inadvertently got caught on the clasp of my bum bag, and as that particular donkey charged off, the furry little shit took me with him.

I don't know whose screams were louder, mine or those of the poor innocent children who suddenly found themselves faced with a crazed, wild-eyed donkey charging towards them whilst trying to shake off an equally petrified, shrieking woman. Thankfully I must have been too heavy a weight for the plastic clasp to take, and after only a couple of yards and a mere few seconds — although it felt like a lifetime to me — the clasp broke, and the head collar came free, releasing the donkey and unceremoniously dumping me, face-down, arse-up, in a crumpled heap in the middle of the car park. The asshole donkey, having realised I was no longer attached and therefore no more a threat to him, got bored of running and wandered off to eat some grass in the field next to the car park. Covered in dirt and straw and momentarily winded by the fall, I found I couldn't move and lay there bunched up, gasping and clawing for my breath.

After several moments, however, I was spurred into action by the sounds of laughter coming from the children who thankfully had not been trampled to death by a bonkers runaway donkey, and now evidently relieved, were finding the whole episode extremely amusing. Somewhat dazed, I, on the other hand, was not. Finally able to breathe normally again, pushing myself up into a sitting position and brushing off some of the drool and muck, I looked up to see Emma running towards me with a look of disbelief on her face whilst also trying her very hardest not to laugh. Knowing my dear friend as well as I did, I could see that her first thoughts were of concern for my wellbeing, but at the same time, she was finding the whole thing ridiculously entertaining. Once she could see I wasn't badly hurt, I saw her struggle and fail to suppress her laughter, and a little titter escaped her lips.

At this point, I, too, couldn't help but see the funny side, and soon we were both giggling hysterically as she began to help me to my feet. It was only then, however, that I registered she was not alone and standing next to her was the most gorgeous man I had ever seen in my life! Still a bit stunned from the whole devil donkey debacle, I found myself staring wordlessly, mouth agape, into his handsome face. Noticing my stupefied state and quickly clocking the reason for my dumbstruck expression, Emma jumped into action and introduced the two of us.

"Oh, erm sorry, Mr Carrington, this is who I was telling you about inside. This is Samantha James, our fundraising manager here at Green Meadow. Sam," she said, turning to me, "this is Ross Carrington, Charles' son. I bumped into him by the refreshments table on my way back out to you. He's going to be joining the volunteer team and he's come along today to see the kind of thing that goes on at a typical fete."

"Hello there," he began and offered his hand for me to shake.

Still reeling from both the fall and the sudden apparition of such an Adonis and unable to arrange any coherent words in my brain, I continued to stare at him like a braindead idiot. Noticing my silence and seemingly unfazed by my inability to converse like a normal human being, he took control and carried on.

"I saw your, erm, incident. Looks like you took quite a knock. Are you quite all right?"

Oh God! He saw the fall, complete with spit on my face and bum in the air resting position. Oh-my-bloody-stupid-effing-donkeys-God! Wishing the ground would swallow me up right there and then, something kicked in, and clearing my throat, I finally found the power of speech again, albeit somewhat strangely shrill and shaky and not my usually calm and measured voice.

"Lovely, lovely, yes, terrific!" I enthused whilst shaking his hand a little too vigorously. "Thank you so much. We always welcome new blood and are so grateful for additional helpers."

Noticing a knowing smile creep onto Emma's face as she could see how taken I was by him, I was keen to end the conversation and run back to the safety of the fete. At the same time, not wanting to scare him off or discourage this gorgeous specimen from ever returning, I added, "It would be wonderful if you could come into the hospice sometime perhaps and meet with me and we could chat about what sort of support you had in mind."

Emma's raised eyebrows said it all, as this isn't usually something that I would offer. New volunteers would simply turn up to a final meeting a few days before an event and opt for a role or agree to work on a particular area. Worrying that she had figured me out, I knew I needed to wrap up the conversation pretty quickly.

"Erm, let me give you my work number so you can call me when suits and we can talk more on the matter," I concluded as professionally as I could manage with a face covered in dried donkey spit and bits of straw stuck in my hair.

Pretty pleased with myself and thinking I had handled the whole horrid situation quite well under the circumstances, I reached into my bum bag and deposited a rather soggy, jam-smeared business card into his sexy, unsuspecting hand. Inwardly cringing all over, but with head held high and as much dignity as I could muster, I made my way back towards the safety of the community centre with a somewhat dented pride and a bum bag full of sloppy, squished Victoria sponge.

Recollection over, my cheeks flushed from the memory of the shameful episode, and with Bobby the Spaniel jumping up and down like a demented jack in the box begging us to continue the ball-throwing and walking, we set off once again speed-trekking through the field. We cross over into the next one and then the next one and then the next one after that too. Vicky is clearly on some sort of record-breaking sprinting mission, charging ahead, chatting merrily away to Bobby, and I'm lagging behind huffing and puffing too much to even contemplate talking.

It's after the next two fields, as we edge further and further away from the village and all visible civilisation, that I wonder exactly how many miles one little doggo needs for a morning walk and will either of them notice if I silently slink off back the way we came and run back down the hill towards the sanctity of home.

Thankfully, however, I don't do this as another couple of arduous, lung-burning minutes later, the three of us reach the end of our mammoth expedition, and I can see that we have somehow quite niftily circled back round to where we started. God! She's a natural at this dog walking lark is my talented and freakishly athletic friend — and quite right about my complete lack of any sense of direction! It seems quite obvious now, so I think the absence of oxygen to my brain must have stopped me from being able to see exactly where we'd got to. I almost pass out with both relief and exhaustion when I spot her specially adapted *Wondrous*

Woofs van parked up waiting for us outside Bobby's house.

"How about we get you inside for a couple of yummy biscuits and a well-earned nap?" I hear her ask invitingly.

"Oh God, yes please," I groan gratefully.

"Not you, you big plum," she scoffs and then it dawns on me she actually intends to squander this special attention on the bloody dog instead.

Tutting my disappointment whilst Vicky is safely securing Bobby back in his bedroom, aka his owner's kitchen, I clamber into the passenger seat of the van and await transfer home.

Home for me is a dinky little one-bedroom cottage, which sits at the far end of Butterford, snuggled in amongst a short row of identical-looking buildings. These old, unassuming but attractive little homes, in keeping with the style of the village, sit tucked behind a low line of neatly trimmed hedges, creating a comforting sense of protection and privacy.

The cottage used to belong to Nanna Rose, but it was left to her only child, my mum, after she passed away. My parents, Pam and Tony, moved out of the village several years ago to pursue a 'reawakening of their youth' as they like to call it. My fleeing of the nest and becoming financially independent from my folks had enabled them to regain their freedom and reboot their social lives. Being walking distance from the shops and restaurants and living amongst the hustle and bustle of the city was something my folks had realised they had been missing during my childhood, but rather than uproot me from my school and friends, they chose to wait until I had grown up.

They must have been keen to get cracking on the next chapter of their lives as pretty much the second I had accepted my place at University, the *For Sale* board had appeared outside the family home, and the box packing had begun. With the sale of the family home, they were able to buy an ideally-placed, brand new, swanky apartment half an hour away in the city, giving them the liberated retirement, they had wished for. Happily settled there now, and living the life of Riley with new like-minded friends and endless enrolments in various clubs and classes, they had no need of my Nanna's lovely little property and were more than happy to gift it on to me. Happy to stay in the village that I grew up in, I jumped at the chance, and the quaint little picture-postcard cottage became mine.

It's a bit crumbly in places, featuring far too many low-level 'bang your head' beams and more chintz than a seventeenth-century dress maker's shop, and without having undergone any kind of modernising, it's not always the easiest to cope with. The pipes rattle and clunk like a mining pit, the single glazed sash windows don't do anything to keep the warmth in during the winter months, and I've had my fair share of problems, such as damp walls and faulty wiring, but it's all mine, my bonny little home-sweet-home. It blesses me with daily reminders and treasured memories of time spent with my cherished Nanna Rose, and for that reason alone, I completely, one hundred per cent love it from top to bottom!

With a slam of the van door, Vicky hops into the driver's seat and starts the engine. Windows down, radio blaring, we both sing at the top of our voices as she expertly navigates the narrow twisting lanes like only a true local can and drops me home before racing off to her next dog walk. That woman has far too much energy for her own good, I decide, and after waving her off, I push open the rusty little gate and attempt to make my way down the wriggly path to my front door.

My body, however, has other ideas, and having made the fatal mistake of sitting still for all of the three-minute van journey, my seldom-used muscles have declared mutiny by tightening and seizing up and are now full-on refusing to cooperate. I'm half-giggling and half-weeping as I waddle like a cardboard penguin towards the door. As I step into the tiny hallway, I spot a letter lying on the doormat. It's an unusual-looking, creamy-coloured envelope with pretty pink flowers all around the edge and also missing a stamp, I notice, so it's obviously been hand-delivered. Intrigued, I instinctively go to pick it up, forgetting that my body has gone on strike.

"Ow, ow, fecking ow!" I hiss, feeling a hot, burning pain in my thighs. Unable to crouch down, and fearing that even if I do manage to reach the floor, I simply won't be able to get back up again, I try in vain to reach the letter with my fingertips without bending my legs, but the envelope catches on the corner of the mat and starts to slide underneath it. After several failed attempts, and much complaining and even more cursing, all I've managed to do is push it further under the mat, so it is now barely visible.

Admitting defeat, I decide that no letter can be that important in this modern world of emails and instant messages, and I leave it where it is to pick up later with a hopefully, by then, fully functioning body. Slowly and painfully, I climb the stairs, mainly on my hands and toes, my legs sticking out straight, stiff and rigid and feeling as if they will snap if I force them to bend.

"Good God! If a brisk little dog walk around some fields can cripple me this way, how on earth am I going to cope with the gym?" I chunter to myself.

I head to the bathroom, hoping that a long soak in the tub might ease my aching muscles and restore my ability to walk. I genuinely don't know how my friend does this day in day out. One march through the countryside and I'm positively done in! My poor little legs couldn't carry me any further, even if Ryan

Reynolds himself was ahead of me, calling me on with a look of longing in his eyes and a plateful of chocolate pastries in his arms.

With great difficulty, I lower myself into the bath and groan with relief as the warmth of the water starts to soothe the sting of my paralysed muscles. Aaahhh, if only I could stay here all day! Responsibilities call, however, and after a blissful, healing twenty-minute soak, I painstakingly push myself up and out of the bath and start getting ready for work.

Chapter Three

Thirty minutes later, munching guilt-free on a cinnamon and raisin bagel, having cleverly convinced myself that it counts as one of my 'five a day', and balancing my water bottle in my lap — why do they never make the cup holders in cars wide enough? — I drive through the hospice gates and look for a parking space.

Green Meadow is a large, two-storey redbrick building with a spacious ground floor aimed mainly at the day care aspect of the hospice and comprises a reception area, lobby, modern restaurant and a good-sized main area used for structured activities and general socialising. This central section is decorated in calming greens and creams, and with many large windows, it has a light and airy, roomy feel. It contains several comfy armchairs, coffee tables, a piano and a TV, and it is easily the heart of the building, where a various assortment of arts and crafts, organised games, talks, and presentations regularly take place, creating a buzzing sense of life and activity.

In the far corner of the room, a narrow corridor links the main hospice to the residential wing, which is made up of patient beds, private bathrooms, a discreet grief counselling room and a nurses' station. French doors lead out from the main room onto the pretty rear garden, decorated with numerous potted plants, cute little gnomes, bird tables and beautiful hanging baskets. The lawn features a variety of fruit trees, shrubs and bushes, and there are several rows of colourful sculpted flower beds dotted about. In summer, patches of wildflowers bloom with abandon around the edges, helping to soften the green metal fencing that marks the hospice boundary.

The upstairs consists of the personnel offices, cleaning cupboards, a conference room, and a compact staff kitchen. As the hospice intake numbers have increased over the years, and the number of volunteers has grown with it, the building has expanded in the form of add-ons, such as detached terrapins and static trailers located in the car park, which are often used as overflow meeting rooms, and volunteer communal areas or storerooms for medical equipment including wheelchairs and walking frames. Amongst these are a small number of useful outbuildings such as greenhouses and storage huts.

It's a happy place, despite its purpose, and thanks to the wonderful nursing staff and selfless volunteers, the mood here is so upbeat and positive it's easy to forget it's a hospice and that people here are often going through the worst times of their lives. It's a place so many people rely on to bring relief and support when in need; every day I drive through the gates, I'm thankful for the opportunity to be involved in such a magical place.

It's five past nine, and as usual, I'm the last to arrive. I can see Emma's road bike chained up against the railings as normal. Even though both she and Adam have the same route into work each day, she much prefers to cycle in, as she thinks it's the best way to wake up the body and start the day refreshed — I'm seriously beginning to wonder how I'm still friends with these fitness-obsessed lunatics I call my besties!

Judging by the cars I can see parked, I know that there are already several volunteers on-site helping to welcome in the day visitors and organise the activities, and the residential nursing staff will be finishing their overnight duties ready to hand over to the day shift. The cooks will have been hard at work in the kitchen since the early hours, chopping veggies, rolling pastry, baking bread, and frantically preparing to feed a hospice full of patients, families, staff, and volunteers. There's always a wide range of healthy and nutritious meals on offer, such as continental breakfasts, light lunches, afternoon teas, and wholesome evening meals. I tend to bring a packed lunch in most days, but it's nice every now and then to treat myself to some freshly prepared quality nosh, even if it's just something simple like an omelette or a lasagne.

I park up, grab my handbag from the passenger seat, and haul myself up out of the car, grimacing as my thigh muscles, suffering renewed stiffness from the drive over, threaten to snap. Hobbling along, I spot Adam, in his overalls and work boots, crouched down in front of the shed sorting through the gardening tools. As groundskeeper, he takes care of anything and everything to do with the outside of the building, from tending the lawns or painting the fences to pressure washing the patio. I can often hear the rumble of his treasured big boy toy — the hospice ride-on lawnmower — as it passes below my office window or his cheerful whistling as he clears the guttering.

He's a bit of a whizz when it comes to maintaining the grounds and anything to do with the outside of the building, and if there's a problem or something's broken, it will be Adam who's called up to fix it. Due to the outdoorsy nature of his job, he has a toned physique and enviable, all-year-round tan, which, when added to the same dark brown hair and twinkly green eyes as his sister, his warm smile and playful personality, makes him a firm favourite with the patients. The older ones especially. On sunny days out on the patio, he can often be seen chatting to them and making them giggle while watering the flowers or sweeping the leaves.

He sees me approaching and gives me a comically over-enthusiastic wave as if we are hundreds of metres away from each other whilst at the same time loudly booming, "Moooooooorniiiiiiing Samaaaaaaanthaaaaaaa!" as if trying to make his voice reach me across the vast, imaginary distance between us. We are, at most, a mere two metres apart at this point, but his strange act is not at all new to me as Adam does this sort of thing most days, as long as there are no visitors about. In fact, this particular silly greeting of his has become rather standard behaviour, much to the bemusement of others, and it never fails to make me smile.

Today I am particularly grateful for the distraction, and I immediately join in the fun, playing my role and waving back with gusto in the same childish manner, sticking my tongue out at him too for good measure. Feigning hurt, he clutches at his heart melodramatically and falls back against the shed in a mock faint.

"You're such an idiot!" I tell him, laughing, and he simply winks at me and goes back to sorting the equipment while I limp into the hospice with a big grin on my face.

I sign in at reception and cheekily take the lift up to my first-floor office, realising any attempt to climb the stairs right now would be futile. I plonk my bag down on the floor next to my desk, switch on my pc, and gratefully sink into my big, soft, comfy chair.

Moments later, Emma pops in to say hi and bring me a lovely hot mug of coffee. We have a quick catch up, and I fill her in on my early morning's torturous adventure with Vicky and subsequently broken body. We don't have much time to chat as she excitedly informs me that she's off out to see a man about a bungee. Apparently, it's something to do with an idea she has for an upcoming fundraiser. I shudder and try not to imagine what crazy plans she might be conjuring up, and we agree to meet later for lunch.

My first tasks this morning involve some general admin and checking of emails, and then I finally take the plunge and call the gym to book my induction session for one evening after work next week. A diary alert pops up on my computer screen, reminding me of the trustee meeting scheduled for ten a.m. in the conference room. The purpose of the meeting is to discuss the declining hospice finances and what to do about them. Having already prepared for this meeting yesterday, I'm ready nice and early, so I take the opportunity to sit back and rest for a moment. The marathon hike this morning, has taken it out of me more than I expected, and I'm actually feeling quite weary. Leaning back in my springy chair like a sleepy baby in a rocker, I make the fatal mistake of resting my eyes for a few moments.

A good while later, I'm woken abruptly by the evil ringing of my desk phone along with the familiar creaking sound of my door hinge as it swings shut. My itchy eyes adjust just in time to catch a glimpse of the back of a man's charcoal grey, pin-striped suit jacket leaving the room.

"Shit, shit, shit! What time is it?" I say, panicked, eyes darting to the clock on the wall. "9.59? Feck!"

Grappling with the phone, I lift the receiver and produce a throaty "Hello?" whilst wiping sleep-induced dried saliva from my chin. It's the receptionist letting me know the trustees have arrived and are making their way to the conference room.

Oh, that's okay, I think to myself, they're only just arriving, and everyone knows the first few minutes of any meeting is taken up by crucial tea making and the opening of biscuit packets. Phew!

Thanking her, I put down the phone and start to gather up my notepad and pen, and it's then that I notice a cute little chocolate chip muffin sitting on top of my paper tray. With it is a bright yellow sticky note which says, 'Thought you could do with a mid-morning pick-me-up!'

My fuzzy brain is struggling to compute, but it eventually whirrs into action, and I come to the conclusion that whoever was in my office a moment ago must have left me the surprise treat. How sweet... and of the cake variety, too. Whoever it was must know me well! Hoping in earnest they didn't spot the unattractive chin dribble, I rub my sorry legs and plead with them to once again loosen up and carry me to the meeting. Shuffling out of the room as fast as I can, I fail to notice that the top drawer of my filing cabinet is open.

I join the trustees in the meeting room, and my heart skips a beat as the first person I see is none other than Ross Carrington.

"Samantha, how lovely to see you!" he says, flashing me a gorgeous smile.

"Oh h-hello," I stutter, feeling my cheeks flush. "What are you doing here?"

"Father mentioned the crisis talk taking place today, and having been a volunteer for a little while now, I thought you wouldn't mind if I came along. I understand things are a little unsettled financially at the moment, and I do happen to know a few rather influential heads of some local charitable foundations. Now, I know that lots of these trusts ordinarily wouldn't consider donating to a hospice, but with a few meetings and conversations with yours truly, they might just agree to sending some contributions our way."

His comments make me feel strangely conflicted. Half of me wants to give him a great big bear hug for this thoughtful gesture, which would have the obvious bonus of copping a feel of what I imagine to be smooth, firm arms and a solid chest under his white shirt. Ross is a broad hunk of a man, and I have the shameful notion that having his big strong arms wrapped tightly around me would make me feel tiny and safe and instantly reduce me to jelly.

I reluctantly tear my thoughts away from this blissful mental image, however, and refocus my mind back to his words as the other half of me, quite frankly, is more than a tad irritated. It doesn't sit particularly well with me that he possibly views me as some sort of maiden in distress who he has come to save. As romantic as it may sound to some, this is not actually how I want him to view me at all! I want him to think of me as a competent, capable woman at the helm of a flourishing charity. I am painfully aware that, in reality, I'm currently responsible for a charity's fundraising department at a time when we are literally about to have a serious discussion about said charity's disturbing lack of funds, and it makes me feel ashamed and embarrassed.

When thinking rationally, of course, I know deep down that no one involved in the hospice is at fault, particularly the fundraising department. Over the years, we have put in more hours than could ever be reasonably expected, and the increase in income has reflected this. The trustees, knowing how hard we work, regularly praise our efforts and acknowledge the amazing results we achieve. The simple fact remains, though, sadly, that times are hard, hospice care is expensive, and donations are at an all-time low. Charles signals for the meeting to begin, so I smile and nod my thanks to Ross, and armed with a drink and a couple of chocolate digestives, I take my seat.

Three hours later, after much brainstorming and lively discussion hashing out some clever ideas to drum up more awareness and — fingers crossed — resultant donations, I'm starting to develop a hunger headache. I risk a dicey think back to the tasty looking muffin sitting waiting for me on my desk and immediately regret it. The image of it inspires my digestive system to wake up, and my stomach juices come alive. My insides begin an embarrassing cacophony of empty-bellied rumblings, which I attempt to mask with some random coughing and shuffling of my papers. The noises are unmistakable, however, and before long, pretty much the entire board room has been alerted to my body's apparent non-negotiable urgent need for food. Seeing the funny side and pleased with our progress so far, Charles suggests that we call a temporary halt to the meeting and book a follow up for later in the week.

Embarrassed by my body's complete lack of discretion, I make a move to slink out before any more shameful gurgles but not before I watch with sheer delight, and blessed realisation as Ross stands up and slips those magnificent arms of his into his expensive-looking, torso-clinging, *charcoal grey and pin-striped* suit jacket. So, it was Ross who had sneaked into my room earlier and left me the little cakey gift. The sneaky devil! I'd rather he hadn't walked in on me possibly fly catching and — oh please, God, don't let me have been snoring too — but the fact that he brought me cake… oh, I could just die with happiness! I knew my irresistible charm would get him eventually. Just wait till the girls hear about this! I think, and with a heart full of joy, I skip out of the conference room, all former notions of aching legs and chauvinistic comments forgotten.

Once inside my room, I realise what a tit I've been and head back along the corridor and down the stairs in a bid to catch up with Ross and thank him for the cake. Before I can reach him, however, I hear someone calling my name.

"Cooee, Samantha, dear."

I look back to see a former-day-patient-turned-occasional-volunteer, Dotty, waving and heading my way. I briefly consider pretending not to see her and ducking into the broom cupboard out of sight but instantly berate myself for such a monstrous thought. Dotty's such a lovely sweet old lady, and I love her company. We've shared many a conversation and silly joke over the years, and she deserves better from me.

"Hello Dotty, how are you?" I ask her, bending down and giving her delicate frame a gentle embrace.

"Oh, I'm fine, dear, thank you," she replies. "You must be so pleased, my dear, now all the worry is over, and everything is all right again with the hospice."

Completely baffled, I start to ask her what on earth she's talking about but am interrupted by the receptionist motioning me over to take an incoming phone call. At the same time, Dotty squeezes my hand and says, "I must be off, deary, as afternoon bridge is about to start in the main room. I'll see you soon, toodle-oo!"

Poor woman. She must be losing her marbles, and I wonder if the cooks are adding a bit too much sherry to the lunchtime trifles.

I finish my phone call and look around in the hope that Ross is still in the lobby. I can't see him and the signing in book confirms my fear that he has indeed already left the building. Disappointed, I accept that I'll just have to thank him for the muffin next time I see him. Another loud burble from my intestines, along with the arrival of Emma back from her business meeting, reminds me that I still haven't had lunch. We head back upstairs together, and I cheerfully tell her all about my secret gift.

Later on, when it's getting dark and time for me to head home, I bump into Adam outside in the car park. He's finished for the day, too, and is packing away his tools into the boot of his truck.

"Looking much perkier than you were this morning, Sam," he says brightly.

"*Feeling* much perkier too, thanks, Adam. I had a really productive meeting with the trustees earlier, lots of new ideas and positivity floating around about how to save the hospice. But the highlight of my day was receiving a perfect little present — the cutest little muffin you ever did see — from Mr Sex on legs himself," I enthuse.

"Sorry, who gave you a muffin?" he asks.

"Ross! You know, ultra-sexy guy, love of my life, my one true love?" Adam stares at me blankly. "Charles' son!" I say, frustrated. Seeing no reaction from him and suspecting he's either messing with me or having some sort of stroke, I choose to ignore him and continue to explain. "He crept into my office while I was... erm... *out*, and left it for me on my desk, and with a thoughtful little note too."

Still nothing. Jeez, what's with him tonight? He's not usually this slow on the uptake. I carry on regardless. "Such a sweet thing to do, don't you think? This could finally be what I've been waiting for, the start of something magical between us!"

A strange look crosses Adam's face, but it passes so quickly I can't tell if I imagined it or not. He doesn't say anything and instead turns sharply back to his loading. It's so out of character for him I'm momentarily thrown off-kilter. Not liking the silence and shocked he isn't jumping at the chance to poke fun at my pathetic love life, I add, "Well, it's been a long day and my poor pitiful body is fit to flop! Best get home."

He produces a half-smile and replies with a simple, "See you tomorrow, Sam." Seemingly unaffected by the lack of our usual banter, he closes his boot, jumps into his truck and drives off. I, on the other hand, am totally unsettled by his unusual behaviour and linger there for a moment, watching him drive away, wondering what just happened. It's usually always so easy chatting with Adam, like I don't even have to try. Feeling like a numpty left alone in the car park, I figure he's just being a mardy arse for some weird random blokey reason, and shrugging it off, I get into my car and head home.

Chapter Four

The following week, the dreaded gym induction rolls around. My aches and pains from my walk with Vicky are long gone, but sadly, they take with them any resolve I might have had, and I am not looking forward to it!

Reluctantly, I root around in my wardrobe, looking for anything remotely resembling fitness gear. Not being much of an exerciser, there isn't a great deal to choose from. I settle on a pair of baggy jogging bottoms and an old, faded Westlife t-shirt, fitting me worryingly tighter than I remember it doing. Feeling blobby and uncomfortable, it's the reality check I need, and remember that this extra weight I'm unhappily carrying is exactly why I booked the induction. Oh, that'll do, for heaven's sake, I think to myself. I'm going to learn how to operate a few buttons on a treadmill, not take part in a photoshoot!

My hair tied loosely in a ponytail and wearing a smattering of mascara — a gym induction it may be, but I'm not a complete peasant — and armed with a water bottle and towel, I shove on my comfy trainers and head out the door, making sure not to catch my reflection in the hallway mirror on the way out.

I park at the gym, walk up to the building, and on the way in, give myself a mini pep talk mainly featuring lines such as, *You got this, bitch,' and 'Keep thinking of those skinny jeans*! I then hesitantly push open the front door and step inside.

I'm confronted with a terrifying sight. There are beautiful people everywhere. Not a joggers and t-shirt combo to be seen, just set after set of coordinated, matchy-matchy, figure-hugging shiny Lycra, all modelled by clone after clone of the same divinely thin modelesque goddess. What was that about it not being a photoshoot, again? Determination rapidly waning, I consider turning around and doing a runner when a small slip of a girl floats over to me effortlessly. She must be all of four foot nothing, and I tower over her, feeling like a whopping great lump. Only five foot five myself, I'm not tall by any means, but her dainty little Barbie body makes me feel like an overgrown freak. I catch a glimpse of the two of us in one of the many floor-length mirrors lining the walls — do they really need to have so many? — and I honestly look like a tired and defeated parent standing with her youthfully blessed, perfectly proportioned daughter. Any minute now, I'm expecting her to ask for help tying up her shoelaces or taking her to the toilet.

Judging by her flawlessly sculpted body, she clearly works here, and I explain the reason for my visit. She checks my details and informs me with her blemish-free, overly made-up face that instructor Max will be handling my induction. Then, with an impeccably manicured finger, she points over to the far end of the room, where an absolute hunk of a man is bouncing gently up and down on one of those large exercise ball thingies.

Thanking her and resisting the urge to pat her on the head and hand her some pocket money, I navigate the obstacle course of scary-looking machines and beautiful gym bunnies and tentatively walk up to Max. He flashes me a welcoming smile and gestures for me to sit down on a separate ball opposite him so we can have a chat. Instantly taking to him, I introduce myself and then try my best to balance on the gigantic ball. If this is how it's going to be, all sitting and nattering, I think I'm going to like this gym lark after all.

Max is exactly as you'd expect from a gym instructor: a twenty-something, perfectly toned beefcake in a muscle accentuating vest and tight little shorts. He has lovely eyes and a masculine jawline, and dazzled by his good looks, I soon forget my worries and insecurities, well almost.

"Hi there, Samantha, is it? How are you today?" he begins, briefly checking his clipboard. "So, you've come for your induction today, although it says here that you joined the gym a few months ago, is that right?"

"Yes, hi," I reply, feeling like a naughty school child who hasn't done her homework. "It's been a while since my last visit to a gym, so go easy on me. I've been meaning to come but just haven't managed to get round to it yet, you know how it is, busy-busy, always someone to help, something to do or somewhere to be and all that jazz."

From his furrowed brow, I can tell he actually doesn't know at all 'how it is' and is probably wondering what on earth could be more important than making time to go to the gym. Back to feeling on edge again, I carry on babbling anxiously.

"Not that you'd ever suffer from that, of course. It's obvious you always find time to exercise regularly being as erm—sort of fit and erm—buff as you are." Of course, he does; he's a bloody gym instructor, you idiot, Sam. I silently berate myself, wincing at my inane waffling and pleading with myself to shut up. He smiles at me sympathetically while I sit there like a loser trying to act cool but failing miserably.

"Don't you worry, we get this all the time," he assures me. "Hop up onto this treadmill and we'll get you started."

Relieved to be moving on from such a cringe-worthy introduction, I eagerly step up on the machine and await instructions. He patiently explains what to do, and with a swift press of a few buttons, the treadmill whirrs into life and I begin walking.

"That's it, a few minutes on this and then we'll move on to the bikes and the cross trainers. Easy peasy," he adds reassuringly. His encouragement and positive vibes are rubbing off on me, and I actually begin to relax and enjoy myself. I've clearly fallen on my feet with this particular instructor and decide that he's a jolly good sort and I most definitely like him.

"There you go," he announces after a short while. "We'll have all that post-baby fat off you in no time!"

I hate him!

He notes the appalled expression on my face and has the decency to look embarrassed, at least.

"Excuse me?" I splutter, forgetting to concentrate on my walking and almost tripping and falling off the treadmill.

"Oh, sorry, it's just that, well, what with the extra weight around the tummy area, I just assumed you'd recently given birth."

As he says this, he screws up his beautiful face a little and gestures to my waist, making a squeezing motion with his fingers as if pinching a roll of flesh. Extremely offended, and stopping myself from leaping off the treadmill, tackling him to the ground and squashing the life out of him with all of my excess fat he very kindly pointed out, I explain to him that there has been no baby and therefore, no pregnancy, and that the fat to which he is referring is the good old-fashioned standard 'I simply eat too much' kind of fat.

Evidently not knowing what to say, but feeling he needs to say something to explain his comments, he continues, "Don't get me wrong, it's not that you're obese or anything. I mean, you're not slim, obviously, but I guess you're not too chubby either.

You're somewhere in between," he says, clearly trying to convince himself more than me. I glare at him, and unnerved by my thunderous expression, he grapples with his words to try and rescue the conversation.

"You're slubby!" he declares triumphantly. "Yes, that's it, slubby!" he repeats as if that's a perfectly acceptable way to describe me. "But don't you worry," he adds patronisingly. "We get women like you in here all the time. You just keep coming here every week and we'll get those extra pounds off, you'll see."

Pleased with himself for what he believes to be an accurate description of me and therefore absolving himself of any wrongdoing, he brings the machine to a stop and directs me over to the static bikes. Needless to say, my and Max's relationship doesn't greatly improve from this point on. I'm angry and hurt but too shocked to do anything other than follow him around like a pathetic groupie listening to his instructions and assurances that he will solve all my bodily flaws.

The more I listen, the more I notice he really isn't the smartest cookie, more *chunk* than hunk, and he seems to have rather a high opinion of himself. I catch him appraising his own reflection in the mirror on more than one occasion while he is supposed to be focussing on me, but to be honest, I'm grateful for his indifference and use it to my advantage to put less effort in. My dwindling verve is pretty much all but depleted now anyway, and I'm just going through the motions.

The rest of the induction goes ahead almost wordlessly and in rather a downbeat mood, the whole thing lasting an agonising forty minutes, and by the end of it, I can't wait to get out of there. Too proud to give up, though, I stick it out to the end and then, being terribly British and well brought up, I politely thank him for the session, and dying a little inside but determined not to show it, stroll across the gym floor and out the door.

Once out of sight, however, I flee to my car, fling myself in, and placing my head in my hands, allow myself a good weep, feeling well and truly sorry for myself. After a few moments, I pull myself together and angrily wipe away the tears from my cheeks. I put the keys in the ignition, and pushing down hard on the accelerator, I bolt out of the gym car park and vow never to return again.

I arrive home deflated and thoroughly fed up! Knowing I'm acting like a teenager having a strop, I storm upstairs, and in complete diva style, I hurl myself face-down onto my bed.

"Stupid bloody gym idea!" I mumble into my pillow. I'm lying there, seriously contemplating never leaving the house again, when my mobile buzzes alerting me to new messages from Vicky and Emma in our group chat. Knowing their messages are bound to cheer me up, I push myself up and sit back against the headboard to read them. The first texts, however, are, of course, questions about how the gym initiation has gone.

An utter disaster! I tell them.

Was foolish to think I could do it. Never going back!

This, of course, prompts a stream of concerned responses from them both with offers to immediately come around bearing mood-enhancing wine and cake. Tempted as I am, I'm whacked from both the physical aspect of this evening and also the emotional turmoil of being told I look like a post-pregnant whale, so thanking them, and whilst agreeing that wine and cake is always a winner, I ask if we can do it another time. Once they're assured that I'm not going to do anything drastic like eat a whole tub of ice cream to myself, we settle on getting together on another night.

I feel like a bit of a party pooper, but all I want to do now is freshen up and have an early night. I strip off my tragic outfit and lob it into the laundry basket where it can stay for all eternity as far as I'm concerned, and then pad into the bathroom. I'm looking forward to a long hot shower to wash away the sweat, and if possible, the lousy memory of the fitness fiasco.

My mood is soon darkened further, however, by the discovery of a broken boiler and a distinct lack of hot water. One of the unfortunate downsides to living in an old cottage.

"Are you kidding me?" I whinge in frustration. "Really? After the evening I've just had? Come on!" I'm sorely tempted to just have a quick rub over with some baby wipes, but I can't quite bring myself to slum it that bad just yet, so I throw on my nightclothes and dressing gown, grab my wash bag and a towel and peg it downstairs and out to my car.

Not wanting to bother either of the girls seeing as I just blew them off and with my parents living that bit too far away, there's only one place I can think of to go and praying I won't breakdown while driving in my PJs, I set off for the hospice. There's a bathroom on the first floor that is solely for staff and volunteer use for after fundraising events or during long shifts. I've used it many times before, and I know no one will have a problem with me using it tonight as it's located well away from the residential part of the building, so I won't disturb any of the sleeping patients.

It doesn't take me long to get there at all now that the rush hour traffic has dissipated, and soon I'm parked up and bounding up the stairs like an excited pupil on a school trip.

Once in the shower, I begin to wash away the earlier stresses and slowly, but surely my mood starts to lift. Belting out pop songs — albeit badly, as I'm a terrible singer — brings me back to my usual happy self, feeling relaxed and refreshed.

Out of the shower, I dry myself and clad once again in my fluffy PJs, and with a towel wrapped around my head, I skip merrily along the corridor to the staff kitchen and start rummaging in the fridge for something to eat. Having not eaten anything since work, my tummy is feeling rather empty, and I'm now suffering from an extreme case of the munchies. Disappointingly, there's nothing in the fridge except for an out-of-date yoghurt, some dodgy smelling milk and a handful of wrinkly grapes.

"Ugh, well that's just not gonna cut it," I declare and briefly contemplate nipping downstairs to the main hospice kitchen for a raid in the pantry. Thinking that would be just a little too cheeky but not wanting to return home to the reality of my broken boiler just yet, I decide to head back to my office and order a takeaway instead. I'm just about to turn around when I hear a voice behind me.

"Didn't know you were such an Abba fan, Sam!"

"Jesus!" I exclaim, almost jumping out of my skin and whipping round to see Adam standing there leaning up against the door frame, smirking.

"Oh my God, you scared the life out of me!" I say and playfully punch him on the arm as punishment.

"Ouch! Oh, and by the way it's 'feel the beat on the *tambourine*' not 'tangerine', silly," he takes great pleasure in telling me.

Feeling a little embarrassed at the thought of him hearing my caterwauling but realising there's nothing I can do about it now, I answer defiantly, "I know what the real lyrics are, I just think my version is better, thank you very much!" and stomp off jokingly to my office.

"Sure you do." He chuckles, following me.

Once in my office, we flop into the armchairs in the corner of the room, and both starting to speak at the same time, we ask each other what we're doing here so late. Adam gestures for me to go first, and I explain all about the shitty gym induction and the broken shower, and then he tells me how he was driving past and saw the upstairs lights on, so thought he ought to pop in and check it out seeing as it should only be the residential wing that's open after hours.

"I just followed the sound of an animal being slaughtered," he teases. Tutting at him and refusing to bite, I tell him I don't really fancy heading home to a cold cottage without any hot water and let him in on my takeaway plans, asking if he wants to join me. Having also not eaten yet this evening, he's quick to agree, and before we know it, we've looked up the nearest restaurant and are ordering lashings of yummy Indian food.

While we wait for the food to arrive, we chat about the hospice and Adam asks me about the current financial difficulties. It's a topic I find hard to talk about but somehow manage to confide in him my worries and the responsibility I feel to make sure we don't fail and have to close our doors.

"It's just too awful to consider," I tell him. "I can't bear the thought of the hospice not being there to provide the patients with their medical needs and emotional support and being left to fend for themselves. It would ruin so many people's lives and completely break my heart."

Adam nods sympathetically.

"I can see how worried you are, and everyone knows how much you care about this place, Sam. How much do you need to raise each year to stay open then?"

"It's around a million pounds with all the services we offer. The cost has been rising steadily over the years and it's getting harder and harder to meet the demand. As you know, it's such a lovely place here and crucial for so many people. The location in these stunning grounds is just perfect for palliative care patients; it's tranquil and peaceful and the building works so well for what we need to provide. It would be absolutely criminal for it to close!" I reply, downbeat.

"Yeah, I totally agree. Do you happen to know much about the origins of the building and grounds, like when it was built and what the land was used for before it had a hospice on it?" he asks.

"A little bit, yeah. I seem to remember hearing something about the land remaining untouched and undeveloped for quite a long time, dating back hundreds of years or something, and then when the hospice was being set up and the founder was looking for a plot of land to use, he came across this particular site that nobody seemed to want and the council agreed to sell it to him seeing as it would be used for charitable purposes. There have been rumours floating around over the years about it once being the site of some sort of early human settlement back in Anglo-Saxon times or something like that. I don't know anything about UK history so I really couldn't say, but you often get lots of speculation about a place's past when it's unknown, don't you, and I'm not sure there's any truth to it."

"Really? I'd love to know more about it," Adam replies, seeming interested.

"Tell you what, I'll dig out my file with all the details from when the hospice was founded if you like. Hang on a mo."

I go to my filing cabinet but am surprised to find the file I'm looking for isn't there. Puzzled, I check again, thinking I must have missed it or maybe it had been put in the wrong place or fallen down the back of the unit, but I can't find it anywhere. Thinking hard about when I could have had it last, I suddenly recall the day of the trustee meeting last week and remember coming back upstairs with Emma for lunch and finding the drawer open. Assuming I'd just forgotten to close it, I had thought nothing of it back then, but now I know there's a file missing, it strikes me as slightly odd. I try to think whether anyone else had been to see me that day and I realise that the only other person to have been in my office was Ross with his secret cake delivery. I guess he must have been looking for some information to help him further the charitable trusts assistance plan and so had taken the file.

I explain this to Adam and promise to lend it to him once Ross has finished with it and given it back. I also make a mental note to ask Ross about it the next time I see him. I'm keen to know if he's had a chance to speak with the other foundations yet and whether they are going to be able to help.

Once the food arrives, we take it into the main day room so we can eat in more comfort and stick the telly on. I have a dig around in the drinks cupboards and find a couple of lagers, which I promise myself I'll replace tomorrow.

Afterwards, with satisfyingly full bellies, neither of us can bear the thought of making our respective journeys home yet, so instead, we move some coffee tables and drag a couple of inviting recliners to a spot right in front of the telly, pop in a DVD from the little collection on the bookshelf, and ease into the chairs. Snuggled under a blanket each, we watch the film and chat away, relaxed in each other's company — effortless and easy, having known each other since our younger years.

A while later, the alcohol has started to take effect and feeling sleepy from a heavy meal on top of the evening's earlier events, I allow my tired eyes to close every now and then, and my head begins to nod. I'm in that strange state of knowing I'm doing it but unable or rather unwilling to do anything about it. I'm just so blooming comfortable I can't stop myself. It seems Adam has the exact same issue, and the next thing we know, the sunlight is pouring through the windows, and we wake to hear the unmistakable sounds of the day hospice waking up and coming to life.

For a while, we both just lie there, enjoying the calm and serenity. The wood of the window frames, make that lovely soft cracking sound as they warp in the sun, the condensation is slowly streaking its way down the windowpanes, and the birds outside are singing their little hearts out, announcing the morning to the world as if their little lives depend on it.

The tranquil moment is short-lived, however, as we soon hear the distant sound of car doors shutting outside and faint voices of the first arrivals at reception. Adam and I look at each other in panic and instantly jump up and set about trying to hide last night's impromptu feast and sleepover. We're almost done tidying everything away and returning the room to its proper layout when the door to the lounge swings open, and in walks Dotty.

Rumbled, we stand there for a moment holding our breaths and saying nothing. Dotty takes a second or two to assess the scene and then, without even so much as a raised eyebrow, creases her lovely face into a friendly smile, says, "Good morning!" cheerily and walks round to the kitchenette to switch on the kettle, ready for the first wave of patients due any minute. Giggling like guilty kids caught raiding the sweet jar but delighted to have avoided discipline, Adam and I quickly echo her, 'Good morning', gather up our empty takeaway dishes and dash out of the room as fast as we can.

Chapter Five

With it not having been my intention to sleepover at the hospice last night, I'm still wearing my pyjamas, and seeing as I don't have a fresh change of clothes with me, I decide the best course of action is to work from home today. That way, I can wait in for an emergency boiler call out as I really don't want to have to go without hot water for too long now that the weather's getting colder by the day as we head towards winter.

I leave a note on reception to forward any incoming calls to my mobile and send Emma a quick text to let her know my plans, and then nip home before anyone else cops an eyeful of my unflattering fluffy jammies. Adam decides to stay the course and carry on as normal, seeing as he's still wearing his clothes from yesterday, and they are mainly hidden under his overalls most of the day anyway. Unlike me, he'll spend most of his time outside, which will spare everybody from any unwashed whiff that might develop on him as the day goes on.

A short while later, sitting on my couch surrounded by giant cushions and fleecy throws, I'm tapping away on my laptop, still waiting for the gas man to turn up when I receive a phone call from Emma. She's called mainly to speak about some work issues. However, the very first thing she wants to know before we get into any work is what happened at the gym yesterday evening, which reminds me that I still haven't explained to both her and Vicky what went wrong and why it was such a disaster. Rather than take up precious work time talking about my woeful introduction to the world of exercise, I promise her I'll gladly reveal all after work and suggest that the three of us meet up later for dinner and a natter. She readily agrees and leaves it with me to get in touch with Vicky to arrange.

First to discuss on our work agenda is how to tweak the finer details of the next event we are due to hold soon, the Winter Remembrance Service. It's an annual affair that takes place in the hospice grounds in the run-up to Christmas where, for a small donation, people write messages to their loved ones who have passed away and then place them on the hospice gates as a memorial. The words are written on simple, plain silver cards and tied to the bars with shiny ribbons, where they line the full length of the front fence and remain there during the entire festive period. It's a beautiful sight when full, and passers-by often stop on their way past to read the heartfelt notes and poems delicately fluttering in the breeze.

In addition to the messages, Emma and I collate the names of the remembered and read them out at the service whilst soothing music plays over the sound system in the background. Today, we are discussing the choice of music for this year, which is no mean feat, as it's so important to select something meaningful and expressive that also has a slow, measured beat and isn't too loud or too quiet and has appropriate lyrics. It must also be different from previous years' choices as we tend to have many of the same attendees each year.

We enjoy ourselves trying out a variety of different pieces from hymns and songs to movie classics and finally settle on a few options we think will be perfect for this year's reading of the names. We also have a practice go, reading out every single name so we'll know exactly how to pronounce each one correctly on the night.

Part of me looks forward to this event every year as it is so moving and poignant, and yet, the other part of me dreads it as I always include a donation of my own and write a personal message to my darling Nanna Rose. We make sure that she features on Emma's list as it would be simply too difficult to read hers out myself, but even so, when I hear my friend say her name, it always brings a tear to my eye. Mind you, at this point in the service, most of the people in attendance are already blubbing, so I don't really stand out.

Once happy with our selections, we move on to other general hospice news, and Emma brings up having bumped into Dotty earlier in the day and a particularly peculiar conversation she had with her.

"Sam, I think she's been on the pop today, you know. She was waffling on quite bizarrely about how good it is that we're 'on the up' now and how she knew all along, that things would 'turn out right again'. Honestly, Sam, I didn't have a scooby what she was on about half the time, and I was just about to march her to my car for a breathalyser test — you know the one I keep in my car for trips abroad — but the little scamp scurried off to join the 'origami for beginners' class being run in the day room. I tell you what, she's pretty nimble on her feet for an old biddy, isn't she?"

Chuckling and thinking back to the day of the trustee meeting when I experienced an equally puzzling moment with Dotty, I reply, "Yes, she said similar things to me too last week. Do you think we ought to mention it to the head nurse?"

"Mmm, maybe. Her ramblings clearly aren't making much sense at the moment, are they? She even said something strange about you and Adam having slept here last night in the day room! I think she's seriously losing it, Sam!"

"Erm, yeah, about that—" I begin, and I am just about to own up and jump to poor Dotty's defence on that particular issue when the doorbell rings, signalling the much-awaited arrival of the boiler man. Quite literally saved by the bell, I quickly tell Emma I have to dash and that I'll call her back to explain Dotty's remark.

An hour later, and with thankfully a newly fixed and fully working hot water system, along with a somewhat depleted biscuit tin and similarly emptied bank account, I call Emma back as promised and give her a good giggle over Dotty catching Adam and me this morning standing like rabbits caught in the headlights, trying to hide all evidence of our unplanned sleepover.

"Well, that explains why I didn't see him at home before I left this morning. I just assumed he was having a lie in and starting work a bit later today. Scoundrel!" she exclaims, gobsmacked. "I'll josh him about that when I see him later. Oh, and next time you're having a secretive little film and food fest, make sure you invite me too, missy!" She scolds me jokingly. "And, to think I was ready to cart poor old Dotty off to the mad house," she adds, laughing. "Maybe she's not that senile after all!"

We chat a bit longer, realising we also need to finalise plans for this year's hospice Christmas party. Some days I feel as if all I do is arrange gathering after gathering!

"How is it that, even though the date never changes, Christmas has a habit of sneaking up on us every year?" I ask her, wondering how it can possibly be that time of year again already.

"I know, I know," she agrees, "but I'm glad it does cause it's the best bloody time of the year, Sam!"

Emma's joy for Christmas makes her already excitable

personality even more fun to be around, and it's so easily infectious that I soon forget any stress of having to arrange yet another get together. Although strictly speaking not a conventional charity fundraiser, it's an important event to put on as it's our way of thanking everybody who has worked so hard for the good of the hospice throughout the year, most of whom do it unpaid.

This year it's being held at The Golden Barrel in Butterford, and thankfully, we had the good sense to book it in their diary weeks ago while they still had availability. That's all we have done up to this point, however, so we get right to it and spend the next ten minutes swapping ideas back and forth — with Emma unnervingly mentioning the word karaoke a concerning number of times — on how we can make this year's bash a 'good'un'. We decide to split the tasks individually, and after the phone call, Emma cracks on with her speciality, the entertainment side of things, while I focus on the guest list, invitations, and menus.

Before I delve into that, however, and the rest of my afternoon's workload, I give Vicky a quick bell to see if she's free tonight for a girly catch up. She jumps at the idea and happily explains that, as it happens, she'll have the house to herself for most of the evening while Will's out with Adam at the squash club. She offers to host and says she'll throw together a nice simple meal of pasta, salad, and garlic bread, and I promise to bring round drinks and dessert. With the evening plans all arranged, I let Emma know and then carry on with my work.

After a long day of admin and planning involving far too much staring at my laptop, my eyeballs have practically shrivelled up and are starting to feel itchy and irritated, and I'm ready for a good break from the screen. It's been extremely useful to be able to work from home, and I'm so lucky to be in the position where I can do that from time to time; however, I'm looking forward to going back into the hospice tomorrow. I've enjoyed spending time in the quiet of my homely cottage, the knocking and banging of boiler fixing sounds aside, of course, but even though it's only been one day, I've badly missed the hustle and bustle of the hospice and its people. My people, my family. Plus, there's always something fun going on and various shenanigans, and I hate the thought of missing out on anything.

Noticing the time, I pack away my work things, and after a quick freshen up and a hunt in my kitchen cupboards for contributions to the wine and cake that was suggested yesterday, I stroll over to Vicky's house in happy anticipation of an evening of food, chitchat, and comfort with my best buddies.

Over dinner, I give Emma and Vicky the grizzly low down, complete with Max's humiliating description of my less-than-ideal body shape, and being the true friends that they are, they immediately show their outrage and disbelief at the treatment I received.

"How dare he say that to you! I've got a good mind to march straight over there and give him a piece of my mind. I thought gym staff were supposed to encourage and inspire people to work out, not put them off going." Vicky exclaims, furious.

"Yeah, I know. I think they forget how much words can hurt when they're safe in their little world with their perfectly formed bodies and general gorgeousness." I reply dejectedly with a sigh.

"So, what are you going to do?" asks Emma gently. "Are you going to go back?"

"Dunno," I answer. "Don't know if I can be bothered to try again, if I'm honest."

"I know it's easy for me to say," adds Vicky, "but I don't think you should let some thoughtless words from a brainless halfwit get to you. You need to try and put it behind you as best you can, forget about him, and carry on with your own exercise regime, Sam. Don't let one muscle head spoil your good intentions."

"I'll think about it," I assure her, wondering if I'll ever feel up to going back there again.

Sensing my low spirits, Emma changes the subject, and we move on to much more important topics, such as potential outfits for the Christmas party. Once we've finished eating, we adjourn to the lounge with our wine and pudding, ask Alexa to play some '90s music and settle down for a good old natter.

Soon after, however, Will returns from squash practice with Adam in tow, and after grabbing a couple of microwave burgers and choc ices like a pair of ten-year-olds, they take it upon themselves to join us in the living room, launch themselves onto the ends of the sofas, and as is very much the custom for the two of them, unapologetically barge in on our conversation. Much to my dismay, I quickly find that I'm the first target of Will's banter this evening.

"So, how's the budding romance going with Mr Fancy Pants Carrington then, Sam?" he teases. "Left the starting blocks yet?"

I'm fully aware he's messing with me and just wants to have a bit of fun, but I can't stop myself from rising to it nonetheless.

"Positively wonderful actually," I counter. "In fact, things are indeed under way, and I am confident we are making great progress, thank you very much."

"Oh really? Well tell all then, girl, don't keep us in the dark from this riveting love story. Has he asked you out? Are you going on a date, finally?"

Feeling a little bit silly now, seeing as my so-called self-declared progress is not nearly anywhere near as advanced as that, I try to backtrack a little.

"Well, there's not actually that much to tell to be honest, except there's definitely been a small breakthrough of sorts as the other day he left me a lovely little muffin on my desk for no real reason at all, and he is also going out of his way to speak to some influential members of some local heavy hitting financial contributors for the benefit of the hospice."

"Not bad, not bad," Will replies, looking impressed. "You'd better slow down though, Sam, or by this time next week you'll be married, ironing his work shirts and packing the little ones into the people carrier to head off to soccer practice every Sunday," he adds with a mischievous smile.

"Ha ha!" I reply, noting his obvious sarcasm and throwing a cushion at him.

"Stop teasing her!" Vicky warns her husband fondly. "She took enough interrogation from me the other week on our walk; she doesn't need you adding to it. Sorry, Sam." She apologises for the both of them.

"It's fine, it's fine," I assure them. Then, suddenly feeling rather silly over it all, I add, "I'm probably just fooling myself anyway. I'm sure he's got much finer tastes in women."

It's shameful self-pitying, but I say it in the hope that Will feels at least a teeny bit guilty for taunting me. Both Emma and Vicky immediately scoff at this, with Emma adding, "Sam, you're gorgeous. He'll see that soon enough, I'm sure! Won't he, Adam? You must have seen him around the hospice and spoken to him a bit. He'd have to be certifiably mad or blind even not to want to go out with our Sam, wouldn't he?"

"Oh my God!" I groan, burying my face in my hands. "I feel like a right lame saddo with you all discussing my miserable love life like this. You don't have to answer that, Adam," I reassure him feeling my cheeks going bright red.

"I'm not really the best person to ask, to be honest," he answers. "I don't think I've ever had a conversation with him. Not important enough for him to warrant his time, I don't think," he snipes, his harsh tone taking me by surprise.

"Well, he doesn't always have a lot of time to spare when he's at the hospice as it's during his free time that he very kindly volunteers for us," I reply, feeling the need to defend him. I don't like the way Adam is making Ross out to be some sort of puffed-up snob, and it's getting my hackles up slightly.

"Sorry, Sam," he continues. "He just doesn't strike me as the right person to make you happy. You probably don't want to hear it, but that's just my opinion, of course."

I'm a little shocked and annoyed by his frankness, and he's right on one thing; I don't really want to hear his opinion if that's what he thinks. I don't want him to burst my lovely, happy, daydreamy bubble of my Mr Perfect.

Slightly miffed, but not wanting to cause a scene, I don't say anything else and just sit there feeling cross like a child who is misunderstood and can't have her way. The mood of the room nosedives a little, and I can see the others are feeling a tad awkward, so I decide to be the bigger person and change the subject.

"Anyway, that's enough about me and my tragic personal life. Let's talk about something else," I suggest. "How was squash tonight then, boys? Did you enjoy thrashing about a court chasing after balls like a pair of school kids rather than behaving like fully grown men?"

This provokes much tutting from the guys, and with everyone happy to move on and talk about easier, more care-free subjects and the mood lighter again, nothing more is said about

Ross and me and our sad, stilted romance.

Several hours later, with the earlier awkwardness forgotten and the usual lively banter reinstated, not a topic has gone untouched, and the world has been put to rights. Tiredness has crept upon us, however, and we're all starting to yawn one by one, so we admit defeat and call it a night. We say our goodbyes, and Emma bundles her bike into her brother's boot, and he drives them both home whilst I walk the short distance through the village to my lovely little cottage.

I'm absolutely shattered, and a good night's slumber is calling me after sleeping in an armchair all of last night, and I just know I'm going to really appreciate snuggling down into my own bed tonight. I will rest soundly in the knowledge that tomorrow morning will bring with it a return to working normality and the promise of a steaming hot shower to entice me out of bed.

Chapter Six

Over the next few weeks, I fall into a rhythm of long, hectic days at work, followed by cosy evenings at home sitting on my comfy little couch in front of the TV. Each night, I easily while away the hours watching mindless reality programmes whilst diligently working through my family and friends' Christmas gift list, *one-click* purchasing like a woman on a mission and single-handedly keeping the internet shopping world in business.

This disgustingly lazy way of shopping is so quick and easy that it leaves me with absolutely no desire to go out to the shops in person, and to this effect, I have turned into a bit of a hermit. Even when I'm not drastically reducing my bank account to unnervingly low levels, fully engrossed in the thrill of ordering the entire contents of Amazon Prime, I'm more than happy in my own company, pottering around the house carrying out enjoyable little odd jobs, such as tinkering with the Christmas decorations, or writing cards. I have also become quite adept at avoiding all notions of attending the gym since the distressing s*lubby* incident.

With winter taking hold and the days becoming increasingly colder and darker, I've convinced myself that there's no point in working out for the time being, as my body is generally swaddled in oversized jumpers or dressing gowns and hardly ever on show anyway. Instead, I've added any kind of exercise to my upcoming New Year's resolution list, along with the recurring attempt at a full year of no swearing — that one's a big ask and features every single year, but I'm yet to achieve it. So, if even the tiniest thought of donning sportswear and heading off to the gym creeps into my consciousness, I rapidly banish it to the back of my mind and refocus all my efforts on burying my head in the sand and busying myself with any other suddenly essential task like the skilled procrastinator I am.

This avoidance technique has its benefits admittedly, as, so far, I've managed to complete all manner of overdue household chores, including steam cleaning the wood floors and kitchen tiles, washing the inside of all the windows, and having a thoroughly good clear out of the cupboard under the stairs. I've found that there are no limits to what I can accomplish when I know deep down, I should be doing something else.

There's no such inclination to apply disgraceful delay tactics at work, however, as the warmth and responsibility I feel for Green Meadow only serves to encourage me to work hard every day with no shying away from difficult jobs. With tasks coming out of our ears and so much to complete still before the end of the season, Emma and I knuckle down arranging the final events of the year, not forgetting those also due to take place in January and February.

Today is the day of the hospice Remembrance Service, which is scheduled to start in a couple of hours' time. It is currently five p.m., and I am sitting in my office, adding the finishing touches to the Orders of Service and the list of names to be remembered this evening. As usual with this event, I won't bother to go home first as there's so much to organise, and I may as well just stay on site and work straight through to make sure we're ready to begin on time. I'm a bit of a stickler for punctuality and ensuring our events start promptly; plus, since it's an outdoor one, it's far too cold at this time of year to keep people waiting around.

I have a knot in my stomach the size of a beach ball, which has been building up all day long due to both the pressure of making certain everything runs smoothly and the fact that this occasion always makes me so emotional. It's during this gathering that I think of my Nanna more than at any other time of the year, and one could easily argue that out of all our events such as the fetes, quizzes, races, walks etc., this is by far the most important. It is this ceremony that reminds everybody exactly what Green Meadow does for the community and why the fundraising team, medical staff, volunteers, and trustees do what we do day in, day out to ensure the continued provision of services.

I check, double check, and triple check the list of names to be read out as it would be just heart breaking for family members as they wait anxiously, listening out for the name of their loved one only to hear it pronounced incorrectly. It's important to make sure all the spellings are accurate, too, as each name is entered into a book of remembrance placed on a lectern to be viewed afterwards.

Once I'm happy that there are no spelling errors or missing names, I place the list in the box of cards and ribbons, which will be tied to the hospice railings later, then head downstairs to go and see how Emma is getting on preparing the day room for the mulled wine and mince pies that will be on offer once the service is over.

On the way, I quickly nip outside to confirm that everything is okay with the outside arrangements and spy Adam working his magic, making the final adjustments to the marquee, sound system and Christmas tree. He's rather preoccupied securing ropes and knocking in ground pegs, carefully avoiding the speaker cables and tangles of string lights, so I don't hold him up by going over to talk to him. I just shout his name and then mouth the question, 'Is everything okay?' and he replies with a bright smile and a comforting thumbs up.

Happy with his response, I continue to the main room and give Emma a hand lugging tables and chairs around in order to accommodate what will no doubt be a large turnout tonight, judging by the number of donations and name entries we've received.

Once that is done, and relieved that everything seems to be on track, I allow myself half an hour to grab a quick sandwich and a drink and then freshen up with a quick spray of perfume and a fresh change of clothes. It won't be long now before people start arriving, and it's time for the service to begin.

A short while later, I'm all set to go and am standing at the door to the marquee, welcoming in a steady flow of people, when Emma rushes up to me with some bad news. She informs me that she has just heard from the volunteer selected to give tonight's readings, who has called to say she's come down with something at the last minute and can no longer make it. I have a momentary panic and am wondering who on earth we could possibly call up at this late stage to take her place when Charles and Ross arrive and wander over to the back of the queue.

"Oh, thank the Lord! Divine intervention," I say to Emma theatrically. Dashing over to them and smiling sweetly, I dive right in, bypassing all unnecessary pleasantries and explaining the problem, asking if either of them would mind awfully coming to our rescue and delivering the readings. Charles, it turns out, has a bit of a lingering tickly cough from a recent cold, so happily volunteers his somewhat stunned son for the role. He pats him on the back and then, chipper as you like, wanders off to mingle. I can see Ross isn't exactly thrilled at the idea of suddenly being launched into the spotlight with no notice or preparation; however, with both his father's assumption that he will step up to the plate and my expectant and hopeful expression, he doesn't really have a choice.

"Erm, I'm not really sure I'm the man for the job really, Samantha. I usually would prefer a little bit of forewarning before any kind of public speaking," he says, a little flustered.

"I understand, I do, only we don't really have any other choice. Please say you'll do this for us!" I plead.

I say this without really allowing him to argue otherwise, thrust a copy of the readings at him, and lead him over to a quiet space where he can familiarise himself with the words for a moment.

"Thank you so much, Ross. This really is very good of you, and well, you're a real hero for doing this for us at such short notice," I tell him, reaching up to him and giving him a quick hug.

I can't help but notice how strong and broad his shoulders feel under his jacket, and I stay there for a moment or two longer than is strictly necessary, enjoying the feel of him and his closeness to me.

"Erm, no problem, Samantha," he replies with a little bluster. "You know I'm always happy to do anything I can for the hospice." He tries to assure me with little conviction, his voice betraying the confidence of his words slightly as he grapples with the idea of this unsolicited challenge thrust upon him.

I leave him to get to grips with the readings and re-join Emma helping her to seat the masses. Minutes later, the service begins, and I look to the heavens and say a little prayer under my breath that all will go smoothly without any further complications.

Thankfully, someone up there is listening, and sure enough, the event passes without a hitch. Ross reads the verses very well, considering his lack of preparation, and Emma and I manage to call out the names without any mistakes, and it's profoundly touching seeing people's relief and gratitude at hearing their loved ones honoured in such a straightforward but powerful way.

Hearing Emma voice Nanna Rose's name is painful, but I manage to stay strong throughout, only allowing myself a little tear afterwards once I have turned away from the congregation. There's almost a unified feeling of relief for everyone when that solemn part of the service is over, and people can relax again and enjoy tying their precious name-cards to the fencing. It's a simple act yet strongly symbolic and a beautiful and therapeutic way to bring comfort to those who have lost someone close.

Emma makes herself useful, guiding people out of the tent to where they can find their cards and then, after tying them to the railings, back indoors to find the refreshments being handed out by volunteers, which leaves me to tidy away the programmes that have been inadvertently abandoned on chairs.

Adam approaches as I wipe the tears from my eyes, and he puts his arm around my shoulders, pulling me into a comforting embrace. Knowing this event provokes sad memories for me, stinging me more than any other, he doesn't say anything, just squeezes me for a brief moment and then slips away into the crowd. I'm thankful for his silent support, and it does the trick bolstering me into action again.

I can see Ross just outside the tent, surrounded by a group of elderly ladies congratulating him on his performance with the readings, and he seems to be enjoying the praise, lapping up the attention. As I approach, I catch a few words as he explains how when he heard there was a situation with a no-show volunteer, he didn't hesitate to offer his services as replacement reader. I chortle a little at his slight twisting of the truth; after all, he did do us a favour by stepping in at the last minute, although I make a mental note that his humility is perhaps not one of his stronger characteristics.

The ladies move away, enticed inside by the Christmas nibbles, and I take the opportunity to ask Ross about the missing file.

"Oh yes, well, I just wanted it for some information to help me with the conversations I need to have with the charitable foundations and trusts, of course. I would have asked, naturally. However, you were in the land of nod when I popped by, and well, you just looked so peaceful, and well, beautiful if you don't mind me saying, and I couldn't bring myself to wake you from your slumber," he explains.

I don't mind him saying it one bloody bit! Thrilled by his use of the word beautiful, I'm ashamed to say my brain basically switches off for a second or two, and I stare at him wordlessly as I drift off into my idyllic dreamland where Ross and I are lovers and spend our lives together in perfect harmony, skipping hand in hand along beaches or gazing into each other's eyes as we sip cocktails by the pool. I spot his brows furrowing slightly, which brings me sharply back to reality, and embarrassed by my reaction now, I feel a little flush of colour rush to my cheeks. I hope to God he hasn't noticed but decide that, if he has, I'll just blame it on the cold air. Reprimanding myself for such a pathetic reaction, and silently telling myself to get a grip, I regather my thoughts and carry on with the conversation.

"Of course, of course, no problem," I enthuse. "You must have access to anything you think might assist you, and do feel free to call me anytime, night or day, if you have further questions or need more details, don't forget." Calm down, Sam, I tell myself, don't act too bloody keen for him to call you all the time. Haven't you ever heard of being aloof?

"Erm, how is it all going, now you come to mention it? Have you had much progress?" I ask him while we're on the subject.

"No, no, nothing to report yet, of course, early days but it's all in hand, no need for concern. I'll tell you when there's anything to report," he declares confidently.

"Sure, sure, of course, as and when, no problem," I reply, a little disappointed that he doesn't have any good news yet but not wanting to sound as if I'm pestering him or doubting his ability to get results. I remind myself I do have a tendency to be impatient — not one of my strengths — and that this is Ross, and I can fully trust that he will come through for the hospice.

"Right, well, I'd better get inside then and help the volunteers with the refreshments. Are you coming in for a quick bite?" I ask him.

"No, no, none for me, thank you, Samantha. I try not to partake in naughty treats this late on in the evening. Not good for the figure, you see," he replies, tapping his stomach area.

"Oh, I wish I had your willpower," I say with a smile whilst trying to shake the image I now have in my mind of a firmly sculpted six-pack I'm assuming lies just under the surface of his top, "but you know me and my unbridled love for cake!"

"Fond of the odd sweet fancy, are you? Not one of those who can't control herself around sugary snacks, I hope."

I'm a little taken aback by this. Surely, he knows my fondness for cake after his gift before the board meeting the other week. Figuring he's obviously just teasing me and remembering I've yet to thank him for it, I reply, "All right, stop messing with me, and thank you so much for the muffin you left on my desk. It was just the energy boost I needed."

With that, I turn on my heel and head towards the hospice door. Then, for some unknown reason that I will never understand, I suddenly think it's a great idea to shout back over my shoulder, "If I can't tempt you to join me, I'll make sure I eat enough for the two of us!" I regret it immediately.

Great going, Sam. Now he'll think you're a right greedy fatso with no restraint who just shovels cake into your gob every chance you get! Quietly groaning and tutting incredulously at my inability to think and act like a sane woman in Ross' presence, I nip inside as fast as I can to hide my embarrassment, marvelling at my skilful ability to yet again make a twit of myself in front of his hunkiness. What can I say, it's a gift!

A while later, after the hordes have gone home, Emma, Adam, and I, along with the remaining hardy volunteers, tidy away as much as we can, packing away tables, chairs, banners, boxes, and sound equipment. The marquee will be dismantled and collected first thing in the morning, but the fairy lights will remain twinkling and glistening on the outside tree as a symbol of love and hope until the New Year.

We shut up the hospice for the night, and exhausted, we all say our goodnights and head home. The service was a great success, with many people receiving the closure or emotional therapy they craved. The donations have been counted, and we are all elated with the amount raised from tonight's event. Another worthwhile contribution to the ever-elusive fundraising target.

As I drive away from Green Meadow through the dark country lanes towards Butterford and my charming little cottage, I'm feeling satisfied with what we've achieved this year and a comforting sense of optimism that we'll raise the amount we need to stay open. With no more official charity fundraisers to stage until January, I can relax a little and take advantage of a few days of rest and chocolate munching over the Christmas break, and of course, I still have the hospice Christmas party to look forward to.

Chapter Seven

One morning the following week, I'm sitting at my desk, absorbed in my work, when a call from the switchboard comes through to tell me Ross is on the line. As always, when he calls, a small shiver of nervous excitement buzzes its way through me like I'm some teenage girl having her first conversation with her school crush. I never feel ready for his calls or visits, repeatedly finding myself a bundle of nerves. I do wonder if I'll ever reach an age where I'll grow out of having reactions like this over a boy, although I secretly hope not as it's a pleasant mini thrill in an otherwise terribly sensible and uneventful life.

I clear my throat, smooth down my hair, and sit up straight, as if he's going to be able to see me magically through the receiver somehow, and trying my best to sound like the professional and alluring office goddess I wish I could be, I whisper seductively into the mouthpiece as appealingly as I can, "Ross... lovely to hear from you, how's things?"

My efforts are totally wasted as the volunteer on the reception desk has got the wrong end of the stick, confusing the two Mr Carringtons, and it is in fact Charles and sadly not his hunk of a son who receives the full force of my fervent voice acting skills. Slumping back down in my chair, I try not to sound too despondent as I exchange pleasantries with him. With the niceties out of the way, he explains the reason for his call.

"Just thought I'd mention that I'll be popping by the hospice sometime this afternoon to drop off some Christmas goodies for you all. Nothing extravagant, just some little chocolates, you know liqueurs, truffles, and the like for you and all the staff to say thank you for all your hard work this year. It's a small token from me and the trustees as we know things have been far from easy. Such challenging times and many more still to come no doubt, but we wanted to remind you that we are fully aware of all your efforts. Please do remember we're here if you need us for any advice or support."

His kind, comforting words and fatherly tone bring a lump to my throat, and I find I can't answer him straight away. He senses this and fills the pause like the true gent he is giving me time to find my voice.

"Anyway, I thought I had better phone ahead and check there would be someone in to receive them, so I don't make a wasted journey. Would that be all right, do you think, in maybe a couple of hours' time after lunch?"

Able to speak once again, I answer, "Of course, Charles, yes, that would be lovely. It's very kind of you to think of us. I'll have the kettle on ready for you. You'll be able to stay for a quick brew, won't you?"

"You know I never turn down the offer of a cup of tea, Samantha. There's always time for that. See you in a jiffy. Oh, and stay on the line as Ross is here and would like a quick word if you wouldn't mind my dear. One moment, I'll pass you over."

And once again, with no time to prepare, I'm thrust into a renewed frenzy of jitters at the prospect of speaking to the object of my desire.

"Hello, Samantha?" God, he sounds sexy! "Could you spare a few minutes? I'd like to pick your brains regarding Green Meadow's current finances. Keen to understand the exact monetary situation to help me with my little quest before I speak with the potential donors."

"Yes, yes, of course, no problem. What do you want to know?" I reply, trying to sound as competent as possible.

We chat for a while with him asking various questions regarding the estimated value of the hospice and grounds, its running costs, budget and the specific target that we need to reach, and he tells me the names of some of the trusts he's making contact with. I actually enjoy the conversation immensely. Talking about the hospice is a passion of mine, and knowing that we are having a private discussion right now, just me and him, united in our fight to save Green Meadow, fuels my romanticism.

I multitask like a boss, answering his questions, providing him with all the necessary information whilst daydreaming, immersed in my imaginary world of what could be between the two of us. His dulcet tones are so soothing to my ears that I'm disappointed when he brings the conversation to an end.

Thanking me for the information, he assures me he has everything he needs. Damn me and my exceptional proficiency! Racking my brains for something to say to keep him on the line, I glance around my room for inspiration and catch sight of my wall calendar with the words *Christmas Party* written brightly in felt tip pen. Yes, brilliant… you genius Samantha! I congratulate myself silently.

"Erm, so I'll be seeing you very soon at the hospice party then, yeah? I hope you're looking forward to it!" I ask him as nonchalantly as I can muster, fingers crossed and praying he'll say yes.

"Oh yes, we'll be there, both father and I. Wouldn't want to miss a good nosh up!" Halleluiah!

"That's great!" I say casually without a hint of fuss whilst, in reality, what I really want to do is run around the room cartwheeling in celebration. I haven't actually tried a cartwheel in years, since primary school, in fact, but I'm feeling that jubilant right now I'd be happy to give it a bloody good try!

"I'll see you there then. Bye for now, Ross, and thanks again for everything you're doing to help the hospice."

I replace the receiver and bask in the lovely warm glow I now have simmering inside. Could this man be any better? I wonder to myself. A smart, well-known, respected man of the community, resolute in helping out the hospice in his spare time, currently unattached, of course, and bloody gorgeous to top it all off. And *I'm* the lucky woman who gets to spend time with him. Happy days.

"Stick with it, Sam. It's all panning out the way it should. You'll get your man!" I say out loud to myself in the manner of a movie villain whose wicked scheme is finally coming together nicely. I can't suppress the urge this image evokes to throw my head back and let out a loud mock evil laugh just as Emma walks in to announce, 'coffee o'clock' and catches me in the act. My refreshingly wonderful oddball friend sees absolutely nothing at all bizarre about my antics, however, and without any kind of reaction or single word, she reaches forward, whips my mug off my desk and leaves for the kitchen.

I sit back smiling, feeling all is well with the world — well… hospice troubles aside, of course — and then, as is customary in mine and Emma's unquestioned morning coffee break routine, I reach into my bottom desk drawer and take out the perpetually replenishing pack of chocolate digestives. A quick chat over our drinks about my lovely little confab with Superstud, and then it'll be back to work for a few hours before lunch.

Time flies, and lunchtime soon arrives, and I decide to stretch my legs and take a leisurely stroll down the road to the little convenience store to buy a sandwich. Leaving Emma to hold the fort, and with her lunch request of a ham and cheese sandwich and a packet of pickled onion Monster Munch scribbled on a sticky note safely tucked into my pocket, I grab my coat, scarf and fluffy ear warmers and head downstairs and out of the building.

We're in the thick of December now, and I feel the biting cold as soon as I walk through the main doors, so I wrap my coat tightly around me, glad of its protective thickness and soft, furry lining. I pass Adam out front performing terribly sensible and grown-up duties, such as checking the grit bin and insulating the outside taps, totally befitting of this raw wintry temperature and exactly the kind of tasks I would, in all probability, completely forget to do until the patients were slipping over and the pipes were frozen solid. I tell him where I'm headed and subsequently add his lunch order of a BLT sandwich and pickled onion Monster Munch — like brother, like sister — to the list.

As I exit the car park and pass the gates, I admire the remembrance cards still tied to the rails, glistening in the bright sun, which sits so low in the cloudless sky this time of year. It takes about twenty minutes to walk to the shop and back, and once returned, I deposit the correct lunch with its correct owner and settle down for a ten-minute break.

The rest of the afternoon ticks by steadily, although by four p.m. I'm clock-watching a little, conscious of the lack of Charles' promised visit. With no phone call to say he'd arrived, I assume something else more important must have come up, work on until about five p.m., and then head on down to the main room to have a chat with the patients.

I try not to interrupt their activities or rest periods too often, but I do like to pop down from time to time to see how they're all getting on and engage in a little chinwag, and I encourage the rest of the upstairs office staff to do likewise. Despite their illnesses, the patients are always so bubbly and chatty, so it's an enjoyable experience in itself, but even so, I'm a firm believer that we'll all instinctively fight for their cause more earnestly if we get to know them as people rather than simply numbers and statistics.

The day room is bustling today with a full turn-out, and I can hear their lively natter as I make my way down the corridor. All organised talks or presentations have long finished by this point in the day, and most people are simply relaxing in the armchairs enjoying each other's company, some hooked up to drips, receiving a dose of their regular treatment, and others being tended to by a nurse.

I spot one of my favourite regular attendees, Jim, sitting near the fireplace with his friends, happily putting the world to rights. He's a fabulous old guy; spirited, charismatic and mildly cheeky, and for the most part, he shamefully yet also quite refreshingly does not seem to possess a single ounce of political correctness. Deep down, though, he means no harm by the occasional outrageous comment, and I love spending time with him. In fact, I see him as the Granddad I never had, with both of mine having sadly died before I was born.

He's slightly frail looking due to the constant battle with his health and the effects of the long-term illness he endures, although with his positive attitude and jokey manner, you'd never guess he was terminally ill and receiving palliative care here every week. I can tell he would have been a rather commanding character in his youth, robust and impressive and a real looker, I'm sure, and it saddens me to think how he has probably deteriorated since becoming ill. He spots me approaching and waves me over.

"Sammy, come over here and sit with us old farts for a bit. We're just about to start a game of Twister actually, care to join in? We could do with a few young fillies like yourself bending and flexing to make it interesting for us old boys," he teases with a twinkle in his eye.

"Now, now," I say, smiling and pulling up a pew next to him, "you and I both know that's not exactly an appropriate thing to be saying nor a responsible game to be playing at your age now is it? Not to mention none of us would stand a chance with your excessive trembling and old decrepit bones clicking and creaking all over the place. You'd probably collapse and knock us all over in the first few seconds!"

I'd never dream of speaking to any other patient in that way, of course, but Jim knows that I'm simply playing my part, dutifully joining in with his jokes, and it's exactly what he hopes I will do. His natural cheeky-chappy demeanour seems incapable of resisting the urge to dish out playful taunts and jibes, fishing for stunned reactions and resultant participation in witty repartee. He wouldn't have it any other way, and the nurses have previously commented on how he always seems so much brighter and happier after a mild bout of teasing and friendly quipping, so they are more than happy to let it continue.

He lets out a loud guffaw at my insulting remark and gives me a gentle pinch in the ribs.

"Indeed, Sammy, indeed! Best not then, eh?" he laments wistfully. "Don't want to give the nurses any more broken bodies to deal with. It'll have to just be safe old bingo instead then if you can take the excitement?"

"Go on then," I reply, "and I agree, that's a much more sensible option, if maybe a little tedious."

87

"Ah, well that's where you're wrong, my dear, as today it just so happens to be good old Batty Barbs doing the number calling so it'll be anything but boring, you'll see!"

Intrigued, I grab myself a card and dabber and ready myself for a few rounds of bingo, which, just as Jim quite rightly warned, turns out to be neither dull nor uneventful. Batty Barbs, it transpires, is a rather eccentric old lady who chooses to disregard any of the generally accepted bingo terms and instead merrily calls out all manner of weird and wonderful phrases at a rate of knots, sometimes without even any mention of the supposed corresponding number.

It's soon clear to see that this version is rather less of a methodical number marking process and more of a panicky 'decode the cryptic clues' guessing game. It's none of your standard calls like 'Legs Eleven' and 'Two Little Ducks', and after a few rounds of trying to decipher phrases such as 'Tickle My Pickle' and 'Snore for Two More', I'm completely lost. She seems blissfully unaware of the confusion she's causing, however, and sees no need to slow down or clarify the numbers called so far. It's hilarious for those of us attempting to play along, and soon we're all in fits of giggles as we try in vain to keep up.

I'm attempting to make sense of the game by cross-referencing my card with Jim's when Dotty enters the room and comes over to speak to me.

"I was just in reception and saw Mr Carrington deliver some presents, Samantha. Do you want me to show you where we've put them?"

"Oh, he's been in? Just now? That's strange. I was expecting him much earlier and he said he would come and have a cup of tea with me. Is he still here, do you know?"

"No, he brought the gifts in and then left straight away. I asked him if he wanted me to come and find you, but he said not to worry and that he's already spoken with you this afternoon. Very kind of him though, isn't it, and he really is a rather handsome chap. I bet he gets all the young girls' pulses racing. In my day, we'd have called him a dish, but I guess you'd call him a spunky hunk or something like that. I can see why you always tend to go a little tongue tied when you're near him Samantha. If I were fifty years younger, I might find myself in a bit of a dither over him too."

I'm still trying hard to keep up with Barbs and her absurd bingo calling while Dotty speaks, so I've only really had one ear on her ramblings. She does go on a bit, bless her, but this last sentence grabs my full attention. My maths isn't great, and I'm trying to work out exactly how ancient she must be to consider herself far too old for Charles when it dawns on me that the two of us may well have our wires crossed.

"Wait, hang on. Who was it exactly that came in Dotty, Carrington Senior or Carrington Junior?" I ask her.

"Mister Carrington Junior, silly! I mean, I know some people think it's fashionable these days to be... what's the word again... a Cougar? But I think I'm a little too old to be swooning after a man in his thirties, don't you?" she says with a tsk-tsk.

Somewhat disturbed by Dotty's use of the word 'Cougar' and the subsequent image it brings to mind, along with her account that it was, in fact, Ross delivering the gifts instead of Charles, I find myself rather flummoxed.

"Erm, did Ross say why it was him delivering the gifts and not Charles, Dotty?"

"No, but why would it be his father bringing them in if the gifts are from him? Are you feeling all right, Samantha? You don't seem to be able to grasp any of what I'm saying."

Ignoring her slightly patronising tone, I explain how the gifts aren't actually from Ross but rather the trustees and that it was Charles who called earlier to say he would be bringing them in himself.

"Oh, well he didn't make that clear, Samantha. I did ask what they were for, and he said as appreciation for all our hard work. I told him what a kind gesture that was, thanked him and then he left. He never mentioned his father or the trustees. Is everything okay though. Did I say something wrong, dear?"

"No, no, of course not, Dotty, it's no problem, I'm just a bit puzzled that's all. Charles must have had something else to do and so Ross delivered them in his place. No biggy," I reassure her. I'm pretty bummed to have missed a visit by Ross and the chance to talk to him in person, but I don't dwell on it for long and am soon back to my old self once I re-join the bonkers bingo. The game is by now a complete shambles and essentially just a room full of bewildered people frantically dabbing away at pieces of card while Barbs continues to reel off at great speed her curious mix of quirky expressions.

Chapter Eight

It's the last week before Christmas, and tonight is the night of the Green Meadow Christmas Party. The Golden Barrel is lit up from the outside like Santa's Grotto with all manner of tacky, shiny metallic Christmas decorations and bright, multi-coloured fairy lights.

The pub is a lovely, solid old building with areas of exposed brick walls and wonky lines. It has a mix of quirky flagstone floors and busy patterned carpeted walkways leading from the bar to the various seating areas. A raging, open log fire in the main lounge is keeping the whole building toasty warm, even with some of the windows open and with the door in constant use from clients coming and going.

The windowsills are cluttered with an assortment of intricate brass ornaments and pewter beer coasters, and the walls are covered with black and white framed photographs of Butterford from times gone by. Mingled in with these are plaques detailing much-revered sporting achievements of various village clubs, such as the local cricket team and bowls club, and hanging up high over the bar in pride of place, is a row of personalised tankards and beer jugs reserved for the more regular and committed punters.

At the back of the building is the main function room, which we have hired for the party, and although we have exclusive use of this area tonight, there are also several other customers here enjoying themselves and freely milling around the other sections of the pub.

There are people everywhere, filling the corridors, beer garden and decking, spilling out into the car park, and at times, they even find themselves taking a wrong turn and wandering into our party room. I don't mind, though, as most of the people here are local villagers or have some connection to Butterford, so it just feels like an extension to the family and a perfect example of 'the more the merrier'.

Overflowing with Green Meadow staff, volunteers, trustees, extra family members and accidental wanderers from the pub, the atmosphere in the room is absolutely pumping! Vicky and Will are here as they are considered much-valued volunteers at the hospice, often lending a hand at lots of the outdoor events, in particular taking charge of the organised sponsored dog walks and dog shows that take place in the warmer months. There's just enough space to squeeze all of us in with row after row of tables lining the full length of the room. A small space has been created in the middle to act as a dance floor, and there's a tiny, raised, makeshift stage at the far end of the room for the entertainment.

My friends and I had shared a table for the first part of the evening but now the meals are finished, people have started to get up and move around the room for various reasons. Some are out on the decking enjoying the fresh air or having a cheeky fag, whilst others are making trips to the bar to top up their drinks. Many people are enjoying a mingle and hopping onto different tables, chatting to new groups, each time facing the challenge of trying to find a space to place their drinks amongst the discarded party hats, cracker debris, dripping ice buckets and empty beer bottles.

Emma, having forged ahead with her karaoke idea, has now left our table and taken her place centre stage, standing in front of the sound system, microphone in hand, encouraging people to venture up and have a go. Much to my surprise, lots of people have been up to give it a go, including a few gifted teenage girls who sound as if they belong on TV talent shows they're that good. There have already been quite a few drunk older men in their fifties and sixties entertaining the room with shouty renditions of 'Come On Eileen' and the like, and in fairness to Emma, the whole sing-along idea seems to be a big hit.

Since the end of the meal, I, too, have left my seat and have been busying myself socialising, making sure to work my way around the room to talk to everyone who has turned up. I spent a long time with all the volunteers, talking with their significant others and families, and it's been nice chatting to them outside of an official hospice event. Jim is here with one of his daughters, his wife having passed away a few years ago, and we had a lovely natter, laughing about her father's frequent lack of filter and how she's often found herself cringing at his outrageous comments over the years. I told her how I enjoy spending time with him in the day room when I can and how much fun he is to be around.

Afterwards, I moved to the opposite end of the room, and I'm currently sitting at a table twiddling some party popper remnants around my fingers and chewing the fat with Charles, Ross and the other trustees whilst doing my very best to remain hidden from Emma's beady eyes as she scans the room looking for her next lot of karaoke victims. I really don't want to be picked. Having had more glasses of bubbly than I can count and enjoying the feeling of being blissfully merry, I still don't consider myself to be drunk enough to have a crack at it. Singing on my own in the shower is one thing but making a tit of myself in full view of everyone, and more importantly, in front of Ross, is not my idea of fun.

I've managed to avoid her gaze so far and am happily pondering whether a second helping of Christmas cake would look terribly greedy when my worst fears are realised, and I hear Emma's booming voice over the noise of the party, shouting my name and summoning me up to sing. Groaning into my champagne flute, I try to ignore her, but Charles has also heard and is now nudging me to do as I'm told. I remain glued to my chair with my eyes closed, hoping everyone will just get bored of nagging me and then Emma starts chanting my name in that incredibly effective and unfair way that makes everybody join in and soon there's literally no way I can pretend I haven't heard. Realising there's nothing for it but to face the music and *sing*, I reluctantly get up, pour myself another full glass of champagne and tip it down my throat. Charles, noticing my reticence, also offers me his glass and says, "Here you go, lass, this'll give you some Dutch courage."

I take the tumbler from him gratefully and knock it back in one, immediately coughing from the burn of the searing liquid coursing down my throat. Charles stares at me in shock, and I realise he probably only meant for me to take a small sip.

"Didn't take you for a whiskey lover, Samantha. Well done, girl!" he says, patting me on the back and with a look of admiration on his face. I splutter a little, croak a quick thanks, then hand him back the glass and reluctantly make my way through the chanting throng.

I reach the stage, and Emma puts her arm around my shoulders and turns me to face my audience. Oh God! So many people! I catch movement out of the corner of my eye and turn to see Dotty waving at me with a big smile on her face, and then she gives me a double thumbs up in encouragement.

"Please don't make me do this, Emma!" I implore her

through gritted teeth.

Completely ignoring my pleas, she brings the mic up to her mouth and asks, "So, what's your particular jam tonight then, boss?"

I don't answer as I'm too busy mentally composing my darling friend's letter of dismissal. After a pause, and with a glint in his eye, Adam shouts, "She's rather partial to a spot of Abba."

I direct my best, "I'm going to kill you!" face at him, complete with narrowed eyes and a shake of my head, snatch the microphone from Emma's hand, and at the same time, swipe her glass from her with my other hand and neck the lot.

"Good God! What are you drinking?" I gasp at her, feeling like I've just inhaled a glass of pure ethanol. I had assumed it might have been something harmless like a white wine spritzer and the sheer strength of the alcohol takes me by surprise.

"Well, it *was* a triple gin and tonic," she answers. "Only, without the tonic."

I'm conscious of the fact that I've just mixed several different spirits and wine like a total lunatic and will no doubt pay for this later, but in my defence, I simply can't bring myself to sing to this many people without copious amounts of alcohol in my system.

"Abba it is then," she declares to the expectant room and reaches over to the music decks, punching in the required numbers for her chosen track. The bouncy intro of Mamma Mia bursts through the speakers and fills the room.

Accepting defeat, I steel myself for the challenge. Feeling painfully on show and trembling all over, I close my eyes, take a deep breath in, and begin. Somehow, I manage to produce some sort of strangled sound. However, my voice is incredibly meek, and I don't think many people can hear me properly over the chatter, which I think for them can only be a blessing really. I'm so nervous, but I can see the encouraging smiles of Vicky, Will and Adam, all watching me, and strangely enough, rather than continuing to feel alone and exposed up here, it actually buoys me along and gives me more confidence.

A couple of verses in, and the prosecco, Charlie's whiskey, and Emma's gin take the desired effect, and I start to loosen up. Digging deep, I manage to channel my inner Agnetha, and before long, I'm actually starting to relax into it and am rather enjoying myself.

By the end of the song, I've lost most of my inhibitions and couldn't really give two hoots what I sound like or what people think of my lack of singing skills. Emma sees the change in me and niftily starts up another track. Hearing one of my favourites, the unmistakable rousing opening bars to Waterloo, I think, why the heck not, and launch into it, giving it my all.

Looking around at the room, I'm pleased to note that people still seem to be enjoying themselves and aren't sitting there wiping blood from their ears, so it's at this point that I don't honestly know what I was worrying about earlier and am wondering whether Emma will let me stay on for a full Abba tribute set.

I sing my heart out, and as the song comes to an end, another one begins, and I carry on happily. A good fifteen minutes and a five-song medley later, Emma — having decided that I've claimed the limelight for long enough now — reaches over and prises the mic from my hands, ready to hand it to someone else.

Somewhat disappointed that my little stint is over but starting to feel a bit woozy from my performance and all the booze I've tanked, I accept her decision, curtsey to the room and receive a loud round of applause and several high-pitched whoops from my best friends.

"See, it wasn't that scary, was it?" she asks, winking.

On a bit of a high from both the alcohol surging through my veins and the thrill of doing something frightening and completely out of my comfort zone, I decide all is forgiven and bellow, "God, what a rush!" whilst hugging her tightly.

Undeniably exceedingly more drunk than before I started, I step down rather wobbly from the stage and look around the room. I know exactly who I'm looking for, and on seeing him, and feeling totally invincible, I sashay right up to him with the confidence of a superstar. Ross is standing leaning back against the far wall, chatting to a rather annoyingly young and pretty waitress.

"So, what did you think?" I gush at him, not caring that I'm interrupting their conversation.

"Sorry?" he replies, looking rather nonplussed.

"Of my singing, silly" I reprimand him, playfully tickling him in the ribs at the same time.

"Oh, yes, it was lovely," he answers, glancing fleetingly towards his companion.

I'm sure I see her smirk at him as if she thinks otherwise, and I'm sorely tempted to smack the tray of drinks she's holding to the ground. The three of us all stand there awkwardly for a second or two, and I wonder what I can say to make this little filly buzz off. Can't she see I want to chat to my intended without her hanging around spoiling the mood by looking all attractive and feminine? She doesn't look to be moving anytime soon, though, so I carry on regardless.

"So, how are you? I haven't seen you in aaaages!" I ask Ross enthusiastically.

"Do you mean how am I since you saw me five minutes ago

at the table, Sam?" he answers.

Feeling a little foggy in the head but seeing his point, I giggle girlishly and continue undeterred.

"Well, yes, yes, but we didn't have much of a chance to talk alone then, did we, with all the other people around. Just thought it would be really nice to have a chat on our own for once, just you and me," I emphasise the word 'own' and glance at the cutesy face waitress, hoping she'll take the hint and go do one. She seems incapable of reading my signals, however, and stands her ground.

I'm getting more and more annoyed with her by the second. Whatever happened to female solidarity? I mean, she can't honestly think she stands any sort of chance with Ross, can she? She must know he wouldn't be interested in her, surely. She can't be a day over twelve!

During this time, Emma has decided to take a break from running the karaoke, and some Christmas tunes are now blasting out loudly around the room. One of my all-time favourites comes on, and with some quick thinking, I grab Ross' hand and whisk him into the middle of the room to the dance floor. Ha! That'll show little miss skinny chops to mess with a real woman. I look back over my shoulder, catching her eye and triumphantly throw her a look that I'm hoping translates to 'how do you like that then, hey?' I'm pretty sure it translates perfectly, as she shoots me an equally dirty look in return and strides off out of the room.

Feeling extremely clever with myself and rather jubilant to have Ross all to myself finally, I hold his hands and start to dance. There's nobody else up dancing with us at this point, but I don't care. I'm high on life after my singing accomplishment and pleased as punch that I didn't make a fool of myself. It's Christmas soon, and I'm currently alone on the dance floor with the most handsome man in the room. I'm practically oozing happiness from every pore and expressing my contentment through my dancing; I boogie with abandon, twirling around and bouncing up and down. Ross is less enthusiastic, I notice, and is currently shuffling back and forth in a rather more stilted fashion — perhaps he's not much of a mover. I guess we can't all be natural performers — but I keep hold of his hands regardless and continue to prance about.

As always tends to happen when someone has done the impossible and courageously ventured onto an empty dance floor, other people, having felt compelled to wait for someone else to make the first move, now feel brave enough to join in, and we are soon accompanied by several others including Vicky, Will, Emma and Adam and together we're all having a total blast.

Well, I am anyway. Intoxicated as I am, I can't help but feel Ross is not enjoying the dancing as much as the rest of us. His face has a sort of pained expression on it. Perhaps I'm imagining it, I reason with myself. After all, I am quite sozzled, and my eyesight is getting rather blurry.

We carry on busting moves and dominating the dance floor, and a short while later, a slow song comes on. Thrilled to bits to be opposite Ross at this opportune moment, I thank my lucky stars, give him my sexiest smile, and throw my arms around his neck.

"This is nice, isn't it?" I say, looking into his eyes. He doesn't answer but stares back at me, and we lock eyes, and I feel his hands rest hesitantly on my hips. In a sudden fit of drunken induced bravery, I lean forward and kiss him full on the lips. I've imagined a moment like this quite a few times over the last few months, and granted, the location is usually different, and we're not surrounded by as large an audience as this, but I don't care.

The kiss doesn't disappoint. His mouth feels both firm and soft at the same time, and there's the faint taste of something sweet on his lips like sherry or rum. Mmm, I could get used to this. It's all over far too quickly, though, as, all of a sudden, I'm aware of him pulling back, extricating himself from my arms and making his excuses to leave. He says something about needing to visit the gents but not to worry as he'll be back soon. Puzzled initially, but on hearing it's only a quick toilet trip, I tell him it's not a problem, and I promise to wait right here on the spot for him.

I'm feeling very tired from all the dancing and rather dopey from my earlier inadvertent cocktail consumption, but I'm so contented with having spent such a nice time with Ross that I'm happy to stay exactly where I am, eyes closed, swaying from side to side while I wait for his return.

It seems to take forever for him to come back, so I open my eyes to see if I can see him. Big mistake, the room seems to have turned into a ship and is now strangely rolling from left to right, making me feel somewhat ill. As it's a slow dance, the masses have left the floor except for people with partners, and I'm now slightly aware of other couples looking at me and whispering to each other so I quickly reassure them that all is well, that I'm simply waiting for my dance partner to return from the toilets. I'm feeling a little self-conscious, though, and I'm not totally sure, but I think I can hear some stifled mumblings and the possible sounds of people tittering about something, so I'm extremely thankful when after what seems like a complete age, I feel a hand in mine pull gently, turning me and guiding me off the dance floor and towards the door.

"Ah finally, you're back," I say, relieved, allowing myself to be pushed from behind through the crowd and out of the pub.

As we step outside, the cold air hits me full in the face, and I falter for a second or two and steady myself by grabbing onto the door frame. Everything just feels so much hard work suddenly. My legs start to buckle, and I have the awful sensation I'm about to hit the deck. Strong arms envelop me, however, and lead me across the car park, and soon enough, we've reached a car door, and I'm being eased into the passenger seat. My clutch is placed on my lap, and I lean back against the headrest. Comfortable and unable to resist the temptation of closing my eyes, I'm vaguely aware of someone reaching across me and fastening my seat belt.

I must doze off for a few seconds as the sound of the car engine starting up jolts me awake, and I come to briefly, but I just can't keep my eyes open any more, so I settle back and allow them to close again. I figure Ross must have noticed I'm a little bit sloshed, for want of a better word and has decided to drive me home like a true gentleman. He's so thoughtful! We edge over the gravel and out of the car park, and remembering that I don't tend to travel well after drinking, I luckily have the presence of mind to ask him to drive as slowly as possible so as not to make me feel sick.

We set off on the ridiculously short journey through the village, which normally I would walk with ease. I'm so grateful for the car, though, as I would never have made it back on foot in my heels and the way I'm currently feeling. The icky sensation in my stomach is bubbling away worryingly, though, and I don't think I'm going to last very long if we continue at this snail's pace.

"Erm, do you think you could drive a little faster please?" I ask politely. I feel the speed pick up a little, but the movement of the car makes me feel even worse.

"Ooh no, slow down, slow down, oh God, brake!" I groan, feeling positively awful, nausea rising up inside me. I feel the car instantly slow, but the braking motion sets me off again.

"Oh God, don't brake! Go faster...! Not that fast, brake! Ooh jeez, stop braking or I'm gonna be sick!"

I hear muttering, and I'm not fully certain, but I think I make out the words, "Make up your bloody mind, woman!"

I open the window and rest my head on the edge of the car door. I'm absolutely freezing, but the hot air from the car heater is making my head feel really groggy. I'm seconds away from throwing up, but I'm using every ounce of willpower I have to hold it all down. I do not want to vomit in Ross' car — I don't think I'd ever live down the shame. I'm not entirely convinced I haven't been dribbling down the outside of the car door, but I'm hoping he won't notice that.

Moments later, we arrive home, and feeling like I'm about to hurl the entire contents of my stomach — Christmas dinner and the trimmings included — all over the foot-well, I roll out of the car onto my hands and knees as fast as I can and take several deep breaths.

After a minute or two, I manage to stand, and feeling slightly less vomitous now that I'm back in the fresh air, but with a pounding headache only eased by me keeping my eyes firmly shut, I find I'm able to stagger into the cottage with Ross' expert handling.

Once inside, I slowly drag myself up the stairs to the bathroom. There's a vile taste in my mouth from the bile that has been threatening to escape, so I reach into the cabinet, take out the mouthwash and swirl around a quick slosh of lovely minty liquid to freshen up my mouth. I'm so tired, and my head is throbbing badly now from all the movement, so I stumble to my bedroom and collapse onto my bed, closing my eyes and willing the pain to ease. I'm aware of familiar sounds around me, such as curtains closing, lights switching off, and what sounds like a glass of water being placed on my bedside table, so I gather Ross has followed me up and is kindly helping me, but I'm far too out of it to open my eyes and look at him.

I'm totally aware that I'm in a bit of a drunken stupor now, and I'm disappointed not to be able to take advantage of his being here in my own home and stay up to enjoy his company for longer, but I am so exhausted that sleep seems the only real option and so very, very appealing.

I mumble my thanks, raise my head as best I can and pucker my lips for another kiss, longing to feel him close again and relive the magic of our time together on the dance floor. There's a small agonising wait, and then I feel his fingers softly lift my chin and then the gentle pressure of his mouth on mine as he tenderly kisses me goodnight. It's a fleetingly brief touch, and it feels so different from earlier when I kissed him fervently as we slow danced. My brain is struggling to process everything now, though, but I know one thing for sure, I'm bloody grateful I thought to use the mouthwash moments earlier. Wouldn't want him kissing me with my breath smelling like a badger's arse.

He slowly pulls away, and I let my head sink back into the soothing folds of my pillow and begin to slip into blissful slumber. As I drift off, I try my hardest to hold onto the wondrous memory of his lips brushing mine and the delicious vanilla scent of his aftershave wafting over me, soothing my senses.

Chapter Nine

Late next morning, I wake with the most horrendous pain in my head and sickly feeling in my stomach. The corners of my mouth are scabby and crusty, and my eyes seem to be glued shut with the smudged remains of last night's mascara. Slowly and painfully, I prise them open and try to focus my vision.

Sunlight is pouring through my crappy paper-thin curtains, and I make a promise to splash out on some funky new blackout blinds as my Christmas present to myself the next time I'm online. It's too painful to keep my eyes open, so I immediately shut them tight again and lie still for a moment, willing the sun to bugger off. Being a stubborn sod, however, and intent on causing me discomfort, it remains firmly in place, streaming into my room with what feels like the intensity of a nuclear laser beam. Fine, I think, I don't need to get up anyway. It's the weekend, so I can just lie here until night time and then get up when it's dark.

Except now, my own sodding backstabbing body has decided to join forces with the sun and is telling me by way of a bulging bladder ache that it's time to get up and go for a wee.

"Aarrgghh, gang up on me then why don't you. Can't you see I'm suffering?" I whinge out loud, regretting it instantly as I try to cope with the effect that the sound of my voice has on my splitting headache.

After another few minutes of persistent bladder pain, I can't ignore it any longer, and so accepting defeat and keeping my eyes firmly closed, I slowly start to lift my head from the pillow and feebly push myself up into a sitting position.

"Ow, ow, bloody ow! Oooh, it hurts so much!" I whimper, but knowing I'm fighting a losing battle with my treacherous bladder, I persevere, edging out of bed and hobbling to the bathroom. The pain seems ten times worse when I attempt to straighten up and walk normally, so I stay hunched over, feeling my way as I go like a blind and crippled old hag. I'd laugh at my pitiful sorry state if it weren't so excruciating, but I'm doing all I can just to stay on my feet and reach the toilet.

Once there, I sit bent forward with my head in my hands, groaning while the pain in my bladder eases, but the pounding in my head intensifies from the effort of the journey. I haven't felt this bad in years. It must be alcohol-induced; that's pretty obvious, but what I must have been drinking to end up in this state is a complete mystery. I rack my brains to work out why I'm feeling so dreadful and try hard to recall the events of last night. Try as I might, though, I can't remember a thing. Maybe it'll come back to me later when I've recovered from this heinous hangover. I figure my brain considers digging around in my memory bank as completely unnecessary right at this minute and just won't allow a task of such magnitude, choosing instead to focus on basically doing all it can just to keep me alive. I realise it's a bit like when you're dehydrated and your brain makes the executive decision to shut down all other non-essential actions, forcing you to conk out for a while so that it can concentrate on its core functions like breathing and keeping the blood pumping.

I sit there lost in thought, marvelling at the impressive capabilities of the human body, and it's only when I notice my toes are tingling from pins and needles, having had my legs pressed into the toilet seat for so long, that I realise I need to get a grip on my wandering thoughts and get moving again. After all, as remarkable as the finer workings of human anatomy are, my appreciation of them is hardly paramount at this precise moment in time, and what I actually need is to get off the bloody bog and crawl back into my bed and die.

I manage it back to bed without incident and allow myself another forty-five minutes of lying dead to the world tucked safely away under my duvet and blocking out the evil sights and sounds of the day, denying any existence of outside life.

Before long though, my ever-operational tummy juices kick in, rumbling and gurgling, and I'm driven from my sanctuary once again, this time in need of food and medication. I'm experiencing that strange sensation of feeling both sick and hungry at the same time, and I'm torn between heading back to the bathroom to spew my guts up and venturing into the kitchen to eat. I decide that attempting to keep down some breakfast will be distinctly more pleasurable than throwing up, and I painstakingly make my way downstairs in search of food.

What I need right now is stodge. I grab a slice of bread, a bourbon biscuit and two painkillers from the cupboard, and with trembling hands, somehow manage to pour myself a small glass of water. I shuffle into the living room and collapse onto the couch. My headache launches into a renewed assault in protest of all the movement, and I sit there for a moment, paralysed with pain. Remaining motionless does the trick, and after a few minutes, the throbbing eases, and I'm able to take the tablets with a few sips of water. I tentatively nibble away at the bread and biscuit combo and sit very, very still.

Thankfully this simple method works a treat, and after a short while, the migraine has lessened, the shakes have subsided, and I'm actually starting to feel human again.

"Never again! I'm never drinking ever again!" I whimper resolutely, knowing full well I've said this many times before and will no doubt find myself saying it again at some point in the future.

Acknowledging that I still need several more minutes before I can contemplate doing anything requiring energy, such as standing up and moving rooms again, I remain sitting there on the couch zombified, staring into space, just happy to be holding my food down and not in any more pain. I'm not really sure how long I remain this way, but I'm jolted out of my comatose state by the muffled sound of my mobile ringing.

It takes me a while to realise what it is and that it requires my attention, so by the time I've fathomed out that I actually need to first find it and then answer it, the ringing has stopped. After a brief pause giving me time to galvanise myself into action, it starts up again, and I stand up gingerly, scanning the room, trying to work out where it could be coming from.

Through the open living room door, I spot my bag in the hallway at the foot of the stairs and realise the ringing must be coming from inside. I manage to get to it before it goes to voicemail this time and see Vicky's name flashing at me impatiently on the lock screen. I swipe the green arrow, croak a raspy hello, and then sink down onto the bottom step and lean against the wall.

"Ah, so you're alive then!" she booms down the line.

"Jeez, not so loud Vics, please," I plead. "I'm somewhat delicate today."

"I bet you bloody are!" she replies, laughing, although in a much softer voice, thankfully. "Had yourself a bit too much to drink last night didn't you, hun? How are you? Have you been sick yet?"

"Managed to avoid it so far, although I wouldn't be surprised if the likelihood of it happening returns at some point so I'd very much love to change the subject if you don't mind."

"Sure, sure. Listen, I know how you're feeling. You and I both know I've been in the same situation many times before. Can I do anything to help? I could come round and look after you for the day if you like. There's not much going on at 'Doggy HQ' today as most of the owners are already off work for Christmas so I'm sure Will can manage without me for a few hours."

"No, no, honestly, thanks for the offer, Vicky, but I think I'll be fine in a bit. Just gotta wait it out really, haven't I? It's just a hangover, it'll pass eventually," I muster like a brave soul.

"All right, well just take it easy though, won't you? You really were quite sozzled last night! Entertaining as always Sam but off your bloody face! Do you remember much of it?"

"Erm, not really, no. I remember the meal obviously and chatting with everyone and then it all gets a bit hazy from that point on. I don't suppose you could fill me in, could you?" I ask her, wavering a little as I reflect that it might actually be better if I don't know what exactly went on. Vicky spends the next few minutes taking great delight in describing the evening's events. She provides me with all the gory details of my drunken antics, from my enthusiastic Abba impressions to my over-familiarity with Ross on the dance floor. I cringe as I hear of my brazen assault, thrusting myself at him, and in her words, 'snogging his face off'.

As she's explaining it all, my memory finally kicks in, and much of it comes flooding back to me in fragments of disconnected images flashing in and out of my head, allowing me to piece them together bit by bit. I am mortified and sit there in complete silence, too embarrassed to speak.

"Are you still there, Sam?" Vicky asks. "You haven't fallen unconscious from alcohol poisoning, have you?"

"Yep, still here, more's the pity," I moan back. "Think it might just be better if I curl up into a ball and die, though, don't you? Oh God, Vics! How am I going to ever face him again after throwing myself at him like that? And everyone else too. I obviously made a mahoosive tit of myself. What must they all think? Was it awful to watch, Vicky, like really, really awful?"

"No, of course not. It was quite sweet how you kissed him actually, even if it was short lived. I think it was a bit of a shock for him though, Sam, I mean a nice one, obviously, but you know, I don't think he was really expecting it and—"

"Nooo, stop!" I interrupt. "No more please, I've heard enough. I can't take the shame of it any longer. I'm going to go upstairs, get myself washed and dressed and pretend none of it ever happened. Thanks for calling, Vicky, and for helping me remember, and I really am so sorry for being such a wally last night."

"Don't be silly. You were fine honestly. We've all been there, so no one will think ill of you, and if they do, they can come and have a word with me." Bless her beautiful soul, my wonderfully loyal friend. "Go on then, go get yourself sorted and I'll see you at Emma and Adam's for our Christmas eve celebrations with the rest of the gang," she adds quickly before I put the phone down.

"Oh God, Vicky! I'd forgotten about that. I don't know if I'll still be alive by then," I moan.

"Don't be silly, you'll be right as rain, and listen, you don't have to drink if you don't want to, if you're not feeling up to it."

"Okay, I'll be there, but only if there's absolutely no alcohol involved, well for me anyway. You guys can drink what you like! Promise me, Vicky, promise you won't let me get into this state again. It's your duty as my friend to look after me and stop me from doing foolish things that I'll only regret afterwards. In fact, I don't even know why I'm talking to you right now, you cretin, seeing as you did such a poor job of it, last night."

Vicky laughs, we say our goodbyes, and I summon the strength to drag myself upstairs to have a shower. Grubby and stinky but extremely weary from both the alcohol abuse and the emotional turmoil of discovering I'm a sexual predator, though, I can't quite face the physical requirements of a shower yet, so I settle for a soothing hot bath instead.

The soak does wonders for my condition, and I soon start feeling much better. The trouble is, as the water washes away the make-up and grime, and the steam clears my senses, my foggy head starts to clear, allowing more details of last night to resurface. I can now also remember being led away from the dance floor, helped into a car, and then put to bed like a right boozed-up lush. I thank my lucky stars that I didn't recall that little nugget when I was on the phone with Vicky. She'd have been able to tell straight away that I'd clocked something, and she'd have found a way to force it out of me. It's bad enough it simply happened, let alone anyone else finding out about it. Even without her knowing, though, I'm burning with the shame of it all so much that I could sit here for hours with the warm water turning freezing cold, and I doubt I'd even notice.

With wrinkly fingers and toes, I pull out the plug, get out and dry myself with a towel. Wanting to apply my body lotion to my dehydrated skin but finding I'm still too wobbly to perch on the edge of the bath as normal, I decide it would be much safer to sit on my bed instead, so I grab the bottle and head into the bedroom.

Crabby and depressed, I'm haphazardly slapping the cream all over my legs when its strong vanilla aroma causes another shard of memory to pierce its way into my mind, lifting my mood in an instant and proving to me that not all my recollections from last night are necessarily bad.

It's a glorious, sweet gem of a memory. A crystal-clear flashback of me lying down in bed, eyes closed, surrendering to the call of sleep, as *he... kisses... me!* Realising this changes everything and that Ross couldn't possibly have been as scared off by my impulsive dance floor grope as I first feared, I allow myself a small smile for the first time since waking up. And seeing as I've got absolutely nothing of any importance whatsoever to do today, I flop back down on the bed, wriggle under the covers once again and submit to a few more lazy hours of dozing, all the while replaying the blissful memory of that kiss — *his* kiss — over and over in my mind.

A few days later, fully recovered from the hangover and with a renewed sense of festive excitement, I hotfoot it round to Emma's flat for our Christmas eve get together. Everybody's there, Vicky, Will, Adam and also some other friends of Emma's from a cycling group she belongs to. I'm true to my word, and the whole time I'm there, not an ounce of alcohol passes my lips.

Despite the lack of booze for me, it's a fun evening with lots of laughing and silly game playing; however, I do unfortunately have to suffer the obligatory mickey-taking session regarding my highly amusing drunken antics from the night of the party. There's no getting away from it, and I have no choice but to take it all on the chin. It doesn't last long, though, and soon it's old news, and we've moved on to other exciting developments such as a new guy on the scene for Emma.

In typical Emma fashion, never able to do anything without some sort of drama, she informs us of her new relationship by introducing her new boyfriend to us all right there and then. The little devil that she is has kept it secret from us all for a few months and has chosen tonight to spill the beans. We're all a little stunned, to say the least, but absolutely over the moon for her. He's a lovely chap called Leo who she met one weekend at cycle club and bonded with through their mutual love of biking.

We learn how they have enjoyed each other's company during several insanely early Saturday morning bike rides racking up the miles touring the local countryside. Leo stands by Emma's side, and they hold hands as they describe their first few encounters. They amuse us with funny tales involving punctures and ill-fitting Lycra and how one time after zooming down a steep hill, Emma didn't change gears quickly enough on the way back up, causing her chain to break under the strain and rendering her bike totally unrideable. The rest of the group rode on, but they were practically in the middle of nowhere, and Leo refused to leave Emma alone. The two of them spent the next hour and a half walking back to the cycle hut, pushing their bikes alongside them and chatting the whole way, the unplanned hike giving them plenty of time to talk and get to know each other better.

I watch them talking so naturally together and seemingly perfectly in tune with one another, each finishing off the other one's sentences and giggling when they accidentally say the same thing at the same time. They make a really lovely couple, and it is heart-warming seeing how happy she is right now.

I look around at my little group of friends, and I don't know if it's because it's Christmas eve or simply because I'm buzzing from Emma's good news, but I suddenly feel very emotional and thankful for such wonderful friends. I'd do anything for this lot no matter what, and I know without a doubt they would be there for me too. As I mull this over, I happen to lock eyes with Adam, who unknowingly reinforces my sentiment by raising his beer, nodding his head, and flashing me the biggest of friendly smiles.

The big day itself arrives and I gather up my parents' presents, pack them into a bag and drive over to their place to spend the day with them. It seems a bit silly doing this at my age, and I'm extra conscious today more than usual that I'm still living alone, not a boyfriend in sight and having to share Christmas day with my folks rather than all loved up and cosy with a partner or family of my own.

I spend most of the day feeling rather melancholy, and although I do my best to put on an act and hide it from my mum and dad, they soon see through the facade and question why I'm so down in the dumps. It's not easy, but I try to explain why I'm just so fed up with always being on my own.

"I dunno," I begin, "I guess I see happy couples around like Vicky and Will and I can't help but want what they have. You know, companionship and a special connection with one other person. I'm starting to think I'll never find *the one.*"

"Oh, there's plenty of time for that, Samantha," my mum says, putting her arm around my shoulders and trying to comfort me. "You're still so young and think about it, you're actually not the only one around you in such a position. Take Emma for starters, she's not found long lasting love yet either has she, mmm?"

"Well, funny you should bring her up, Mum, as I found out just last night that she's recently got a fantastic new boyfriend and they're clearly made for each other and currently super loved up. So, in actual fact, it's looking more and more like I'll end up the old spinster of the group." I can see that this unexpected revelation somewhat shatters my mum's argument, and she's momentarily at a loss as to what to say next.

"Maybe I need to try something different like online dating," I suggest.

Being in the age group that didn't grow up with much technology in the home and still viewing the internet at times with distrust and fear, my parents see the world of online dating as a frightening concept fraught with risks and danger. The idea of their only child entering into such a world, which, in their eyes, is made up entirely of rapists and serial killers, fills them with utter dread.

I catch my mum shooting my dad a panicked look forcing him to join the conversation and help her out. Never a natural at this sort of thing and probably very much preferring not to be involved in any talk of his daughter's love life, happy to leave such matters to the womenfolk, he clears his throat with a little cough and rather unwillingly and under my mum's penetrating glare, he joins the conversation in his own unique way.

"What's the matter with you Sam? Boys aren't everything. You've still got your legs, haven't you?"

I can't help but laugh. For some unknown reason, this is a favourite saying of my dad's, and I've heard it many a time growing up. Any problem or worry that I had, my dad would always reason that it was never as bad as all that if my legs were still attached to my body. I don't know exactly why he thought there was such a possibility that I could indeed lose my legs so easily. Maybe it's something to do with his generation and needing to be grateful for not living during wartime under the constant threat of being bombed, perhaps. Whatever the reason, he must have thought it a worthy piece of advice at one time and has stuck by it.

Seeing me laugh, he sits back with a triumphant look on his

face assuming the issue has blown over now and his daughter is happy once again. Unfortunately for him, his victory is short-lived, and he receives a sharp rebuke from my mum.

"Really Tony, the legs thing again?" she tuts, shaking her head at him in despair. She takes over again, trying to steer the conversation back on track.

"I think what your father's trying to say is, well, not to worry for starters. You'll be just fine if you don't have a certain somebody in your life for a while and that you mustn't try to rush it. You can't force love, Sam, it's got to come naturally."

Always the voice of reason, my mum, and well-versed at interpreting my dad's kooky phrases. She gives him another pointed look, and he bravely tries again.

"Yes... um... well, your mum's right, Sam. No point going in gung-ho and dating just for the sake of it. You'll end up with a bunch of weirdos and deadbeats and that won't get you anywhere. Bide your time. My daughter deserves a prince, not a frog!"

"Yeah, I guess so," I mumble, smiling at my dad's outdated fairy tale references and feeling like a small child again. I'm unconvinced, however, and determined to wallow despite my parents' wise words.

"I'm just not sure my prince — *nope, too cheesy!* — my *one* is out there and if he is..." all thoughts in my head turning to Ross at this point, "...whether he's fully on board with being with me."

Desperately wanting to help cheer up their only child but pretty much all out of any other logical reasoning or words of wisdom, my parents look at each helplessly. Doing the only thing he can think of to cheer me up whilst staying on the subject, my dad launches into several cringe-worthy stories from when he and my mum were young and courting each other and how love didn't always run smoothly for them. I love hearing them reminisce about their time together as young sweethearts, and although it doesn't solve my problem, it does go some way to cheering me up in the short term.

I try not to dwell, and we end up enjoying a lovely slow-paced day full of scrumptious food, naff Christmas films and old battered board games and later that evening as I sit on my parents' settee laughing with them at the usual festive comedy repeats on the telly, I realise just how lucky I am. I'm still feeling a strong sense of loneliness and longing for a soulmate, but I have a real genuine appreciation for everything else that I have in my life. Amazing friends, loving parents, and as my dad quite rightly pointed out, my legs!

Chapter Ten

December comes to an uneventful and peaceful end, with me opting to forgo any notion of New Year celebrations this year. It's just after nine-thirty p.m. on New Year's Eve, and I'm warm and cosy in my little cottage, happily snuggled up on the couch, feet resting on the footstool. I'm watching endless re-runs of Friends whilst sipping lemonade from a wine glass and munching through a sharing box of Maltesers.

I'm not the only saddo of the group staying in tonight. Vicky and Will are in, too, with a full house of dogs boarding overnight whose owners are all out on the lash enjoying the festivities. Vicky and I spoke earlier in the day when I called to wish them both Happy New Year, and I could hear several of the dogs in the background barking and yapping away, and it honestly sounded like they had the cast of 101 Dalmatians around.

New lovers Emma and Leo have also decided to stay home for the evening together at his place for a couple's date night. Emma, having the heart of gold that she does, did ask me if I wanted to join them, concerned I'd be lonely on my own. I appreciate the sentiment, but the thought of playing gooseberry in such a new relationship is not my idea of a good time, so I politely declined. I'm not really sure what Adam's plans are, but I think Emma mentioned something about him wanting to grab an early night's sleep so he could make the most of the bank holiday tomorrow. He's recently become rather interested in British history apparently, and he's keen to spend the day indoors for once, researching online about ancient artefacts or something or other like that. It seems like a strange way to spend a day off to me, but then each to their own.

I obviously haven't heard anything from Ross since the party, which is to be expected really as I don't think we've ever actually spoken with each other outside of hospice gatherings, so I'm not too bothered by his lack of contact. I'm looking forward to seeing him sometime back at work, though, and I've been spending far too much time reminiscing about our secret kiss and wondering if he's been thinking of it too.

A couple of hours, and several more Friends episodes later, I'm starting to feel sleepy and in danger of nodding off on the couch, but I'm determined to stay up and see in the New Year the old-fashioned way, just like my Nanna always used to. It seems only right with me living here in her former home. I turn off the TV, tidy up the lounge, put my glass and somewhat depleted Malteser box in the kitchen, and walk towards the front door.

There's a few more minutes to go until midnight, so I lean against the wall by the door and scroll through some of the messages I've been sent on my phone. As I do this, I reflect upon my evening and realise that I've actually rather enjoyed myself tonight even though I've been on my tod. In the past, I would have found it strange not to be out partying with friends, and I feel proud of myself for not needing to be surrounded by others or having someone right there with me on such a notable date. I guess growing older is teaching me that actually I *can* be happy on my own at times, and I don't necessarily need someone there twenty-four-seven to feel secure.

I hear the village church bells start to chime and open my door wide to welcome in the new year. Seconds later, having considerably underestimated the chill of the night air, I quickly shut it again, reasoning that a couple of seconds is ample time for the new year to enter. Looking out instead through the small glass panel on the door and gazing at the moon for a brief moment, I ponder my new year's resolutions of exercising more and swearing less and add looking forward to the future with more optimism to the list.

Satisfied with my newfound ability to 'adult' and my positive new outlook on life — and not loving the cold draft I can feel squeezing through the letterbox — I lock the door, turn off the lights and trundle off to bed. As I climb the stairs to the sound of distant fireworks, I feel significantly more relaxed about my current situation than I did on Christmas day and a teensy-weensy bit excited about what this year might have in store for me.

January bulldozes in, predictably grim with its cold, grey days of persistent rain and biting wind. We're teased by the occasional fluttering of snow, but they're mostly disappointing, half-hearted flurries mingled in with sleet, and it's never quite enough of a fall to stick.

During the first few days at work, I knuckle down to organising the new batch of events set to occur over the next few months. The first on the schedule is an annual ten-kilometre run around a large country park a few miles away from Sandlefirth. The name of the event is Ice Dash, so-called due to the difficult wintry weather conditions that typically come to pass when the race takes place.

It's an extremely popular event, baffling me every year by its high turnout. As I understand it, serious runners happily brave these challenging conditions, keen to fit in as many races as they can, building up to the longer courses and marathons later on in spring and summer. Even with having been informed of this, the fact that anyone would willingly choose to don shorts and a vest and leg it around a park for mile after mile in such cold temperatures is completely beyond me!

Race day is on the last Saturday of the month, so I have a couple of weeks left to finish off the final preparations. So far today, I have arranged for numerous volunteers to assist in all sorts of roles such as car park stewards, race marshals and time-keepers. There will also be first aiders on site, although I'm very much hoping they won't be needed or, if they are, that it's only for the odd sprained ankle or out of puff runner.

Due to the outdoor nature of the event and harsh weather conditions, it's a tricky one to man as it takes a certain type of person to cope standing in the cold for so long or lugging heavy boxes of post-race bananas around, for example. Although we have an abundance of kind-hearted, eager hospice volunteers ready to help at the drop of a hat, they do tend to be mostly of the grey-haired, elderly variety. But, as this event is rather hardcore, it's resilient helpers we need on this occasion, so we always tend to be a bit short of assistance on the day.

As often happens with large scale fundraisers, such as this one, other staff members are roped in to lend a hand; otherwise, it would just not be possible to manage the event properly. Emma will be working her magic on the registration stand, signing people in, handing out race numbers and answering any questions. An arduous job in itself as a great many runners arrive tense and nervous and consequently end up acting rather needy and demanding. Emma is more than capable of dealing with them, however, and I have no doubt at all that her confident and jolly manner will have them all feeling calm and reassured and ready to race when the time comes. At the sound of the starter's gun, she will then make her way to the halfway marker, ready to hand out water bottles and energy gels. I've also delegated her the job of hiring a fitness instructor to lead the pre-race warm-up routine along with a willing volunteer to don the costume and play the role of *Penguin,* the official Ice Dash mascot, whose job it is to work alongside the instructor mimicking the exercises and encouraging the crowds to join in.

Adam will also be helping out on the day, and I've assigned him the job of handing out goody bags and participation medals to the runners as they cross the finish line. The plan for me is to stay unattached to any specific task so that I can move around freely overseeing everything and be on hand to step into any unmanned roles or sort any problems that should arise which, in my previous experience as a race organiser, they invariably do.

As is often the case with the first month of the year, some days can seem rather long and dull, especially compared to the business of December, so I try to brighten them up a little with occasional trips to Butterford's cake shop on my way to work, bringing in a different selection of sweet treats for Emma and me to munch on as we plough away at our desks. I always remember to pick up enough for any impromptu volunteer visits or other members of staff popping into our rooms, and I like to let Adam know so he can come in and grab one when he's on a break. It's always nice when he nips in and has a chat for five minutes between jobs. I know he appreciates the quick sugar fix and a warm up by the radiator before heading back outside again.

These little moments are so simple but very effective in breaking up the long drag of January, and together with a busy schedule and a steady flow of work, the rest of the month goes by relatively quickly. Powered by our love of the hospice and copious amounts of sugar, we all work hard, and when Ice Dash day arrives, the whole team is ready and raring to go.

Emma and I travel to the venue together, regroup with the volunteers in the car park, and then wait for Adam to arrive with the events trailer, which is loaded with essential supplies and equipment such as portable tables, camping chairs, runner information packs, two-way radios and Hi-Viz jackets.

As expected, the weather doesn't deviate from past form and could be accurately described as Baltic. In fact, that would be putting it rather mildly. I'm dressed in precisely eight layers of clothing, including a full set of thermals and several fleecy jumpers, and I look like a big fat potato or when actors wear those hilarious fat suits to make them seem larger than they actually are, and even in all that garb, I'm still freezing my tits off!

I brief the helpers, ensuring everyone knows their role and where they need to be, and with immaculate timing, Adam arrives just as I'm rounding off, and we all muck in unloading the provisions and setting up.

Whilst we're preparing the various stations, competitors turn up in their droves. It's a sight to behold with revealing spandex and Lycra all over the place, complete with an obscene amount of unfortunate, unsightly bulges. I try as best as I can to avert my eyes from these disturbing visions, but much like with car crashes and accidents, I often find myself drawn to them and then unable to look away.

It's not all young athletes, as one would assume for a sporting event such as this either. There are all types taking part, from elite runners to complete newbies, some who look like this is the first time they've ever put on a pair of trainers, let alone completed a ten-kilometre race in the freezing cold. I recognise many of the usual participants from previous years and smile at the familiar faces as they hover in groups, discussing race techniques and comparing PBs. As always, I can't help but feel a pang of sympathy for the shell-shocked first-timers who stand horrified, shivering in the freezing cold wearing only the thinnest, stretchiest of outfits, wondering what on earth they have signed themselves up for.

We finish setting up, and Emma and two volunteers take their position at the enrolment table to deal with the queue of keen competitors that has already formed and is starting to snake its way around the park. So far, the preparations are going well with everything in hand, so there's not much I can do now before the race starts. I take the opportunity of a five-minute breather and grab a quick snack from the park kiosk. The heavy lifting of all the tables and gazebos has taken it out of me a little, so I choose a chocolate bar and a can of full-fat Coca Cola to give me the necessary sugar boost and caffeine kick.

I'm reclining on one of the camping chairs in the corner of the main event tent, my feet resting on a box of spare running vests, happily munching away on my calorific goodies when the fitness instructor for the warm-up chooses that exact moment to walk in. I recognise his face in an instant and am mortified to see it's none other than Max, the obnoxious trainer from my mortifying gym induction. Of all the moments for him to arrive, he picks this one! I think to myself incredulously.

He slowly surveys the scene in front of him, taking it all in, starting from my horizontal position in the chair to the half-eaten chocolate bar in one hand and the can of fizzy pop in the other. His eyes skim the length of my fat suit body and then return to settle on my horrified face. I'm pretty sure I see a glint of judgement flash across his smug expression before he pipes up and introduces himself.

"Hi, I'm Max, your warm-up instructor for the race." He

pauses briefly before furrowing his brows slightly and adds, "You look very familiar. Do I know you from somewhere?"

Hurriedly dropping the rest of my snack and drink into a rubbish bag on the floor, I leap up out of the chair and stand up as straight as possible, brushing flakes of chocolate off me and attempting to flatten down my gazillion layers. I try my best to erase the image of a lazy blob idling on her backside, shoving calories down her throat, and hopefully replace it with one where I look as if I might just belong at an active event like this.

"Hi, Max, did you say?" My childish pride takes over as I pretend to be unsure of his name and hence deny any recollection or significance of his existence.

Seemingly undeterred, however, he replies, "Yes, yes, I remember now. Didn't you come in for a new member induction a few months ago? You wanted to get rid of your… erm—" The memory of his previous pregnancy weight blunder suddenly dawns on him, causing him to falter and stumble over his words mid-sentence, keen to avoid the same mistake. "—Your erm… extra pounds." Composing himself after his little slip, his overabundant self-assuredness returning once again, he adds, "I wondered where you'd got to. Figured you'd decided it was too much effort, given up on exercising and cancelled your membership."

Feeling my anger begin to bubble and wondering if just once it might be possible to have a conversation with this guy and *not* want to smack him in the face, I take a deep breath and remember I'm here in a professional capacity on behalf of the hospice and that perhaps it wouldn't be the best move to punch our specialist help in the jaw no matter how thoughtless and upsetting his comments are.

"Oh right, that was you, was it?" I ask, continuing my little dig of not knowing who he is. "No, not given up, not at all. Just been rather busy with work, that's all," I add, pleased with my restraint.

"Sure, sure, well if you find you have some time on your hands again and want to give it another try, just pop back in and we'll get cracking. You might want to rethink your diet though," he adds with a little nod to the bin bag containing my snack wrapper and drinks can. "All that sugar's not great for weight loss you know. Those extra rolls won't shift with exercise alone, I'm afraid."

Dumbfounded by just how tactless one person can be and biting my lip hard to stop me from unleashing a well-justified tirade of abuse on him, I take a deep breath, rearrange my face into a smile and lead him out of the tent to show him where he'll be performing his warm-up. I've had just about as much as I can take of this idiot with his careless remarks and holier-than-thou attitude, and I want shot of him.

"Thanks for coming, Max. I'll show you where to set up," I say with the control of a saint, pointing over to the raised grassy knoll by the start line.

"Great stuff!" he replies, no hint of perception on his face that his stinging words have wounded me yet again. "Don't forget to send your polar bear over in time for my instructions."

"I'm sorry, what now?"

"Your polar bear! Your costume thingy... to help with the routine. When I spoke on the phone with the lady who booked me for this event, I explained the need for a helper, and she assured me your race mascot would be available to lend a hand. I do hope you've got someone fit and healthy who won't have trouble keeping up with the moves," he says, looking me up and down as if to suggest that person can't possibly be someone as fat and out of shape as me.

Knowing better than to rise to it but unable to stop myself, I hear myself reply with, "*I'm* actually the mascot for today and I'm sure I'll be more than capable of keeping up with a few warm-up exercises."

The words sound confident, but my mind is screaming at me: what are you doing, you daft cow? You're letting him get to you. Rise above it, woman! It seems my mouth and my mind have most definitely parted ways, however, and I find myself continuing on in the same vein, saying the exact opposite of what I know I should, in fact, be saying.

"Give me a moment to find my costume and I'll be right there," I assure him with as much authority as I can muster. "Oh, and by the way, it's a penguin, not a polar bear."

"I'll show him… the sanctimonious tosspot!" I mutter immaturely under my breath as I storm off towards the registration stand to speak to Emma.

I march up to her with a face like thunder, and on noticing immediately that something's wrong, she excuses herself and steps aside to see what the matter is.

"I need the penguin suit, Emma. Do you know where it is?" I bark grumpily, still fuming from my interaction with Max.

"Sure, it's just here under the table. I was waiting for a lull in the registrations so I could take it to one of the younger volunteers to wear. Are you okay, Sam? You look like you want to murder someone!" she asks worriedly.

"I'm fine, I just had to endure a conversation with that odious excuse of a man over there. You do realise you only went and booked that self-righteous plonker from my gym induction, don't you?" I snap, practically biting her head off as I struggle to control my emotions.

126

"Oh, God, no! I'm so sorry, Sam. I didn't think to check when I booked it. I take it he remembered you, then? Has he been a complete arse again?"

"You could say that. Long story short, he was more than happy to point out that he doesn't think anyone as obese as me could be at all capable of keeping up with his poxy little fitness routine, so I somehow ended up telling him that he's got nothing to worry about seeing as *I'm* the mascot for today and I am wholly competent in matching his moves. I mean, how hard can it be? A few jumping jacks and knee bends and we're warmed up, surely."

"Oh, Sam, this is all my fault. Again, I'm so sorry for bringing him here. If only I'd thought to check his name with you first."

It's clear to see how guilty she feels, and I know it was an innocent mistake on her part, so I quickly apologise for snapping and reassure her that everything's okay.

"Listen, no harm done. It's all peachy, Em, really. I just have to put the outfit on and jump up and down for a few minutes that's all. That should show that irritating little fool, and you know as well as I do that shit happens and this is exactly why I stay unassigned to any particular role on the day, so I can jump in and sort out any unexpected issues. Do me a favour though and radio through to that volunteer to let them know they won't be needed after all and ask them to help some of the others instead, will you? Then come and give me a hand to get this blasted costume on," I say as I drag it out from under the table.

As we lug the disconcertingly large and heavy penguin outfit across the grass, slipping and sliding on the mud and almost dropping it a couple of times, I allow my anger to subside a little and find myself on the verge of giggling. Emma, feeling the same but not wanting to show it in case I'm still upset, is trying hard to keep a straight face. We make the fatal mistake of looking at each other, and soon we're sniggering like naughty school kids.

"Oh my God, what the hell is this thing made of?" I exclaim in between laughs. Reaching the row of portaloos but realising instantly we're not going to fit in a standard one-person cubicle, we head to the disabled loo and somehow manage to squeeze both the costume and us inside.

Several minutes later, after much grappling, wrestling, and howling with laughter, we emerge from the cubicle. Emma looks somewhat frazzled and beaten but still in human form at least, and I, hidden beneath layers of black and white fluff and mesh, am one wholly unmistakeable, humongous jumbo penguin!

"I can't see a bloody thing!" I exclaim to Emma whilst peering through the tiniest of eye holes inside the giant wobbling mask.

"Who cares?" she cries. "Sight's overrated. You look amazing!"

"Erm, I think you'll find being able to see where I'm going might be just a tad more important," I reply sarcastically, but before I can moan any more, Emma takes my flipper and starts leading me over to the section cordoned off for the mass warm-up. It is insanely difficult to move in such a massive costume, and every step requires great effort to lift up each heavy foot in turn and then swing it around and forward whilst at the same time keeping my balance on the other foot. I'm knackered just from the short journey over and seriously starting to wonder what I've got myself into.

Emma deposits me in front of the already gathered and patiently waiting crowd. She wishes me good luck, pats me on the back, and moves to the side out of harm's way. I can hear her laughing, but I've lost sight of her as I can only see anything that is directly in front of me and even then, it's only about twenty-five per cent of the full image, so I'm far too nervous to twist to the side in case I lose my balance and topple over.

I'm seriously contemplating sacking the whole thing off and abandoning my plan of proving my point to that narcissistic cad when I hear him approach, bellowing enthusiastic instructions to the crowd through his headset, his irritating voice reverberating through the speakers and across the park.

He grabs hold of me, and muffling his mic, he whispers, "Right, just do what I do, follow my lead and try to keep up if you can." He says this with such disdain, it's exactly the stimulus I need, and with my resolve to prove him wrong fully returned, I immediately ditch any plans of doing a runner and brace myself for action.

The music starts, and Max launches into action, throwing himself energetically from side to side and forwards and backwards at great pace. I do my best to follow his every move, but the costume is so cumbersome there's almost a delay with every single move I make. Each limb weighs a ton, and as soon as I manage to get the necessary body part raised and then coordinate each component into the correct position, that particular manoeuvre has finished, and he's on to the next one.

Despite the freezing temperature, it's sweltering inside the costume, and I'm sweating like a pig. I can feel sweat droplets trickling down my neck and cleavage, and I'm already painfully out of breath. The lack of vision I had originally is further compounded by the steam of my hot breath fogging up the plastic lenses of the penguin's eyes and I've completely lost my bearings and now have no idea which way I should be facing.

Determined not to fail and prove Max right, I press on,

knowing I'd rather drop down dead trying than give him the satisfaction of giving up. Deciding I'd be much better off ditching Max's unrealistic routine and doing my own thing, I stop bouncing around like an idiot and stand still on the spot instead, performing a series of stretches I've seen people do over the years. I find this remarkably much easier to achieve and spend the next few songs reaching, lunging, extending, and sweeping. I lean forward, swinging my flippers alternatively from toe to toe and then move onto bending them at the elbow and placing them on my middle, twisting my waist around to the left and then the right.

I carry on like this, coming up with different moves every few minutes and find that this is much more pleasant, and I actually start to enjoy myself whilst feeling the benefit of the controlled and rhythmical stretches. I may look like a six-foot penguin on the outside, but I feel like a lusty, bendy babe on the inside.

I can't see for toffee, but I can hear well enough, and I pick up on the crowd starting to chant something. I realise they're shouting my name, well, not *my* name exactly, but rather "Penguin, penguin, penguin," over and over. I wipe the fake eyes with the tips of my flippers and can just about make out a disconsolate looking Max standing on the side of the area, arms folded, being ignored by the group, every single one of them having turned away from him and his overly exuberant routine and now happily following my lead instead.

Their adoration fuels me, and I carry on entertaining the hordes with umpteen different comical positions for a good while longer. Embarrassed that no one's paying him any attention, Max sidles off, leaving me the sole centre of attraction. "Ha, how d'you like that then Maxy boy? They love *me*, not you!" I declare triumphantly, watching him walk away defeated. He can't hear me, but it feels good to say it, nonetheless.

The music comes to an end, and after several hugs and high fives, the runners leave and head on over to take their positions at the starting line. Emma rushes over and helps me ease the mask off.

"That was bloody brilliant, Sam!" she gushes. "You were so funny to watch, a great big penguin doing all those funny stretches and poses like a human being. You really got people following and copying you. Did you hear them chanting?"

"I did," I reply, smiling. "But, more importantly, I think I showed *Mister Loves Himself* over there that just because he's some brawny fitness freak and I'm just a lowly overweight penguin with a fat head, it doesn't mean he's any better than me, even if I couldn't quite keep up with his moves in the end. It's sad to think that, even though I'm the one standing here in this ridiculously gigantic costume, his big fat egotistical swell head is still infinitely bigger than mine!"

With Emma's arm hooked around my enormous flipper, we slowly waddle back to the tent, laughing and rejoicing all the way.

Thanks to the help of everybody involved, the rest of the event unfolds without a single hitch. Happy runners leave positive feedback, and I feel immensely relieved to have completed another great fundraiser for the hospice.

As I finish packing up my car with any extra gubbins that won't fit in the trailer, I glance at the donation buckets resting on the back seat, knowing that, along with the runners' entry fees and any further sponsorship we may receive, we'll have a nice tidy sum to add to Green Meadow's bank account. Another job well done.

Chapter Eleven

The feeling of elation from our recent accomplishment is unfortunately far too fleeting as, the very next day, probably down to both the cold weather and physical exertion, I come down with some sort of nasty flu type virus and end up spending most of February really quite poorly.

The illness takes a strong hold, and I snuffle, wheeze, and cough, hour after hour, without a hint of improvement for days. I take some time off work to recuperate and lose several days to falling in and out of sleep, alternating between bouts of hot, feverish flashes and uncontrollable body shivers. Each night, I go to bed early, wrapped up warm and rattling with painkillers, hoping to God that I will wake the next morning feeling better than the one before, but it never seems to happen.

Fed up to the back teeth of spending each waking moment feeling like death warmed up, I try out all manner of self-help methods, such as leaning over bowls of steaming water to clear my sinuses and drinking hot toddies to soothe my burning throat, but nothing seems to help, and as the weeks pass by and the desperation creeps in, I even give a few old wives tales a go, no matter how strange they seem, in the vain hope that they will help me recover. I reach my lowest point one day as I apply rashers of raw bacon to the front of my neck in a bid to cure my sore throat and rub onion all over my chest in a futile attempt to clear the mucus from my lungs. Needless to say, they don't work, and I simply add, 'stinking like a pig in a compost heap' to my list of complaints.

By week three, the bodily aches and pains eventually start to ease, and I find I'm strong enough to venture back into work. It's a quiet time events-wise, thankfully, so I shut myself and my stinky germs away in my office and struggle away at my desk in pitiful solitude, not really feeling up to seeing anyone, and equally, with nobody wanting to spend much time with me either, understandably. I tell Emma to stay away and keep to her own room, knowing she can call or email me with anything workwise while I focus all my efforts on upcoming events with special attention to the Easter fete in April. Emma and Vicky both phone me regularly to check how I'm doing and to make sure I haven't shuffled off this mortal coil.

Against my advice, Adam pops in regularly to bring me mugs of hot chocolate and interesting news stories from the outside world, but I'm too worried I'll inadvertently infect him as he breathes my contaminated air, so I never really let him stay for long. It's so lovely of him to make the effort, though, to keep me feeling cheerful and sane while I'm at death's door, and it means a lot to know I'm not totally forgotten about as I wait out the illness in my solitary confinement.

Luckily, there's been no call for any important trustee meetings lately, and any business that Charles has wanted to discuss has been easy enough to do on the phone rather than face to face. I've resisted the urge to ask after Ross during our conversations, as I haven't wanted to risk Charles putting him on the line should he be there when I call, or, worse, sending him to me in person. I couldn't bear him seeing me in this state with permanently bloodshot and streaming eyes and a nose that insists on tormenting me by flitting between being horrendously stuffed up one minute and uncontrollably runny the next. I look rotten and feel rotten, and I can't honestly remember what life was like pre-virus, when breathing wasn't an effort and wiping away mucus wasn't my only pastime, and I'm longing to be well enough to get outside again and re-join the world of the healthy.

Mind you, the weather is so bleak at the moment, with relentless drizzle and sunless skies, that there's so little happening socially either at the hospice or even out and about in town, so I'm not missing anything. Most people are just concentrating on getting through the winter, hopeful of reaching the other side and the much-anticipated arrival of spring, with its warmer, sunnier days and the potential for more interesting plans.

Today, I'm having a particularly slow day at work, updating the hospice's various databases and trying hard not to make my nose bleed with my incessant sniffing when the receptionist brings up a mysterious looking package with my name on it. It's a brown cardboard box, which in itself is not abnormal; however, my name is written on a white sticky label in large, swirly, purple glitter handwriting, and rather than the conventional brown parcel tape, it's sealed with bright-coloured craft ribbons and decorated with a pretty pink pull bow. On top of this, it lacks any kind of postage markings whatsoever, so I know it must have been hand-delivered.

The receptionist explains how she was away from her desk when it arrived, so she has no idea who it is from and then, not wanting to stay any longer than absolutely necessary to avoid being infected with my germs, she quickly slides it onto my desk and rushes back downstairs to the safety of her pure, non-contagious atmosphere.

The kind of post I receive here normally tends to be pretty boring, run of the mill type letters or invoices, and then there's the usual unsolicited junk mail, such as those freebie catalogues trying to sell me all sorts of weird and wonderful gadgets from battery-powered nose hair clippers to automatic bagel slicers. This, along with the occasional money bag of hard-saved pennies or raffle ticket stubs and cheques from generous donors, is about as exciting as it gets on the mail front, so to receive an unexpected package like this is really rather peculiar.

Seeing as I haven't gone anywhere or done anything remotely interesting for weeks now, I'm really intrigued to open it and find out what's inside. I promptly push aside the ribbons, lift up the cardboard flaps and peek inside to see a lovely assortment of goodies. There are all sorts of get-well gifts, from cold remedies, including throat sweets, decongestant sachets, and packets of painkillers, to lovely little titbits like tissues, powdered soup packets and chocolate bars.

Along with the medicines and food supplies, there are other thoughtful presents, such as a heat-able neck wrap and a hot water bottle, plus a joke book and CD of soothing sounds to aid sleep. It's a veritable treasure chest of drugs, sweet treats and carefully thought-out offerings, and I'm bowled over by the effort that must have gone into it. I carefully lift each item out like a fine art collector unpacking priceless breakables, enjoying the process immensely and wanting to savour the moment for as long as possible.

As I remove the last object from the box, I see a small hand-written note lying on the bottom, which says, *From your number one fans and all who love you at Green Meadow x.* Having felt so poorly and stuck wallowing in my own self-pity for so long, this unexpected, kind act stirs up my emotions big time. My vision clouds, but for once not solely due to the build-up of congestion from this crummy illness but mainly the realisation that those lovely people downstairs, volunteers and patients, each with their own more serious problems, have taken the time to put this lovely gift set together just for me.

Taking a tissue from the new packet — one of those more expensive, fancy ones with softening balm too, as opposed to the cheap sandpaper versions I usually buy — I dab my eyes and vow to go and thank them all in person the very minute I am both germ and snot free again.

I start to see an improvement over the next few days, thanks to the help of my magical little box of cures, and one day right at the end of the month, I finally feel well enough to enter into the land of the living once again. Checking in with the head nurse first to show her I am, in fact, now safe to mingle with the patients, I pop into the day room to give them my thanks.

Always happy to do the talking, Dotty jumps at the chance to explain just how sorry they'd all been feeling for me locked away upstairs, imprisoned in my 'room of sick', all alone and with no one to care for me. I try to take it all in as she gabbles at me full tilt in her own special, rambling way.

"We were having a little volunteer meeting of our own, you see, and someone mentioned how long you'd been ill for, but that you were still making the effort to come to work when so many others would have just stayed at home in bed and then that lovely young, handsome chap, that he is, came up with the idea to make you a treat selection from all of us to try and cheer you up and help you get better faster. As soon as he said it, we all thought straight away what a good idea it was and that we wanted to contribute." Then, lowering her voice to a whisper, she adds proudly, "It was my idea to add in the CD. There's nothing worse than not being able to sleep when you're feeling ill don't you think?"

My pulse racing, I replay her words in her head, focussing

on one phrase in particular — 'that lovely young handsome chap' —, and on hearing that it was a volunteer meeting, I realise that it must be Ross she's on about and hence whose initial idea it was to send me the package. I, for one, certainly can't think of any other volunteer or patient here that fits that description. As much as I love the other old boys, and even with Dotty's somewhat loopy train of thought, I very much doubt she would describe them in such a way as 'young and handsome'.

As it's been so long since I've seen Ross, what with there not being much call for volunteers in January and my illness pretty much taking up the whole of February, I've been starting to think that what happened the night of the Christmas party was all in my head or, worse still, that he simply regretted the kiss and has been doing his best to keep his distance.

But now, with Dotty's thrilling intel, albeit sketchy and possibly unreliable at times, I'm feeling extremely hopeful once again. Just when I was beginning to think things had been way too quiet for him to be genuinely interested, and any notion of him and me was a complete lost cause, he pulls a real whammy like this, something so incredibly thoughtful and kind, and sucks me right back into the game. Oh, my poor, rattled, romantic heart. How much more of this roller coaster ride can it take? I muse, while Dotty continues to prattle on to deaf ears.

March arrives on a bright sunny day, and I say a happy 'good riddance' to my illness riddled February. It's always a bit of a shitty, 'do nothing' month, but I'm extra keen to see the back of it this year. Feeling light and skippy and fully appreciative of my newly restored health, I'm enjoying the simple pleasure of being able to breathe through not just one but both of my nostrils at the same time.

My newfound happiness doesn't last very long, though, before being abruptly shattered a few days later by the tragic news of a patient death at the hospice. One ordinary weekday afternoon, as I sit at my desk and power through my work high spirited and energised like a four-year-old on a doughnut-fuelled sugar kick, I'm interrupted by one of the nursing staff who comes to tell me that our beloved Jim has passed away during his post-lunch, pre-bingo nap.

She gently explains how he didn't suffer and was happily lounging in one of the great big day room armchairs surrounded by his pals. He simply closed his eyes without bother or fuss and quietly, comfortably, and peacefully slipped away.

For the first few moments, I can't quite compute what she is saying, and I sit staring at her, simply too shocked to react. Aware of my close friendship with Jim and knowing how difficult it is for me to fully digest the news, she leaves the room to go and find Emma, to tell her what's happened and to see if she can be of more comfort to me.

Emma arrives and takes over from the nurse, freeing her up to continue her difficult journey through the hospice, alerting unsuspecting others to the terrible news. I'm still too shocked to speak, so Emma simply sits down next to me, takes hold of my hands, and waits for it to properly sink in. And when it does sink in a few minutes later, it hits me hard like a violent punch right in the guts. Jim, my brilliant banter buddy, my honorary Granddad, my friend… has gone.

The crap of the last few weeks of constantly feeling under par has drained me, and with today's added distress and anguish of losing Jim, it suddenly all feels too much to bear. Utterly heartbroken and overwhelmed with grief, I burst into tears. Without words, Emma wraps her arms around me and lets me sob on her shoulder for several minutes. She softly strokes my hair and makes calm, soothing sounds like a mother to a child while I let it all out and bawl like a baby.

Later, my eyes sore from crying, the two of us head down to the day room to sit with the remaining patients and members of staff, and together, united in our grief, we spend the rest of the day quietly mourning the loss of a brilliant character and a much-loved friend.

A week later, the funeral is as expected, a difficult and extremely sad affair, but also very beautiful, with Jim's friends and family taking it in turns to share memories of a life well-lived. Stories are told, tears are shed, and hugs are in abundance as we all do our best to support each other through.

Afterwards, the family go home to grieve in private, and the rest of us return to the hospice and pile into the day room for our own special mini wake and celebration of Jim's life. We read meaningful poems and sing hymns, and as is usual for this lot, put on a good old plentiful spread of food to help distract us from our sorrow and eat our way through the pain.

It's always a strange time when a patient at the hospice passes away. Even though the atmosphere is mainly positive and upbeat most days, the possibility of death is strong for many for obvious reasons, and another life lost brings about the inevitable renewed sense of worry that death could come for any of us at any time and no one is guaranteed another tomorrow.

However, on the other hand, I've found during my time here over the past few years that, despite being clearly rattled by the loss of a cherished member of their community, the older members don't tend to dwell quite as much as you would expect. They seem to accept more readily their departed youth and how much closer to death they are themselves, which in turn gives them a real sense of appreciation for the lives they have had and a real pragmatism in recognising a need to get on with things and enjoy the time they have left.

I see a perfect example of this way of thinking and positive attitude not long into our little function as Emma is whirled about the room by one of the older patients to the tune of an old-fashioned waltz playing loudly on the hi-fi system. Throwing me a bemused look, I'm not sure she has much say in the matter, but as it seems to be making the patient happy, she's going along with it for now.

I, on the other hand, am steering well clear of any dancing activity, and trusting in the old adage of comfort eating and its therapeutic qualities, I am currently coveting the cupcake section of the buffet, wondering which one... or two... to pick.

I notice Dotty and Adam chatting in the corner of the room, and as to be expected today, in stark contrast to their usual cheerful conversations, they're both looking a little downcast and gloomy. I select a handful of cakes, pile them up high on my plate and head over to them to see if a hefty helping of sugar and carbohydrates can make a small difference towards cheering us all up.

As I walk over, I notice that they seem to be talking rather quite seriously about something, almost secretively, in fact, and on seeing me approach, Dotty seemingly hush-hushes Adam, and the two of them cease talking immediately and then turn to me and smile. It's all a little strange, and Adam, in particular, has the grace to look rather sheepish. Slightly unnerved by their shifty behaviour, I hover nervously, feeling as if I've just interrupted a private conversation. After an awkward second or two, Dotty budges up and pats the seat in between them, gesturing for me to sit down. Hiding my suspicions behind a smile, I do as she wishes and then offer them both the plate of cakes.

We chat for a while about the service and about Jim, and it all seems very rational and normal, well, as normal as any conversation can be when Dotty's involved, so, figuring I must have imagined something that simply wasn't there, and more to the point, feeling way too tired and without the necessary strength to deal with anything problematic after such a horrid day, I decide to forget about it.

Not long after I've joined them, however, Dotty jumps up and makes some random excuse to leave, muttering something about the two of us needing time to ourselves. As she's walking away, and mistaken in thinking I'm not paying attention, she glances back at Adam, and with all the subtlety of a drill sergeant, winks at him in a most comical, over-exaggerated way that wouldn't look at all out of place in a *Carry On* film.

"What was that all about, then?" I ask Adam once she's out of sight.

"No idea," he answers with a shrug. "You know Dotty, though. It would be weird if she wasn't a little kooky at some point in every day!"

"Mmm, I guess you're right," I say, tending to agree with him.

Still slightly unsettled, though, and not quite able to shift the nagging feeling that the two of them are hiding something, but knowing that this is not the time nor place to question friendship and risk having an argument, I decide to let it go for now, and instead, we sit together in companionable silence, thinking of Jim and his family, and robotically munching through our mountain of cakes.

Chapter Twelve

After such a dreadful, few weeks, I'm desperate for things to pick up again. I need a do-over, a fresh start, a rebirth, if you will, some way to renew that sense of optimism and hope I felt when I made my well-intentioned resolutions on New Year's Eve.

I think back to that moment at the start of the year and the lovely positive outlook I had. I remember the warm feeling it gave me simply by believing the right mental attitude would help me to cope better with life's stresses, effortlessly navigating any bumps in the road and smacking unexpected curve balls right out of the park. Granted, it hasn't exactly worked out for me so far, so I'm a little sceptical, to say the least, but longing to have that feeling back again and intent on leaving the tears and pain of the last few weeks way behind me, I force my doubts to the back of my mind and give it another try.

Over the next few days, motivated and fired up, I put my traditionally lax willpower to the test and focus all my energies on channelling good vibes only. I'm not naive enough to know there won't be more testing times to come, but if I can take active steps towards tackling them with the right attitude, then surely that's a move in the right direction.

One of the first things I do is buy myself a beautiful calendar full of inspirational quotes, a different one meant for each individual day, and I diligently read one every morning before starting work, staring hard at the words as if I can absorb the positivity right off the page. It seems to be working well for now, although, if truth be told, the hardest things I've had to overcome so far have been running out of paper clips and coping with the occasional tricky paper jam in the printer. So, for the moment, I guess I've yet to put this new positive attitude fully to the test. The important thing is I'm trying and therefore managing to uphold at least one of my resolutions.

Not totally unsurprisingly, I've already failed the *more exercise* and *no swearing* ones. The most exercise I've managed lately has been dragging myself to work and back, my body still weak from last month's debilitating illness. And, with regard to the wholly unrealistic aim of getting through life without the use of obscenities, well… all I can say to that is there were definitely a few dark days during the height of my sickness when my cursing levels were known to reach critical level. However, I cut myself some slack because, as my new calendar buddy is quite happy to point out, 'one shouldn't dwell on past mistakes when striving towards a brighter future', or something naff and cheesy along those lines.

The following week, my commitment to positive thinking seems to pay off, and I receive some unexpected, favourable news. A manager from a local beauty salon has been in touch to say they have chosen Green Meadow as their nominated charity for this year and would like to offer their services in the form of a series of fundraising pamper sessions at the hospice. It's not the first time we've received an offer from a company with its own specific event idea as it's often a nifty little way for businesses to donate to charity and simultaneously raise awareness of their own organisation whilst also sticking within their comfort zone and doing what they do best.

On this occasion, the salon manager is proposing that, in exchange for donations to the hospice, members of her team will perform various spa-type therapy, such as massages, facials, and makeovers, and all we have to do is supply the rooms, take care of the advertising and source the customers. My interest is piqued as this type of activity hasn't been done here before, and we need constant variety with our events to attract a wide range of clients and potential donors. Not to mention the icing on the cake with this one is that all hospice patients and staff will have the chance to experience some luxurious therapy without having to venture outside or pay astronomical fees on spa retreats.

Conscious of having been gifted a unique and enticing event involving very little legwork on our part and in which we're also lucky enough to participate, I welcome this rare occurrence with open arms and gratefully accept the offer. It goes without saying that both Emma and I will be working the event, and towards the end of the evening, when things quieten down, and most of the customers have gone home, we will have the opportunity to sample some of the treatments on offer, no doubt spending an exorbitant amount of money on miracle-promising beauty products while we're there. It's super timing for me after everything that's gone on as I could really benefit from being pampered and fussed over, so, as moving on techniques go, this one will do just nicely.

We set a date for the first session for one evening at the end of March, giving us enough time to make preparations and drum up sufficient interest. I immediately get to work planning the layout of the room and designing and printing the tickets whilst Emma focuses on the promotion side, producing flyers and posting shout-outs on social media and local radio.

Our combined marketing efforts work a treat, and word soon gets around with tickets selling like hotcakes. It seems I'm not the only one in need of some indulging, and within days, the event is completely sold out. Just like an impatient child awaiting a promised trip to Disneyland, I excitedly count down the days and enjoy crossing them off my happy little calendar one by one, with the biggest marker pen I can find.

This lush sounding pamper night dropping magically into our laps is just the tonic I needed, a much-appreciated change in fortune, albeit rather small scale, but a change in fortune nonetheless. And for the first time in weeks, I allow myself to once again believe, only a little, as it wouldn't do to get too carried away just yet, that there might be something to all this positive thinking business after all.

With not much going on socially, the next couple of weeks threaten to move by so slowly, and I begin to think the pamper event is never going to arrive. The monotony is broken up nicely, however, by some spontaneous game night sessions after work with Emma, Leo, Adam, Vicky and Will, involving several hours of playing cards and board games late into the night, a few too many fattening takeaways, but a good healthy amount of belly laughs and memory-making, feel-good moments. Time spent with my friends makes the remaining time fly by, and with the days successfully counted down, Emma and I spend the hours leading up to the pamper evening readying the day room, emptying it of all its heavy furniture and squeezing everything into any rooms where we can find space before moving on to decorating the windows and walls with silky voiles and hanging beads in calming pink and purple pastels.

The salon team arrive in good time, and we stand back and watch in awe as they wheel in an endless collection of fancy-looking equipment such as electronic massage tables, pop up changing rooms and spray tan booths and expertly and swiftly assemble and arrange them all into neat, clearly defined sections around the room.

Each separate area comes complete with its own modesty curtains and individual seating areas, some with padded armchairs and others with enormous squishy bean bags adorned with velvety cushions and sumptuous throws, and there are little corner tables in every section, on which sit a variety of trinkets such as fat little Buddha ornaments or moon and salt lamps.

In the beauty stations, there are sparkly cosmetic trolleys and light-up mirrors and a fabulous array of tools and instruments — some rather torturous looking — the likes of which I have never seen before. Someone has put together a welcome table at the entrance to the room with a large dish of complimentary mints and several glasses of non-alcoholic punch at one end, and a list of treatments and therapies on offer at the other.

Soothing sounds of panpipe music softly fill the room, along with the unmistakable spiced aroma of a burning incense stick, but I have absolutely no idea where either of them is coming from. The main day room stereo has been unplugged and moved to another room, but I haven't seen any other sort of music device brought in, and I am as yet to locate any evidence of perfumed smoke. Having witnessed such slick, committed and quite frankly scarily flawless behaviour from these perfectly polished professionals over the last few minutes, I wouldn't be at all surprised if it is indeed the therapists themselves emitting such wondrous sensory delights, although quite from where I really wouldn't like to envisage.

Stupefied and seriously impressed, I have watched this entire scene created in the blink of an eye, something akin to what you would expect from a secret government agency called in to avert a national crisis, and it's evidently clear this skilled crew have done it many times before and know exactly what they are doing. Used to lugging around battered and broken second-hand hospice gear and having to make last-minute emergency repairs out of duct tape and twine, Emma and I look on with a mixture of admiration and envy, wishing our own events would set up as smoothly as this.

With such a competent and capable team, we find ourselves superfluous to proceedings for once and spend the next few minutes wandering around, feeling redundant and looking for something to do. It's an odd sensation for us when we are usually run off our feet and attempting to do the job of ten people. The therapists assure us all is in hand with the treatment side of things so, once we have welcomed all the customers and the sessions are underway, we make the most of the unusual situation and sit down to relax for a while.

Having snapped up a ticket, Vicky is also here tonight, and in between her treatments, the three of us enjoy a much-needed therapeutic natter. It's been ages since we've had a chance to get together, and we are well overdue for a catch up. We chat about all sorts of things with Emma depicting beautiful scenic images from her recent cycling adventures around the county and Vicky having us in stitches as she describes the latest shenanigans from some of the more mischievous patrons at *Wondrous Woofs* but it's not long before the conversation inevitably works its way around to the topic of Ross and me.

"So, how did it go when you broached the subject of the Christmas kiss?" asks Vicky while sipping her punch.

"Erm, we haven't really got round to discussing that yet as erm… well… we haven't actually spoken much since the party," I admit, a little embarrassed.

"What?" she spits, astonished, almost choking on her drink.

"You haven't talked about it yet... and what do you mean by 'much' exactly?"

"Erm, kinda... not at all... I guess."

"Woah, hang on a minute! Do you mean to tell me that you haven't spoken to him since you kissed back in December?"

"Erm, yep, that would be affirmative, captain," I confirm reluctantly, then brace myself for the verbal attack I know will surely follow.

"Bloody hell, Sam!" she exclaims in disbelief. "Did you know about this, Emma?" She turns and demands rather accusingly of our poor, mutual, unsuspecting friend, dragging her into the middle of the discussion. I roll my eyes and mouth 'sorry' to Emma. She means well, our Vicky, but she does have a tendency to become rather forceful at times, particularly when she's outraged by something. Pretty used to her occasionally interrogative style of conversation after all these years, though, Emma doesn't take it personally.

"Yeah, I knew," she answers calmly. "But, in Sam's defence, Loverboy hasn't been around the hospice since then, I don't think, and even if he had been, she hasn't exactly been in the best shape for romancing what with the illness and well... everything else that's gone on lately."

All three of us know straight away that Emma's 'and everything else' specifically means Jim's sad passing, and Vicky's demeanour softens in an instant.

"Of course, sorry, Sam, it's just that, well, that's almost three months now. Don't you think you ought to speak to him before too long passes, before it hits that really awkward stage?"

"I think that ship has sailed, unfortunately," I answer, somewhat dejectedly.

"Rubbish!" Vicky replies, reanimated. "You just need to take the initiative and give him a call."

"Yeah, I suppose so, but okay, so I didn't get in contact with him, what with January being so manic at work and then February being so shit and all but he didn't call me either, and he is the bloke after all, it's more his job than mine," I argue, instantly regretting voicing such an old fashioned, sexist view in front of Vicky and flinching as she pounces on my unforgivable howler.

"Come on, Sam, I know at times you're the soppiest of romantic sods that Butterford has ever seen, but it's not the fifties any more. What happened to women's rights and girl power and all that, hey?" she remonstrates me softly.

"I know, I know, but it's just that I'm getting a bit fed up with never really knowing where I stand with him, you know? He blows hot and cold all the time. One minute he's leaving me little cakes, organising get well parcels and kissing me on the dance floor and then the next minute, he's distant again as if it all meant nothing to him. Although, I do think it was actually more of a blessing in disguise that he didn't contact me when I was ill as one look at my snot-riddled face and he'd have done a runner!"

"Mmm, fair point," Vicky agrees, "but if you want my advice." She continues all seriously, and headmistressy, and Emma and I bravely risk a quick grin at each other, knowing full well I'm going to hear the advice of our well-meaning but sometimes bossy best friend, regardless of whether I want it or not. "Stop waiting for him to make the next move, dig deep for that sassy chick assertiveness I know you've got lurking inside you somewhere and take control of the situation."

"You're right, you're right, I'm just not very good at that sort of thing. You know me, Vics, I'm less of an assertive take-what-I-want badass and more of a I'll-swoon-and-you-come-catch-me kinda girl," I admit with a shrug.

"Bloody men, hey? Too much hard work! Think I'll just get a few hundred cats instead and be done with it," I add, trying to both lighten the mood again and encourage the less serious Vicky back to the fold. I love her to bits, but she's so darn practical and logical and always so quick to seek a clear solution to a problem; she sometimes forgets not everybody's wired the same way as her and doesn't understand when we don't act as she would. She's right; I am a romantic at heart and slightly old fashioned in some respects. It's my natural way, and as much as it might make my fearless feminist ancestors roll around in their graves in disgust, I've never really wanted to do the chasing in relationships, so far always wanting the guy to take the lead and come to me.

Still, mistaken as she is when it comes to how I wish for my love affairs to unfold, as a caring friend, Vicky's the absolute best, and she really does just want what's best for her friends. Her loyalty is unquestionable, and when she becomes riled on our behalf, it's a testament to how much she cares about us.

"Second that!" Emma chimes in. "Well, not to being a loser cat lady, but bloody men and their weirdness for sure."

Eager to switch the focus from me and concerned there may be an issue with her and Leo's relationship, I quickly ask her what she means. "What's going on? Not trouble in paradise with you two lovebirds, is there?"

"No, I'm not on about Leo, all's fine and dandy in that area, thankfully," she replies, smiling happily and suddenly looking all glassy-eyed and goo-goo, twiddling her hair around her fingers.

I fear she's in danger of drifting off somewhere inside her head, picturing images of the two of them together in some sort of sublime and sickly bliss, so I swiftly drag her back to reality with a little elbow nudge.

"Um, earth to Emma? You were in the middle of explaining something?"

"Oh, yeah, no, erm, it's not Leo, it's that strange brother of mine. He's just been acting a bit unusual lately, moping around the flat in a grump and when I ask him what the matter is, he just clams up and walks away. I reckon there's a girl on the scene or something romance-wise bothering him. I've only ever seen him like this once before and that was a few years back, remember when he had his heart broken by that super bitch who just up and left him one day for that other guy at her workplace?"

"Oh yeah, what was her name again? Felicity or Tiffany or something? Dumped him for a suited and booted, posh out of towner type, didn't she, if I recall correctly?" asks Vicky.

"That's right, yeah, Felicity, the cow! It knocked him for six if you remember, totally crushed him. He went super quiet and wouldn't talk about it for weeks after."

"So, do you think something like that's happened again? I didn't even know he was seeing anybody," I say, confused.

"Well, that's just the thing, he *isn't* seeing anybody as far as I'm aware, and hasn't been for a while now, but he's acting in a similar way, well at home he is, anyway. He seemed a lot more upbeat at our game nights and he's sometimes back to himself at work but he's not been around as much as usual, has he? Almost as if he's hiding away most days and keeping to himself."

I think back over the last few weeks, and it dawns on me that I, too, have seen less of Adam around at work, and when I have, it's just been odd glimpses of him working away in secluded areas, either down at the bottom of the garden or tucked away in his shed. Not totally unexpected given the nature of his job, but now I come to think of it, it's been a while since I've seen his cheery face smiling at me through the window or since we've

151

shared a playful repartee, and apart from Jim's funeral, he hasn't been inside the day room much either, chatting with the patients like he normally does. There were those lovely snippets when he popped in to see me those times in February during that wretched virus, but I can recall now how, in the mornings, as I would scurry into work, head down and hidden beneath scarves and woolly hats in a bid to reach the confines of my desk unnoticed like an outcast leper, I never really had the issue of dodging Adam in his usual spots like the car park or the front lawns. She's totally right, I think. He hasn't been about as much as usual, and I feel really guilty now for being so wrapped up in my illness and my own life that I haven't noticed anything unusual going on with him before now.

"Now you come to mention it, Em, I've hardly seen him around either and not just because I've been keeping my distance from everyone else. Do you think there's something wrong, then? Should we ask him if he's all right?"

"Oh, there's definitely something going on, I'm just not sure what, but if you held a gun to my head, I'd say it's most likely something to do with a woman. Trouble is, he won't talk to me about it, but then I'm his sister so I'm probably the last person he'll open up to when it comes to matters of the heart. Probably a bit too awkward."

"What about Will then?" Vicky suggests. "I could ask him if he knows anything."

"I guess so, yeah, probably worth a try," Emma says, "as long as we get all the juicy details of who she is afterwards. It's not necessarily a bad thing remember. Might just be Adam being a drama queen and wanting to keep his new fancy woman to himself for a while. I guess I did a similar thing with Leo, didn't I? But if there *is* a new special someone on the scene, I want to know about her, and equally can't wait to meet her! You can never have too many awesome girlfriends and sisters in your life, hey?" she declares, raising her glass to the three of us.

I clink my glass with theirs and mull over in my head everything Emma has just said. I'm unnerved by the odd sensation I'm feeling. My thoughts gallop away with me as I try to find a reason for it. So... a new love interest for Adam, possibly, and one he's being all cagey about, so possibly something serious. It's bothering me, and I can't work out why. I should be pleased for him, I know that, but it's as if I can't quite make myself feel it. Almost as if I'm jealous or threatened even. But why, though? It's not like *I* want to go out with him, for God's sake! He's my friend, that's all, but then perhaps that's the reason why. Maybe I'm worried a new special someone in his life might unwittingly upset the dynamics of our friendship group or take him away from us. Or, even more worryingly than that, what if Adam finds himself in a serious relationship just like the others, leaving just me, Little Miss Spinster, all alone and heading straight for Crazy Cat Lady Town?

Oh, shut up, Samantha, I tell myself sharply. You're being incredibly childish and selfish about all this. You need to stop being oversensitive and all weird and possessive, and be happy for him instead, you daft bint. I force myself to stop thinking about it and bring myself back to the conversation with Emma and Vicky, which I notice has now moved onto a lively debate about the merits of cycling versus running, obviously a topic I won't be at all involved in.

Later on, as the pamper session begins to draw to a close, Emma and I, as anticipated, are invited by the therapists to sample a few of the services that have been on offer all evening. I go down the more holistic route to start with, opting for a hot stone back massage followed by a soothing and relaxing head rub, and Emma chooses some beauty treatments, including a manicure, eyelash tint, and an upper body spray tan.

Then, all three of us finish off with a refreshing facial cleanse and hydrating mask treatment. We each lie on a bed next to each other in a row while the beauticians skilfully and rhythmically stroke and caress our faces with their fingertips. Then, with our foreheads, cheeks and chins thickly coated with soothing Aloe Vera, they leave us to bask for a while as the lotion soaks into our skin, purifying our pores.

I should treat myself to these more often, I think, as I lie still in the quiet room, chilled to the max with a completely rested mind and then BAM! Out of nowhere, my treacherous little brain wrenches me out of my tranquillity and returns my thoughts to the troubling picture of Adam and his possible new faceless girlfriend. I know, deep down, there's no reasonable excuse as to why this image should bother me so much, but for the rest of the night, I find myself struggling to shake it off.

Chapter Thirteen

The next day, I arrive at work uncommonly early for me, pulling into the hospice car park at the exact same time as Emma. She speeds through the gates on her bike like an Olympic track sprinter, saluting at me as she whizzes past and then free-wheeling across the car park towards the entrance. As she nears the building, she does that impressive thing that all proper cyclists seem to do so easily, and while still moving, she swings her right leg over the bike frame and covers the last few metres of the journey standing up and balancing on the left pedal like a total pro.

I slowly drive in after her, feeling like a right boring old codger in comparison to her super-elite level sportswomanship and park up in one of the multitudes of empty parking spaces, completely spoilt for choice. It's an experience I am most unaccustomed to, seeing as, event days aside, I rarely arrive at work this side of nine a.m. and before the majority of spaces have been taken.

Our accidental coordinated arrival time is a combination of both me being unnaturally early and her being refreshingly late. The reason for my uncharacteristic punctuality I easily put down to a terrible night's sleep. For the entire night, my body and mind were at complete odds with each other. My body is floppy and relaxed thanks to yesterday's massage angels, but my brain is still agitated by all the talk of Adam's new secret romance that, for all we know, could be nothing but a fabrication anyway.

The result being I tossed and turned for the majority of the night, and finally admitting defeat at some ungodly hour of the morning, gave up on trying to sleep and dragged myself out of bed. Aided by a large mug of strong black coffee, my body slowly, stubbornly, and with much protest, began to wake up. I didn't blame it, to be honest, seeing as it had been torn away from a very comfortable bed and forced to join my restless lunatic of a mind, which in total contrast had been having a whale of a time at an all-night rave inside my skull.

My limbs felt heavy and slow, and when I asked them to do something, there was a small delay as if they needed a moment to interpret the request. It reminded me of those odd instances you get some mornings when you wake up to find you're paralysed and can't move a muscle or even open your eyes, so you go straight into major panic mode for a second or two, assuming that this will be the very moment an intruder decides to break in and attack you as you lie in your bed screaming inside your head, unable to fight back. And then, seconds later, you wake up for real this time, and it turns out you're not paralysed at all but that actually you weren't properly awake the first time; you just thought you were because you were coming to faster than your brain could cope with. It's all very complex at times the human brain... a marvel, a scientific wonder! But then, when it won't switch off and instead latches on to some random unimportant issue in the middle of the night and won't let you go to sleep, it's a right bloody pain in the arse!

Once up and moving, however, I soon discovered the merits of having got up so early and found I had an extraordinary amount of time to myself before needing to be at work. I started with something simple, such as showering and getting dressed and then fixed myself a hearty breakfast of scrambled eggs on toast, providing me with enough fuel to take a gentle stroll around the village. It was actually a surprisingly lovely time to be outside, still dark at first, but serene and still and without another soul to be found. I wandered the length of Butterford from edge to edge, and having somehow timed it with accidental perfection, I watched, awestruck, as night turned to day with the most sensational gold and amber sunrise.

It was a beautiful sight, and I felt very grateful to have borne witness to it. I often take walks around the village but usually in the early evening to help digest my dinner and stretch my legs after a day of desk work, so to have experienced this morning's walk, so different from what I'm used to, was a real treat, and it certainly made up for my dreadful night's sleep. That mesmerising view of the sun rising up over the countryside made me more appreciative of the beautiful world we live in and how lucky I am to be part of it all. I thought back to the chat with the girls the night before and realised life's far too precious to take for granted or to simply waste by being too scared to take chances, and I decided there and then to throw caution to the wind and follow Vicky's advice to contact Ross.

Although somewhat unusual for her, too, Emma's late arrival is rather easily explained. It isn't a totally brand-new occurrence, having happened quite a few times already over the last few months, with the simple reason being that on the days when Leo stays over at hers, unsurprisingly, she finds she has a lot less inclination to get out of bed.

"Good morning, you wanton harlot!" I say to her as she locks up her bike. "What time do you call this? Finding it tough to tear yourself away from the love nest, I see."

"I have absolutely no idea what you mean," she replies demurely but has the decency to look rumbled at least.

Both laughing, we walk together to the entrance, and I fill her in on my unusual morning and how I intend to call Ross as soon as possible to arrange a meetup.

"Attagirl!" she replies, seeming genuinely proud and pleased for me. "Good luck! Let me know how it goes, although I'm sure it will be just fine. By the way, that facial we had last night was out of this world, wasn't it? I don't know about yours, but my skin feels so soft today, like a baby's bottom. Here, have a feel, do you see what I mean?" she asks, taking hold of my hand and placing it on the side of her face.

"Yeah, it's lovely, mine too. I noticed it after my shower this morning and almost didn't moisturise it felt so smooth. Touch mine, see?"

We must look quite strange standing there stroking each other's cheeks, but it's really only brought to our attention with the arrival of Adam, who walks up to us with a look of amusement on his own face.

"Interesting greeting you've got going on there, girls," he says with a grin and in his usual playful way. "You can stroke mine too if you like, but I skipped a shave today so I must warn you I'm a little stubbly."

"Be quiet, you douche bag!" Emma fires at him before jabbing him in the ribs, just like little sisters do. "Actually, what do you think to this, Ads? Sam's plucked up the courage to take the bull by the horns and ask Dreamboat Ross on a date. He'll like that, won't he? Men love it when women get all assertive, don't they?"

Oh God. "Emma!" I cry, feeling my super soft cheeks redden violently all of a sudden. "Do you have to? I'd really rather my love life isn't discussed with all and sundry if you don't mind."

"It's not 'all and sundry' you dope, it's just Adam and he

doesn't mind relationship talk." Then addressing him directly, she says, "You're open and honest when it comes to girls and chatting about the opposite sex aren't you, bro, mmm?"

I know exactly what she's doing, the little minx. She's trying to goad Adam into talking about his apparent mystery woman. I admire her for her enterprising methods; only I'd much rather she tried it without using me and my failing love story as her way in. I see straight away that Adam isn't at all comfortable with this topic of conversation, and he visibly stiffens as she attempts to draw him in. Quick as a flash, he makes his excuses and all but marches off, and I see with my very own eyes exactly the behaviour that Emma was describing to us yesterday.

"See?" she says, turning to me the second he's out of earshot. "Weird or what? Did you see him bristle the moment I brought up relationships and girls and look how he couldn't wait to slink away rather than stay and talk about it. It's not like him at all. There just has to be a girl involved, surely?"

She stands there with her hands in the air, notably frustrated at her brother's odd behaviour, and seeing as I'm also rather baffled by this sudden change in his personality, I regrettably have no explanation to offer her. Instead, I shrug my shoulders in sympathy and then head on inside to start work with an annoyed and concerned Emma following closely behind.

Once at my desk, I check my to-do list for today, and staring up at me written in my own handwriting, I see the words, 'Fete final check today— don't forget!'

I obviously know myself well as I did indeed fail to remember that I'd previously booked this afternoon as the Easter Fete venue check. Bugger! I'm way too tired for this today, I think, and contemplate postponing to another day but seeing as the fete is next weekend and knowing I'll have to get it done at some point soon anyway, I suck it up and keep it as it is. After a quick phone call through to Emma to remind her also of the plans, I crack on with work.

After an hour or so, as promised, and before I lose my nerve, I pick up the phone and call the Carrington household. It's a cowardly move as it'll likely only be Charles who'll be there given that it's a weekday morning, and I imagine Ross will be at work rather than visiting his father, but I'm nervous as hell about calling him, and this feels like a gentle way of easing myself into it. It's also been a while since I've spoken with Charles, so it won't be a wasted call anyway.

Feeling sick as a dog, I dial the number and then sit fiddling with the chord, twisting it around my fingers and pulling it tight, practically cutting off my blood supply. I listen to the rings and try to take deep breaths as I anxiously wait to hear who will answer. I'm under the impression that Ross sees his father regularly, so there is always the chance he will be there with him today and may pick up the phone. Go on, girl, you got this! I remind myself encouragingly, thinking any minute now I'm going to slam down the receiver before the call can be answered.

As expected, though, it is indeed Charles who answers, and I sigh with relief, even though I know it will probably only be short-lived as I've got to put my big girl pants on at some point and make the call to Ross. God… why am I being such a wuss about it?

"Samantha, so nice of you to call, how are you?" he booms down the line.

"I'm fine, thank you, how are you?"

"Yes, all's fine here thank you, my dear. Lucky you caught me actually. Not long back in from a nice early bird round of golf. Just the nine holes today… not as sprightly as I used to be, alas!

160

What can I do for you today?"

"Oh, nothing specific, just calling for a quick catch up. Is Ross there with you today?"

Please say no, please say no…

"No, he isn't, I'm afraid."

Whoop whoop!

"I should imagine he's at work. I'll no doubt be speaking to him this evening though, would you like me to ask him to give you a call?"

"No, no, it's okay, it's nothing urgent. I have his number though anyway so I can always call him on that."

"Good stuff! Now tell me, how are you getting on with improving those hospice finances? I take it you've got everything in hand, have you? Only it's year-end soon, as I'm sure you know, and the trustees and I are really hoping you'll have some good news for us soon."

Jeez, talk about getting straight to the nitty-gritty. No flies on him today, I think, now wishing I hadn't been such a pathetic little scaredy pants and had just rung Ross on his mobile instead. That'll teach me.

"Yes, well, we've been doing extremely well with the events so far but as you know it's going to take a little more than just that this year, but don't worry, I'm still working on it and I'm hoping for good news soon, too."

"That's the ticket! Just what I wanted to hear, Samantha. You know how the board feels. We're convinced if anyone can save the hospice, it's you, my dear."

Oh God, not too much pressure then.

"Thank you, Charles. Right, well I'd best get back to work now, I think."

"Right, yes, yes, jolly good. Keep up the good work then and

I'll see you in a few days at the fete. Bye for now, dear."

After the phone call and Charles' comments about the hospice finances, I have the weight of the world, or rather the future of the hospice, on my shoulders and am feeling pretty down and depressed. I try to put those worries aside for the moment so I can get this blasted call to Ross out of the way — curse that well-meaning Vicky and her bloody sensible advice. I give myself a firm talking to, tell myself to stop acting like a big baby and then, like the cowardly, yellow belly chicken I am, pick up my mobile and send him a text message instead.

It takes me about twenty minutes to compose the damn thing, making sure to have the tone just right. Interested yet casual, professional yet friendly, and not forgetting, of course, to use perfect punctuation and grammar. I'll happily ignore language regulations in group messages with my mates, but I have the feeling Ross might be the kind of person who expects standards in any kind of written message, and I wouldn't want him thinking I don't know my semicolons from my colons or how to apostrophise correctly.

I make sure to sound casual and keep it light, asking after him and what he's been up to, and I even mention the favour he's been working on for the hospice and whether we can meet soon so he can update me. I don't want to scare him off by just talking about the two of us, but similarly, I don't want to make out it's all about the hospice either. It's not an easy task, and I'm mentally exhausted afterwards and then instantly terrified I've done the wrong thing. Throwing my phone down on my desk like it's a hot stone, I then spend the next few minutes freaking out and wishing I'd never sent him the wretched text. Then, with the most melodious little ping, my phone alerts me to his wonderful reply.

'Hi Sam, that would be great. Maybe over lunch towards end

of April? Might have some exciting news for you by then. R x

Thrilled to bits, I immediately text Vicky to tell her the good news.

Took your advice and asked Hunkychops out on a date, well not a date as such, but a meeting to catch up and guess what? He said yes! AND he even suggested lunch. You're an absolute legend, babe, my very own Cupid! Thanks for pushing me. Love you xx

Not long after, I receive a short reply from her congratulating me.

Brill news hun! Proud of u! Catch u l8er, hard 2 type atm, dog walking x

I quickly buzz through to Emma's room so that she's up to speed with my romantic masterstroke, then get straight back to work. I've already spent far too long on my private life this morning, and I really need to crack on if we're going to have time for the fete recce too.

Charles' gentle reminder of Green Meadow's financial strife has frightened and inspired me, and I knuckle down for the rest of the day, applying for grants from numerous charitable bodies, making sure not to step on Ross' toes by contacting the organisations he has already taken charge of. These grant applications often have many stages to get through and can sometimes take months to process fully, so even though I haven't received anything from them yet doesn't mean he hasn't been successful in his bid or that they aren't still in progress. It would look extremely unprofessional and disorganised of the hospice if I were to request financial aid from them also whilst they're already dealing with Ross. It's been a good while now, though, since he kindly offered to deal directly with them on behalf of the hospice, so they could well be nearing the final stages. Fingers crossed, he'll have a positive update for me on our upcoming lunch date.

"Okay, so the inflatables will go there over by the far wall, next to the crazy golf, and then the retro games and sports day section will be just to the right of that, but on the grass. Gotta make sure people have a soft landing if they fall over in the egg and spoon and three-legged races," Emma informs me, looking extremely efficient as she walks around with her clipboard, pointing at various spots in the grounds of the community centre.

"Wow, that really is a pretty physical set of pursuits you've arranged there, I see," I say to her as I follow her around while she explains the proposed layout of the Easter Fete's activities section. I'd left Emma fully in charge of this side of things once again — much to my extreme concern — but she promised me unreservedly that this year there would be categorically no donkey, or indeed, any other type of animal involvement, and assured me I would therefore be safe from a repeat of last year's humiliation.

"Well, the more fun they have, the more money they'll spend, surely?" she says with a hint of panic in her voice and looking at me pleadingly like I'm a grumpy parent about to take her Xbox away and make her read a history book.

"Don't worry," I say reassuringly, "it all sounds fab so far, and as long as I don't see Eeyore and his mates turn up this time, I'll be happy."

It's just after lunch, and having wrangled with Emma's bike for an embarrassingly long time trying to squeeze it into the back of my car — I think the bike came out victorious as I'm covered in oily marks and grazes — and then driven us both over to the community centre, we have begun the fete layout preparations and are now double-checking that everything will fit nicely so we can have as smooth a set-up as possible on the big day.

We get to work, making sure we'll have room for each stall, not forgetting the music equipment, mobile eateries, and seating areas, and also take care to count the power outlets and inspect cable lengths for all the generators.

It's a large-scale event with over a hundred different stands, each requiring adequate space for at least one table but with a fair amount of them also requiring extras such as electricity or gazebos. We painstakingly take into account each stallholder's individual needs to make sure they will be happy with their allocated slot, and thankfully, we've been given permission by the community centre to mark out the relevant areas with chalk and pegs as they haven't got anything else booked in between now and the day of the fete, so they won't get in the way.

With so much ground to cover and so many other little jobs to do, such as putting up signs and posters, and where possible, the odd bit of decoration like banners and bunting, and completing other necessary duties such as risk assessments and health and safety checks, it takes us a good few hours, and we're there until late on in the evening.

Happy with our progress and feeling pretty well-prepared for next weekend, we decide to call it a day and head off home via the fish and chip shop as a little reward for all our hard work. It's always enjoyable and exciting preparing the location of an upcoming event, but it's also tiring, and a little brain-ache-inducing, and neither of us are particularly in the mood or have any energy left to go home and cook.

Twenty minutes later, having dropped Emma home and clutching my disgustingly large, mouth-watering bundle of battered cod, chips and jumbo sausage — I defy anyone who is capable of visiting a chippy without buying a whopping great chunk of sausage — I walk through my front door, flop down onto the couch and stuff myself satisfyingly full of glorious salty carbs in front of the TV. Dinner fit for a queen or, more accurately, a knackered, sleep-deprived fundraiser at the end of a very long and draining day.

Chapter Fourteen

Fete day arrives, and my trusted, dedicated volunteers once again willingly abandon their warm, cosy homes out of the sheer goodness of their hearts to come and help Emma and me get everything prepped and ready. As usual, a buzz of excitement filters through the group, and just like smiles, it infectiously spreads from one to the other until each and every one of them is practically bouncing up and down like school kids on a snow day as they await our instructions.

Out of all the events, it's always this one that seems to generate the most enthusiasm. I'm not totally sure why, but I'd hazard a guess that it's mainly to do with the time of year that it takes place; that, and all the chocolate eggs, of course.

April's warmer weather and longer days give a lovely sense of renewal and hope, but mainly relief at finally leaving the gloomy chill of winter behind. People seem to associate the fete with the change of season and improved weather and see it as one of the first real opportunities of the year to spend time outdoors without needing to wear a coat that resembles a sleeping bag.

The countryside is enjoying its new lease of life. All around the hospice grounds, pretty spring flowers are sprouting up, and out in the town, beautiful pink and white cherry blossom trees flourish without warning, overnight almost, their buds bursting open with a 'ta-da' at daybreak. Sandlefirth's streets are lined with tree after tree of cotton candy explosions that surrender silently to the gentle breeze, covering the ground with their petal confetti. And, in between each short, sharp rain shower, the puffy clouds give way to the bright, faithful sun sitting in its cool, cerulean sky.

It is the early hours, and whilst most sane people are still blissfully tucked up in bed, the team and I are hard at work on event set-up duty. There's no Adam today, however, as he's apparently had to head down to London at short notice for something else more important. I'm not sure what exactly, some sort of antiques roadshow or something along those lines. It sounds a bit dull if you ask me, and I can't imagine why he'd choose to go to something like that today of all days. To be fair, I'm sure this new hobby of his is all very interesting and all that, but I was only half-listening when Emma told me this morning as I struggled to look past the fact he wasn't coming, period, let alone the reason why. I mean, how can a few old bits of junk be more important than this? Obviously, he can do what he likes, but I'll admit I was a little miffed to hear he wouldn't be helping out today. He knows how much there is to do on days like this, and it's not like him to not make himself available.

I wouldn't mind so much, but he's always such a bloody good help when he's here too, as he's extremely efficient and practical and really great at problem-solving. Not only that, but seeing as he's usually so bubbly and jokey too, he's quite nifty at keeping the mood light and has a knack of calming me down when things get a little stressful. I'm really going to miss him today.

Armed with copious amounts of wake-up juice in the form of hot cups of tea and coffee from the local drive through coffee house, the volunteers, Emma and I, start by collecting the usual hoard of essential event gear from the fundraising offices. We carry it down, box after box, stacking it in neat towers outside the entrance, ready to be packed into the trailer and then transported to the community centre. We work tirelessly together, making journey after journey, passing each other like a well-practised, perfectly-coordinated little colony of worker ants.

Then, having already loaded all the larger units, such as the folding tables, roller banners and industrial-sized tea urn into the trailer the previous evening, we bundle our tower of boxes and other smaller items, including donation buckets, power cables and extension leads, and several hundred books of multicoloured raffle tickets into any remaining available space, cramming in as much as we can. Once the trailer is full, we overflow into any other car that will also be making the trip, and when we're finished, we stand back and admire our efforts. There are several different cars and vans of all shapes and sizes, each stuffed full to bursting, colourful bits and bobs pressed up against doors and poking out of windows and through boots half-closed with elastic straps. I say a little prayer that any passing police officers will turn a blind eye to our set-up as there can be absolutely no doubt that we're in serious breach of at least one of the highway codes. Not one of our drivers can see out of the rear-view mirror.

With the final car loaded, we lock up the hospice, and with the look of a travelling circus, we head off to the community centre, the trailer in pole position, followed by one jam-packed vehicle after another, a long, proud procession of fearless fundraisers bubbling with energy, nervous excitement and irrefutably dangerous levels of caffeine in the blood.

The route to the community centre is rather short and straightforward, so we arrive a few minutes later, still managing to maintain our group convoy. We complete the last part of the route down a lengthy street rammed with traffic calming

169

measures. Its speed bumps and chicanes cause the volunteer who's driving the trailer, and consequently, each vehicle in the line behind, to edge along painfully slowly, giving us the appearance of some sort of poor man's street parade. Except instead of fancy, bright-coloured, and highly decorated carnival floats with escorts of uniformed scouts and guides marching beside us, we're rather more of a ragbag bunch of battered old estates and two-seater vans. Our entourage comes in the form of extra volunteers making their own way to the fete on foot and who just happen to be turning up at the same time. We look like a Z-list celebrity street tour, only we don't have anybody famous taking part or anybody bothering to cheer us on.

We park up and get to work immediately, unloading all the paraphernalia and assembling endless stalls throughout the premises. We lay long rows of tables inside the hall and across the tarmac outside, leaving the green areas mostly clear for the outdoor activities and as free space for people to sit in the sun and enjoy the goings-on.

The external exhibitors and hired entertainment crews arrive in due course, and Emma mans the car park entrance, ticking them off her attendance list and directing them to their specific zones. Soon after, it's a frenzy of organised activity, with gazebos being erected, inflatables being inflated, and numerous stands, each being individually and lovingly furnished with all manner of interesting items for sale.

As per usual, we have a few minor issues along the way with missing tent ropes or wrong length cable ties, for example, but nothing that a good root around in our event boxes can't solve. There's also the odd verbal scuffle amongst some of the private stallholders who, in a bid to bag the most sales, are having animated disputes over certain stall positions, comparing likely footfall and possible advantages. It's nothing Emma and I haven't seen before; in fact, we like to see a healthy amount of competition between sellers as, if properly contained, it will only help to drive sales and ultimately increase hospice donations. It's also easy enough to fix with some composed mediating, and simple layout tweaks, and sure enough, all new stall placements are happily accepted, and harmony is swiftly restored.

All in all, it doesn't take long for the whole thing to come together, and after a busy hour or two of constructive teamwork, the set-up is complete. For another year running, just as everybody has now come to expect, the community centre has been cleverly transformed into Green Meadow's fun, vibrant and highly anticipated Easter Fete. Rows of tables are stacked high with merchandise, each with its own smiley-faced human ready to sell the treasured wares, chocolate eggs galore, and of course, my favourite... the incomparable heavenly cake stall and even a charming little pet corner, full of real live hopping bunny rabbits. They're not donkeys, I'll admit, but animals all the same, so I'll be having a word about that with that sneaky little assistant of mine later. With the whole place surrounded end to end with brightly coloured festival bunting flapping softly in the breeze, it's a truly splendid sight to see — the very picture of a spring extravaganza!

With everything in place and only a short while to wait before the gates open up to the first customers of the day, I breathe a huge sigh of relief and exchange a look of satisfaction with Emma. I'm proud of all our hard work and careful planning in the weeks leading up to today, and as set-ups go, and we've experienced a good few, this one hasn't been too bad at all. I reckon we must have somehow unwittingly absorbed some of the ninja-level skills of the pamper crew the other night.

Like normal for huge-scale events such as this one, I have a little fret beforehand that no one will turn up on the day and we'll have put all of this effort in for nothing, but once the fete opens with hundreds of people turning up, I see that this particular little concern of mine can be happily ignored.

When it comes to worries, I like to scribble them down on a piece of paper and then rip them up into lots of tiny little pieces, stuff them into a tiny transparent sandwich bag and then carry them around in my pocket, so if ever that particular worry should reappear, I can take out the bag and look at the pieces reminding myself it's no longer a valid concern; it's simply a pile of shredded paper. I've picked up this funny little ritual from my mum, who has her own similar technique, only, instead of ripping them up, she shoves them in the freezer and then forgets about them. There was many a time when I was younger when I'd be helping out with dinner, and I'd reach into the freezer to find several little scraps of paper stashed away at the back between the chicken nuggets and potato waffles. I'd make sure she wasn't looking and then read each one in turn, giggling at her concerns, which, at the time, seemed to me so trivial and silly.

Sentences such as 'Worried Samantha might hurt herself on the school outdoor pursuits trip' or 'Worried Tony's gout will play up again just before the holiday'. I don't think she specifically tried to hide the fact that she did this regularly, but she certainly didn't talk about it openly, and Dad and I didn't feel we could bring it up either. Back then, I secretly ridiculed her method, telling my friends and laughing at her expense — the typically selfish actions of a naive and care-free child, I guess — but now I know just how right she was and how important it is to deal with stresses in whatever way it works for you. To give my mum her due, I've since found that the system really does seem to work for me too.

The most satisfying part of this odd little custom is that when the worry has passed and is no longer relevant, you get to discard it once and for all, however you see fit. I usually like to stick them in an ashtray and burn them. I mean, there's really no coming back from that, is there?

I'm nearing the stage, where I can forget all about my concern of nobody turning up as the place is heaving, and everywhere I look, people are smiling and laughing and seem to be having lots of fun. I see a mix of familiar faces from Butterford neighbours, including staff from the Green Barrel and the village cake shop to people I've seen out and about around the town. There are also several newcomers, people I've never seen before, who have maybe never been to one of our events until now or some who have even travelled from further afar having seen our posters and decided to give it a try. Looking around at the crowds and also the long queue of people waiting to enter, I take great satisfaction in removing my little bag of 'worry words' and dumping them in the nearest bin.

An hour or so later, I take a little walkabout to check everything is in order and find Emma demonstrating some of the activities in the inflatable games section. She is currently dressed head to toe in a very fetching, bright-yellow padded Velcro suit and is repeatedly flinging herself at an inflatable wall, also covered top to bottom in Velcro, with the aim of sticking to it as high up as she can. It's hilarious watching her run, flip, and splat herself onto the wall, and she's doing a great job of encouraging several punters to have a go too, mainly young kids and their dads, not surprisingly. It looks like a lot of fun, and I'm tempted to join in myself, except I happen to spot Ross and Charles in the distance, browsing the stalls together. Emma sees me, so I wave to her and gesture that I'll be back soon and head over to the Carringtons instead.

As I walk over, I can't help but notice how handsome Ross looks. In contrast to the smart business attire I'm used to seeing him in, today, he's dressed stylishly casual, and it really suits him. He's wearing a white polo neck and a deep red open-checked shirt with the collar turned up on his top half and light-blue stonewashed jeans, which fit snugly over his lean legs and toned bottom — is it possible to be envious of a pair of jeans? — and he finishes the look with a chunky pair of tan worker style ankle boots. He looks like a lumberjack… a really muscly, labourer type dude. The kind you see depicted in movies chopping down trees in a forest, all strong and sexy. All he needs is an axe, an unruly head of hair and a little bit more in the way of sideburns, and he could easily pass for Wolverine from X-Men.

I'd be lying if I said I wasn't enjoying the view as I walk towards him, slowly taking it all in, rugged good looks and that hunky woodcutter thing he's got going on, and my mind wanders off into fantasises of a passionate woodland affair between a logger and his lover.

They both see me approach, so I hastily push all raunchy thoughts aside, smile as innocently as I can and concentrate hard on keeping my face neutral. It's not at all easy, especially with Ross looking directly at me, and any attempt at an indifferent expression is completely sabotaged the moment I notice he's sporting a new look — a neatly trimmed but incredibly manly, swoon-inducing beginnings of a beard. Oh, dear Lord above! And rather than my intended virgin-nun-in-a-convent expression that I was going for, I'm pretty sure I'm now nailing the sex-mad-hen-at-a-male-strip-show look.

"Hello both, having fun at the fete?" I ask as nonchalantly as I can.

"Oh, hi, Samantha, yes, I always enjoy a little mooch around. How are you?" Charles replies whilst Ross smiles and nods his hello.

"Good thanks, busy though, you know, overseeing this lot. Making sure it all goes swimmingly."

"Of course, yes, a tough job, I'm sure. Oh, but do excuse me quickly, I've just this minute spotted someone I must talk to but I'm sure you two youngsters will be all right on your own for a minute, mmm? Won't be a jiffy." And with that, he strides away, leaving Ross and me standing there together.

Feeling nervous and like I'm on an awkward first date, my mind goes blank, and I can't think of anything to say. I simply stand there for a moment, twiddling my thumbs, my eyes briefly catching his and then darting away and settling on an extremely interesting stain on the floor and staring at it like a right brainless numpty. Ross appears to be slightly less bothered by our impromptu one to one and starts up a conversation with me, albeit a bit of a tame one, as if we've only just met.

"So, it's all going well then, by the looks of things. Quite a large event, isn't it? Must have been a great deal for you to organise, something as elaborate as this, I should imagine."

My filthy mind starts to wander again as he speaks, and I watch his mouth move with each word. Good God woman! What has got into you? Get your thoughts out of the gutter and focus! He's going to think you're a right bimbo if you just gawp at him like a lovesick puppy.

"Yes, yes, it is… well it was… erm… well, I mean, both, yes ha, ha," I stutter and stammer like a total nitwit.

He looks at me blankly, and cringing inwardly, I try again.

175

"So, just having a relaxed wander today then, not looking for anything specific I can help you with?" I ask, gesturing to the stalls with a sweep of my arms like I'm some sort of shop assistant whose store he's just walked into.

The corner of his mouth twitches a little like he's trying to stifle a smile, but he holds it back and answers my question.

"I'm just here accompanying my father really. He's much more of a fete goer than me, and well, he asked if I'd come along with him today. This sort of thing isn't really my scene, a bit too much of a jumble sale affair for me."

There's another uncomfortable pause as I consider what he's said and find I'm torn between wanting to agree with him, even though granted it came across as a tad snobby, but also wanting to explain just how much money events like this raise for the hospice and how loved it is by many of the locals. My heart's not really in it to talk about it negatively.

I'm starting to feel tense and a little disappointed. This clumsy small talk and one-line answers seem stilted and a little bit like too much hard work. I'd like to think it's the raw chemistry or heightened sexual charge between us that's making it feel unnatural and awkward, but if the truth be told, something feels a little off.

Ross is at least coming across like a normal human, whereas I have the distinct impression I might be acting like a bit of a weirdo that can't handle social situations, but something feels strange, and I can't work out why. It's almost as if we don't know how to talk to each other any more, or we don't have anything to talk about, no common ground or connection. How can that be, though? We both really like each other. The kisses at Christmas and our upcoming lunch date prove that, surely? Maybe it's simply down to the fact that I still get a little bit giddy when I try to talk calmly and rationally to him. It is *Ross,* after all, the man I've been pretty preoccupied with for a whole year now, and as always, my insides are anything *but* calm and rational. Either that or I'm having a stroke!

Thankfully, we're both soon saved from any more torturous prattle by the timely appearance of my parents. Probably for the first time ever, I'm actually glad to have a private moment with him interrupted. There's no denying on this particular occasion that I really was making a right old hash of it.

After the introductions, Ross politely excuses himself and walks away to go and find his father, leaving me with my folks, and I wonder why that little meeting was so strained and why I seem so incapable of just having a normal conversation with him. It's almost as if I forget how to talk, like any normal person of sound mind would. God, I'm such a plum! I'll have to look for him later, and see if I can show him I'm not the socially inept imbecile he must now think I am.

Their unsuspecting rescue success aside, it's really nice to see my parents. I always appreciate it when they come along to hospice events. They always tell me they like to attend fetes and bazaars, regardless of whether their own daughter is the organiser, but I don't fully believe them as I'm sure deep down they're mainly here to support me, no matter what they say, and I do love them for it.

"Hello, boss lady," my dad says, giving me a big hug. "Looks like another humdinger you've organised here again, Sam. Going well, is it?"

"Yeah, seems to be for now. A good turn out and not too many problems as yet."

"That's good, love," mum says, giving me a squeeze. "Now, tell me, who was that good looking fella you were talking to?

What's his name and what does he do, and more importantly, is he single?"

Not wanting to get into the whole saga of mine and Ross' relationship — or rather *lack of* — right now, I niftily dodge her interrogation by pointing out the games section over on the grass.

"Come on, I'll show you over to the fun zone where Emma is, and you can quiz her all about her new man Leo. And you'll be pleased to see we've got crazy golf here today. I know how much you love a game."

"Indeed, we do, come on, Pammy," my dad says joyfully, taking my mum's hand and almost skipping off like a little boy.

Emma's busy helping people get on and off the inflatables, so I leave my parents happily ensconced in crazy golf and start making my way around the stalls, checking if any of the floats need replenishing. I'm almost finished when I spot Ross again over by the car park entrance talking to an official-looking woman in a smart trouser suit and heels. Thinking her outfit is a little strange for a charity fete and being naturally nosey, I wonder who she could be and whether she's here in more of a business capacity to do with the hospice.

Then I have a brainwave and realise she could well be a representative from the charitable foundations that he's been dealing with. It would make perfect sense for her to visit one of our fundraisers if they're strongly considering us as it's the ideal place to see how much the hospice means to people and how willing they are to raise money for it.

I keep my eye on them and decide that if they're still talking by the time I've finished my float check, then I'll jump in and introduce myself and see if I'm right. After all, Ross did say he might have some good news for me, and so it would make sense for me to start getting involved now.

Just as I'm getting close, however, their conversation comes to an end, and Ross heads off in the opposite direction. Blast! Oh well, there's no reason why I can't still go over and acquaint myself with her, I think. As my dad reminded me, I am 'boss lady', and strictly speaking, this is my event at the end of the day, so it wouldn't be out of place for me to do so. Happy with my logic giving me a valid reason to endorse my snooping, I walk up to her, offer a handshake, and start to speak.

"Hello there, good afternoon. My name's Samantha and I'm one of the managers at Green Meadow hospice. I don't believe I've seen you at any of our events before and just thought I'd come over, introduce myself and welcome you to our fete."

"Good afternoon, Samantha, I'm Helen. Nice to meet you. This looks fun, is it one you've been involved with?"

"Yes, that's right, me and the rest of the fundraising team, which is my assistant Emma — she's over by the inflatables at the moment, and you might just be able to spot her jumping up and down on the bouncy castle — and our wonderful band of hard-working volunteers. Couldn't do it without the volunteers. I see you already know one of ours, Ross Carrington. I saw him talking to you just before I came over." Ooh, impressive linking skills there, Samantha, I think to myself. Smoothly done.

"Oh, yes Mr Carrington. I didn't realise he volunteered for you."

Okay, strange. I wasn't quite expecting that particular response from her.

"Oh, didn't you? Sorry, do you mind, can I just ask which charitable foundation or trust you're from, are you local, or national?"

"I'm sorry, I think there's been a slight misunderstanding. I'm not from a charitable trust, I'm from Prentin Associates,

Chartered Surveyors."

"Oh, right, I see," I say, except I really don't see at all. "So erm, sorry, I'm a little confused as you can probably tell," I add with a little nervous laugh. "How is it exactly that your company will be helping the hospice financially then, if you don't mind me asking? I'm not familiar with your charitable-giving history, I'm afraid."

"I don't mind at all, only, it seems as if there's been some miscommunication between you both somewhere along the line. As Chartered Surveyors, we're not really in the business of providing financial aid to hospices. Mr Carrington came to us a few months ago to request a valuation and survey of Green Meadow Hospice for his latest property development project."

Chapter Fifteen

I can't think straight. This woman's not making any sense. Why on earth would Ross want to have the hospice valued and surveyed? My brain's telling me that, whatever the reason, it can't be good, but this is Ross we're talking about here, so I'm totally conflicted. I need more information.

"You don't happen to know the particular details of his development project, do you?" I ask her, not totally sure I want to hear the answer.

"My information is rather limited I'm afraid. I'm really only here to tell him that the survey has been completed and to hand over the findings. I spoke with him on the phone this morning and he explained he was here and asked if I'd mind dropping it in. I take it you aren't aware of any of this, then? I do hope I haven't said something I shouldn't," she says worriedly.

"No, it's fine, you haven't done anything wrong, but it's just that I'm struggling to see why he would want a valuation and survey done in the first place."

"Well, in my experience, there's only ever really one reason, and that's to make a purchase. Then, once he's the proprietor, he can, of course, use the building and the land for whatever plans he has."

I think I might actually vomit, right here, right now. I'm starting to feel terribly hot, and I can feel beads of sweat on the back of my neck. My heart is pumping so strongly that I'm pretty sure any minute now it's going to burst out of my chest and smack poor Helen right in the face. I think she can sense I'm not coping with this new information too well. Probably the look of utter bewilderment that I imagine is currently on my face, mixed with panic, disbelief, and rising anger as I gradually digest everything she's saying.

She touches my arm gently and starts talking in a soothing manner.

"Listen, it seems as if this is all rather unexpected news to you, and well, I've probably said too much already, so I think it would be best if I go and leave you to speak with Mr Carrington directly. It's probably just all one big misunderstanding and I'm sure everything will be cleared up in no time."

It's obvious she wants to extricate herself from the situation, and I completely understand. It *is* rather awkward, and none of this is her fault. She's probably wondering what on earth she's walked into.

I take a deep breath, force my face into a smile and hold out my hand again for her to shake.

"Yes, I think you're right, Helen, probably just some silly mistake. So sorry to have bothered you with all my questions, and erm, thank you, you've been very informative."

With that, I turn and walk away as quickly as I can. My eyes are stinging with tears, threatening to spill over any minute, and I really don't want her to see that. We both know the truth of my feelings weren't very well hidden behind my fake smile, but I've got too much pride to let her see me cry. I feel stupid, embarrassed, and furious all at the same time, and my hands are shaking so much that I have to bunch them into tight fists to try and stop them. I'm not sure where I'm heading, but I need a minute to process everything she's told me and to try and make some sense out of it. She must be mistaken, surely. He can't want the hospice for his own profits... can he? Oh God! There's that sicky feeling building up inside again. Keep it down, Sam, I tell myself. Please don't throw up in front of everyone.

I charge towards the community centre in a sort of half-walk, half-run, desperate to flee the crowds and find somewhere quiet inside where I can sit alone and compose myself for a moment. My mind works overtime, trying to come up with a plausible theory as to why Ross may have ordered the survey, but try as I might, I can't come up with anything. The more I try, the less sense it makes, and the angrier I get, and by the time I reach the doors, I'm considerably riled. I catch sight of myself in the windows, red-faced and looking thunderous; the only things missing are the cartoon style puffs of steam coming out of my ears.

There are people everywhere, so I head to the toilets and lock myself inside a cubicle. Not the greatest of places to sit, granted, but I need somewhere I won't be disturbed so I can gather my thoughts.

I close my eyes and practise a breathing technique I learned when I was at school. It was during an assembly aimed at teaching students how to manage nerves and calm the mind before an exam. Big long, deep breaths in through the nose... out through the mouth. It actually does work, and I soon find the nausea fading away and my pulse rate slowing to a non-cardiac-arrest pace.

After a minute or two, when the trembling in my hands has subsided, I take out my mobile from my pocket and text Adam. I don't know why I specifically think of him straight away, but it feels right. I know that Emma's got her hands full at the gaming section, and my folks are in the middle of crazy golf. and if I contact Vicky, she'll quite possibly go straight to outraged-on-behalf-of-her-friend default mode and immediately call me with all sorts of well-meaning advice. It's wonderful, loyal, and so supportive of her, but it's not what I want right now. I don't need any more rage; I need calm advice. I'm not exactly sure what Adam's up to right now, but I can't imagine it's anything too pressing if he's just at some sort of antiques market thingamajig, so I figure he might be available to listen, or, in this case, read, as I'm not in the mood to talk to anyone just yet so I'm texting only.

I send him a few lines explaining what has happened and ask him what he thinks I should do, then sit back and wait for his response. I don't have to wait long at all before he texts back.

Hells bells, Sam, that's weird! Are you okay? I think you should ask him what's going on. I'm nearly finished up here, so I'll be heading home really soon. I'll come and find you when I'm back, and we can ask him together if you like.

I reply to let him know I agree. It's the only obvious thing to do, really. I knew that deep down before texting him, but I guess I just wanted to vent and ask his point of view too. I thank him for his offer of coming with me but tell him that I need to do this on my own. It's not a conversation I want to have. I'm dreading it, in fact, and I still have hope that there's a reasonable explanation for it all or that Helen just had it all wrong. I'm probably clutching at straws, but I'm still finding it extremely hard to see Ross as a bad guy. I'm prepared to give him the benefit of the doubt and hope that this is all just some innocent mistake.

I mull it all over for a few more minutes in the hope of a solution; however, I just end up going round in circles and getting nowhere. I'm torn between my protectiveness of the hospice and my feelings for Ross, constantly flitting between hating him for what he may or may not have done and then believing I'm probably just getting worked up over nothing and that he'll be able to clear up all this nonsense straight away. Realising that I certainly won't get any answers if I hide out here all day, I take a few more controlled breaths and then leave the cubicle. I give myself a little one-to-one pep talk in the mirror, check for any smudged make-up, and then emerge calm and collected and ready to face Ross.

Preferring to speak face to face but having no clue where he might be, I figure I'll just have to make my way around the whole fete until I find him. I make a detour past the cake stall for some confidence-boosting power food in the form of a lovely little chocolate brownie and then continue my search. It doesn't take too long, and I soon find him sitting with Charles outside on one of the picnic tables near the food tent.

I walk directly towards them with purpose, weaving through the crowd and making sure to avoid eye contact with anyone else. I'm ready and focused on the task at hand, but I know that if I stop and chat with anyone on the way, I'll lose my courage. I need to be as assertive as possible, which I fear is going to be hard enough as it is when I get up close if past experience of my chats with Ross is anything to go by. I've not always managed to stay the most clear-headed when talking to him, and I need to make sure I remain impartial and see the full facts of the situation, not just what I want to see simply because of who he is.

Once there, without preamble and with a straight face and as strong a voice as I can muster, I ask Ross for a word in private. Charles, probably unused to seeing me looking and acting so firm, seems to sense something is up and immediately asks me if everything is all right. Not trusting myself to say any more than I have to, I try a small smile of reassurance and simply repeat that

I need to borrow Ross for a moment or two to talk hospice business, and then I turn around and walk away from the table, indicating for him to follow. Charles seems unconvinced but thankfully stays sitting while Ross makes his way over to where I'm standing, just to the side where we can talk without being overheard by anyone. Okay, I think to myself as I wait for him to catch up, first part done. Now I just have to confront him before I lose my nerve.

"Ross," I start nervously, willing my voice not to falter. "I was wondering if you could clear something up for me. I've just had an interesting conversation with Helen from Prentin Associates, and she tells me she came here today to give you the report for the survey you had carried out at Green Meadow."

I stand and wait with bated breath for this gorgeous man, who I've adored for so long, to deny all existence of the survey and happily tell me there's been an innocent little mix-up, that it must be a survey for an entirely different property. How wonderful for the problem to just melt away and for us both to chuckle at the absurdity of it all.

I'm looking beseechingly into those beautiful eyes of his, eyes I've seen looking back at me in my dreams so many times before. I'm too scared to move a muscle for fear of breaking this fragile spell of hope, a few seconds of security before hearing any possible adverse revelation.

The moment of promise ends quickly, however, and I'm bitterly disappointed, as I watch his face take on a look of shock at first, and then clear guilt as he realises he's been rumbled.

"Ah right, I see. Let me explain, Samantha."

"So, you did request it and the valuation?" I ask him firmly, my heart breaking with every word.

"Yes, I did, but you see, I didn't mention it as I thought you might be against it."

"No, really? Why would I be against it, pray tell? Surely only good can come from you wanting to know the financial worth of the hospice and then presumably trying to buy it," I snap at him sarcastically. It's the first time I've ever spoken to Ross in that way, and it pains me so much to do it, but I'm so angry and hurt by what he's done.

"Look, I've seen the figures and been involved in the crisis meetings. It's not looking good for the future of Green Meadow now, is it? It's only a matter of time before you fail to bring in enough money and the place has to close."

His use of the words 'you fail' cuts me to the quick, almost rendering me speechless, and I continue to listen, horrified as he attempts an explanation.

"I'm just being smart and thinking ahead. I'm always on the lookout for new business opportunities, and well, this could be a real earner, Samantha, you must be able to see that. If the hospice is on its way out, then I want to make sure I'm at the top of the list of potential buyers."

I'm absolutely livid. How could he even think of doing this to Green Meadow, the patients, and their families? How could he do this to me? He was supposed to be helping me save it all, not working on his own selfish plans. Then something else dawns on me, making me feel sick to my stomach, but I somehow find the words I need to question him.

"Ross, you told me you wanted to help by talking to local charitable foundations and trusts on behalf of the hospice. That was months ago now. Please don't tell me that all this time you were lying just to cover up what you were really doing."

"No, of course not."

Phew! That's something at least, I think to myself, relieved.

"Well, not initially anyway."

Shit!

"I did intend to speak with them at first, but when I read the file and came to a better understanding of the age and size of the building and grounds, well I couldn't help but think what an amazing opportunity it would be if I developed the land instead. I mean, think of the possibilities, Samantha. Once the hospice is demolished, the land would amount to a vast area, large enough for several new modern family homes or a sizeable block of contemporary apartments. It's a developer's dream plot."

"Okay, so let me get this straight. You didn't try to find us any financial aid at all, but you simply spent months prying into the hospice's worth to further your own goals instead. And what about the patients, Ross? Did you think about them at all? What do you assume will happen to them, if you take away the place they receive their vital medical care?"

"Well, yes, I know there's the possible tricky side to rehousing them all, but there are other hospices and residential care centres around, not too far away I imagine, and they'd soon find a place in another one, I'm sure."

"Oh, it's as simple as that is it? It doesn't work like that, Ross," I say to him despairingly. "The hospice is their home, their family — can't you see that? And when did you even have the survey carried out?" I ask, still not quite sure how I could have missed all this going on right under my nose.

"In February, when you were feeling a little under the weather and at home for a few days. I thought it would be a good time to have it done then, so as to work it all out myself beforehand and then tell you afterwards. In fact, that's actually the good news I mentioned in my text message the other day when you asked to meet up. I had an inkling the survey would turn up positive results and I wanted to fill you in on my exciting plans. You see, if my bid to the board is successful and they do indeed accept a purchase offer from me, then all your worries would be over. Yes, no more hospice, but that also means no more spending your time trying to save a sinking ship. You could accept defeat and move on to brighter shores. It's plain to see it's no fun always being so behind and struggling to meet targets. This way, you can cut your losses, sell up and move on. As far as I can see, Samantha, there's no other way. No one else has shown any interest in buying the place and at least this way you get to leave before the hospice fails."

I stare at him in utter disbelief, and I suddenly feel so massively ashamed of myself. All this time, I was so blinded by my obsession with him I just didn't see what was going on and who he really was. How on earth could I have been so wrong about him? He's looking at me defiantly, and I have the awful impression he really believes he hasn't done anything wrong. On the one hand, I'm distraught at losing him, but on the other, I instantly feel refreshingly free, like a weight has been lifted. Funny how that can happen. It's as if I'm no longer shackled by my fascination with him and my desire for him to like me back as much as I've liked him. The realisation that he isn't the man I thought he was quells my anger, allowing me to accept the loss of him more easily.

"Well, it's a good job you've told me now, Ross, as we won't be meeting up any more, not now I know what you've been doing behind my back. You and I and our relationship has hit a pretty big brick wall, don't you think?"

"I'm sorry you feel that way, Samantha, although I'm not really sure what you mean by 'our relationship'. I can't say I was aware that we were ever in one."

After all the near starts and never really knowing where I stood with him, this comment frustrates me immensely, but I remain calm, keeping my voice low as I respond, as there are still plenty of people nearby, and I couldn't bear them to hear what's going on between us.

"Well perhaps not a relationship as such, but whose fault is that? I can't keep up with your mixed messages all the time, Ross. One minute you're keen, leaving me thoughtful little gifts and then the next thing I know, I don't hear from you for weeks. And just so you know, I don't go around snogging *every* man I come into contact with, and I did think that maybe you were someone I could eventually enjoy being in a relationship with, especially after our kiss at the Christmas party and then the second one back at my place. Don't worry though, I'll let you off. I can see now that your priorities lie more firmly with your money-making career and heartless business transactions rather than with real, meaningful relationships with other people. You'll be pleased to know you don't owe me anything and I'm giving you formal notice that our upcoming date is cancelled."

My blood is boiling, but I'm staying composed, and it feels good to tell him to get lost.

It's an incredibly small victory, however, and I'm not feeling triumphant for long because what he says next leaves me feeling more than a little puzzled and unsettled.

"I can see you're incredibly worked up at the moment, Samantha, so I think it would be in both our interests if I left you alone for a while. However, there is one thing I feel I must say before I go, just to set the record straight. I'm not sure exactly what you think happened between the two of us at the Christmas party; only, the kiss on the dance floor wasn't exactly mutual, if you understand my meaning. I think it's safe to say I was a great deal less inebriated than you were at the time and you did rather fling yourself at me. You're a lovely girl, Samantha, but I just don't see you that way, I'm afraid, and even if I did, I don't think you and I would be a very good fit. I did try not to embarrass you at the time, of course, by not pushing you away, but it was rather unexpected, as I'm sure you can imagine. Oh, and as for this second kiss you mentioned, well, that one's a complete mystery to me, I'm afraid, as I've actually never been to your house, Samantha."

With that, he turns and walks away back to his father, and I'm left there feeling like a prize idiot. I want the ground to open up and swallow me whole. How embarrassing! And just as I originally feared when Vicky was describing what happened on the dance floor. So, I did throw myself at him, then, and my feelings weren't reciprocated. I can feel my cheeks burning, and I know they must be bright red with shame. I'm totally baffled by what he said about the kiss in my bedroom, though. How can that be? I guess I must have an amazing imagination when I'm drunk, then, because that kiss felt very, very real!

I start walking back towards the stalls and glance over and see that Ross is now back with Charles, and they are talking like normal, as if the last few minutes didn't happen. Ross doesn't seem bothered by it at all and actually looks remarkably carefree and unaffected. I, on the other hand, am still reeling. Mind you, I do have the presence of mind to acknowledge that at least it's going to be easier from now on to openly hate him for his betrayal of the hospice now that there's absolutely no hope of anything romantic happening between us. How could I have been so wrong about him? And how dare he assume that the hospice is going to fail, and the board are just going to roll over and allow someone like him to buy it and demolish it for some poncy, flash apartments? Over my dead body. I, for one, will fight to my last breath to save the hospice from a travesty like that. Thankfully, I've known Charles and the other trustees for a long time, and I know for a fact they'd never agree to it, not in a million years. Wow, how different can a father and son be? Poles apart. I'm sure it would really hurt Charles to know what his son has been up to, and I really don't want him to find out, but if it comes to it, and I have to tell him for the sake of Green Meadow's future, then I'll do it without a second thought.

I'm almost at the community centre doors again when I bump into Dotty walking along with her arms full of knitted dolls and teddy bears.

"Oh, hello, Samantha, dear," she says, giving me a hug. "It's just wonderful here today. You've done a smashing job again, top banana, as you young folk say."

A rush of emotion escapes, thankfully only as a laugh, probably down to her unexpected turn of phrase, but it's strangely shrill for me, though, and makes me sound slightly unhinged. The confrontation with Ross and all its horrid revelations has left me in a delicate state where I need a release, and it's either going to come out as a laugh or a cry, and I've got no idea which one it's going to be. If Dotty continues to say kind things to me, I have a feeling it will be the crying version, and once I start, I'm worried I won't stop, and I really don't want to break down here in front of everyone.

I thank her and try to move on, but she reaches out and takes hold of my arm.

"You look a little bit troubled, Samantha. Is everything all right?"

I can't possibly go into the true details of why I'm upset with Dotty right now, so I tell her a little white lie, saying something vague about it being the usual hospice money troubles in the hope she'll just accept it and leave it at that. It doesn't work, however, and keeping hold of my arm, she tries to console me.

"Now, now, you're not still worrying about the hospice, are you? I've told you time and time again everything's going to be all right, haven't I? The donation last year will have sorted out that problem with the finances. I did think you might have mentioned something about it before now though, maybe in the fundraising newsletter, or at one of the volunteer meetings perhaps. You know, as a good news story or something to lift everyone's spirits."

Here we go again. I really must see the nurses about poor Dotty and her confused ramblings.

"Sorry, Dotty, I don't know what you mean. Did you say something about a donation?"

"Yes, from my brother Bernard, silly! The legacy he left the hospice in his will when he passed away last September, God rest his soul. Ooh, you are forgetful sometimes Samantha. I *have* told you about it a few times now, *and* that dozy assistant of yours. Head in the clouds, that one!"

Ha! Good job Emma's not around to hear her say that. "She never seems to listen to me, that girl," continues Dotty. "Don't know how you put up with her, Samantha."

My brain catches up with what Dotty is saying, but I'm still none the wiser, so I check I've heard her correctly.

"Wait, sorry, hang on a mo, Dotty. Did you say a legacy from your brother… as in from his estate? I don't recall receiving anything like that, Dotty."

"Yes, dear. He was a patient here, as you know of course, and he wanted to leave a little gift, or I should say *big* gift, really, shouldn't I? To say thank you to the hospice after he died. He checked with me first, of course, with me being his only remaining relative, and with it being such a large contribution, but I didn't want any of it. What would I do with all that money? I'm happy with my little lot. Not looking to up sticks and move anywhere else now at my age, that's for sure."

She's on a roll now — a Dotty special — talking pretty much without breathing in between sentences, but she's grabbed my attention, and I'm now listening intently and concentrating hard on everything she's saying.

"Back in... ooh, let me see, when was it? Yes, October that was it. I popped the cheque through your door myself. Didn't want something that important to go missing with all the other post and junk mail we get these days so I thought it would be safer that way, you know, if I hand delivered it to your house instead. You did get it dear, didn't you? It would have been easy to spot, rather a memorable envelope, one of those pretty handmade cream ones from the card stand in the hospice reception with a lovely pink flowery border on it."

All of a sudden, I have a flashback to the day I went dog walking with Vicky and ended up coming home stiff and sore, hardly able to bend my legs. I remember there being some post on the floor when I got home, but I couldn't reach down to pick it up, and there was this one letter in particular that kept sliding out of my reach...an unusual looking cream one... with a pink flowery border.

Oh my God! The doormat. I pushed it under the doormat, trying to pick it up. It must still be under there.

"Dotty... you're a bloody angel!" I declare, grabbing her by the shoulders and giving her a big smacker on the cheek. "I have to go right now. Can you do me a massive favour and go and tell Emma over by the inflatables that I'm nipping home quickly for something, but that I'll be back as soon as I can, please?" Without waiting for her reply, I spin on my heels and sprint as fast as I can to my car.

Chapter Sixteen

I race home as fast as I can. I'm amazed that, despite my eagerness, I still manage to drive carefully, only slightly edging past the speed limits on some of the bigger open roads. I repeat Dotty's words over and over in my head. 'Big donation, large contribution, all that money.' My brain is working overtime, wondering what all this could mean, grey matter firing synapses all over the place like a firework display on bonfire night. So, if I've understood this correctly, and she's saying what I think she's saying, her brother Bernard's donation is currently lying under my doormat and has been all this time, and it's a pretty hefty one too, a big fat whopper of a legacy left to the hospice in his will. Oh my God! This could be it. This could be the answer to Green Meadow's financial problems, the way out of the gloom finally. No more money issues… problem solved, yippee! I *have* to find that blinking letter.

The excitement is building up inside me big-time, but as is typical for me, I've also slipped deep into panic mode with endless what-ifs zooming around my mind. What if the letter's not even there? What if I imagined seeing it, and it was never delivered? What if it *was* there, but I threw it away in a fit of cleaning one day? This particular scenario makes me laugh out loud, and I immediately scratch it off the list. Be realistic, woman; even in December, during my gym avoidance inspired housework phase, I still didn't think to clean underneath the doormat.

By the time I reach my cottage, I'm a nervous wreck. I park up, leap out of the car, and run down the path like Usain Bolt. I push open the door, jump over the doormat so as not to step on the all-important cheque, and quickly close the door behind me. Without a second thought, I reach down and whip away the mat. Bits of gravel and dirt fly across the floor, and a mini dust cloud puffs up, making me close my eyes and turn my face away. God, I'm a grubby cow at times, I think to myself with disgust, wafting away the dust with my hands. I really must start lifting things up when I clean instead of just wiping around them.

I turn back and look down at the rectangular patch marking the mat's usual resting place, and there, lying on the floor, rather grimy and with a couple of hair strands stuck to it, is Dotty's glorious letter. Just as she described, all delicate and elegant complete with the pretty pink floral edging.

"Yes, yes, yes!" I cry, picking it up by the corner and brushing off the filth. Now, knowing it's been hidden there all these months while I've been walking over it day after day, totally unaware of its existence, I'm keen not to waste any more time, so I walk to the staircase, plonk myself down on the bottom step and slowly tear it open along the seal, being careful not to rip the contents. I peek inside and see the delightful tell-tale shape of a bank cheque along with a little handwritten note. Unable to wait any longer, I ignore the note and slide out the cheque, my eyes darting straight to the small box containing the value. Then, as I read the numbers taking in the true sum of this crucial donation, I can't quite understand what I'm seeing. Convinced I'm mistaken and that I must be reading it wrong, as surely there's a zero or two missing, I move across and read the words as well just to be sure. Sadly, I have to acknowledge the unfortunate truth of the situation, and my heart sinks. Drat! £20,000. A really lovely gift, an extremely generous amount of money to donate, in fact, but not the windfall Dotty had led me to believe it was, and nowhere near enough to solve the hospice's problems. Hopes completely dashed, and sighing heavily, I pull out the other piece of paper and read the note.

Dear Samantha,

Please find enclosed a contribution towards Green Meadow's upkeep from the proceeds of my late brother Bernard's home, minus any outstanding mortgages and debts.

Best wishes,

Dotty Banks.

"Dotty, Dotty, Dotty," I say out loud to my empty hallway. "You're a beautiful sweet old lady, and I do love you so, but you're just a teensy bit behind the times when it comes to today's economy."

Oh well, it was a lovely dream while it lasted, but it's back to square one again now, I guess, and time to get back to the fete too. Emma's going to be thinking I'm a right slacker today. I lean forward, pick up the mat and put it back in its rightful position in front of the door. Then, cheque in hand, I head out to the car, and at a much steadier pace than just a few minutes earlier, drive back to the community centre emotionally drained and crestfallen.

What an absolute shitter of a day this is turning out to be. I seem to be unintentionally working my way through a range of exhausting emotions, what with Ross' double whammy of betrayal and rejection and then Dotty's short-lived ray of hope quickly turning to despair. I'm disappointed beyond belief and frankly not quite sure how much more I can take.

Dotty and her knitted animals are waiting for me as I pull into the car park. She's standing with her hands clasped together, looking excited and proud. I can't possibly be honest with her and explain that her brother's kind donation, albeit still a great deal of money, won't even make a dent in the hospice's yearly target. Instead, I hug her and thank her profusely without going into too much detail about how it might help and assure her that it will go straight into the charity bank account on Monday morning and be put to good use immediately.

"It really is so very kind and generous of you and Bernard, and I'm just so sorry it took me so long to open it and acknowledge it. I'll make sure there's a mention of it in the next hospice newsletter."

"Oh, I am glad, Samantha, and Bernard would be very pleased to know he helped save the day. See, didn't I tell you all would be okay in the end? You just have to have faith, dear."

"Very true, Dotty, and I do try but it's not always easy, some days being harder than others," I say, sounding more downcast than I intended.

"Is today a difficult day for you, deary? Is the event not going to plan?" she asks, genuinely concerned.

"No, it's not the fete, Dotty, just having a bit of bad luck in the old romance department, that's all. Found something unexpected out, and well, rather unpleasant about someone important to me earlier and it's kind of put a kibosh on the whole thing between us unfortunately."

"Oh, it's that kind of difficulty, is it… matters of the heart, is it? It'll come right in the end, my love, you'll see," she says softly, patting my hand reassuringly like a kind grandparent. My eyes fill with tears, not only for my shitty excuse of a love life and realisation of Ross' true character but also in memory of my precious Nanna Rose and how, now more than ever, I wish she was here with me to help ease the pain. And not for the first time today, I have to fight really hard to hold back my tears.

Seeing my emotion threatening to bubble over, Dotty tries to lift my mood with more comforting words of wisdom but actually ends up doing that confusing thing that so many elderly, more experienced people seem to do at times like this and spouts mysterious, cryptic clues instead, leaving me feeling puzzled and confused.

"You know, Samantha, love, sometimes we spend far too long looking in the wrong direction or barking up the wrong tree. You might think I'm too old and senile to see things clearly any more, but I'm not blind, my dear, and if I'm right with my assessment of your particular circumstances, then today is a good day for you and you'll come to see that soon enough, I'm sure. No point dwelling on past mistakes. It's time to open your eyes a little wider and see what's right in front of you."

I literally haven't the foggiest what she is on about except that maybe she doesn't think it's such a bad thing that I've had my heart broken. Who knows? After all, it is Dotty, Queen Waffler, that I'm dealing with here, God love her. Still, it does serve a purpose of some sorts in that rather than simply wallowing over today's crappy events, I spend the next few minutes focusing on trying to decipher her mysterious monologue of advice instead. Dotty, looking immensely satisfied that her work with me here is done, squeezes my hand and then walks away, leaving me alone and incredibly non-plussed.

The rest of the fete passes incident-free, thankfully, and after several more hours of games, activity and much moolah-raising-fun, it's time to call it a night and start packing everything away. Most of the customers have gone home, and the majority of the external stallholders and outside entertainment squads have already begun to shut up shop and leave. Emma and I have split into two teams for the clear up, and supported by the same volunteers from this morning, we work on clearing our separate areas.

She's currently tackling the inside of the hall, and I'm focusing on the outside. It's mid-evening, and the sun is going down fast, making the temperature drop rather notably and giving a distinct chill to the air. After a while, even with all the physical work I'm doing, I'm still feeling pretty cold, so I check some of the event boxes nearby to see if there are any spare fleeces or jackets I could wear. I have a good rummage but only manage to unearth a selection of lightweight charity tabards and luminous yellow vests used for street tin collection sessions. I nip inside to check if Emma has a spare layer that I could borrow, and she tells me she doesn't but that she did notice one of her brother's old work fleeces lying on the floor of the event trailer earlier when she was looking for some cable ties. I skip over to the trailer and spot the fleece lying on the floor, just like she said. As soon as I see it, I recognise it as being one of Adam's, having seen him in it many times before working outside on the grounds of the hospice. It's old and tatty and a bit mucky, but that's no problem as it's no catwalk show here anyway, and I'm feeling pretty yucky myself after a day of fundraising. I'm in dire need of a wash and a change of clothes, and I can't bloody wait to get finished up here, go home, de-bra, have a shower and get into my pyjamas.

I start heading back to my half-finished job, throwing the fleece on as I go and instantly feeling the warmth from the thickness of the material and fluffy inner lining. It's far too large for me, but I don't mind as beggars can't be choosers, and I'll be happy enough as long as it does its job and keeps me warm. I zip it up, right to the top, the collar closing around my neck and reaching right up to my ears. I breathe in the lush scent of a man's cologne, Adam's cologne, obviously. It's a gorgeous smell, vanilla, sweet and creamy almost. Very soothing and ever so familiar. Where have I smelt that before? I wonder as I head back to my half-packed away stalls and boxes. Mmm, it's making me feel all relaxed and sleepy and… oh… hang on a minute! My hands shoot to my cheeks, and I freeze as a vision suddenly appears in my head. No, it can't be, surely, I think to myself, well and truly shellshocked. I tell myself to stay calm but fail miserably and remain frozen like a statue, my hands clamped to my face, but my eyes darting around in panic as if waiting for some magical explanation to appear.

"It wouldn't be the first time you've added two and two together before and come up with five, so let's not jump to conclusions," I say to myself sensibly and with confident authority. One of the volunteers has noticed my strange behaviour and is now watching me intently, no doubt wondering what the hell I'm doing. It's no good, I think, this just can't wait. I smile and wave at the volunteer to reassure her I'm not having some sort of mental breakdown, then turn around and run back towards the community centre to find Emma.

"Ah, you found it then, that's good, feeling warmer?" she asks as she sees me approach.

"Erm, yep, just the ticket, thanks Em," I reply. Then, having rushed in without giving myself time to work out what I'm going to say, I stand there like a lemon just looking at her.

"What's the matter? You look really weird and spaced out, like you've seen a ghost, or you've had too many magic mushrooms. What's up?"

"No, nothing's up… erm… I was just wondering if I could just pick your brains quickly?"

"Sure, fire away."

I make sure there's no one in earshot and then start to ask her a couple of questions. I'm trying to be nonchalant and indifferent, but the odd nervous laugh escapes and I know I must be coming across a little strange.

"Nothing major, just… erm…well… erm…"

"Oh, spit it out, Sam, you're acting like a right moron! What's got into you? Have you hit your head or something?" she asks, rapidly losing patience. "I don't want to be rude or anything but you're slowing me down a bit and there's still rather a lot to do. I wouldn't mind getting back home at some point tonight you know!"

"Yep, yep, sorry, it's just that, well, I need to ask you something but it's rather embarrassing so… oh feck it! Okay, here goes… you know the night of the Christmas party? Well, you didn't happen to see me and Ross leave the party at all did you, at the same time I mean, you know after the whole kissing-on-the-dance floor caper and all that?"

"Yeah, sure, I saw you both leave, why?"

"Oh no reason, erm… okay thanks Em, that's erm, yeah… groovy I guess."

"Samantha, seriously, what the hell has got into you? Do you need a sit down or something?"

"No, honestly, it's fine now, thanks. I just needed to check something with you, but I must have just made a mistake, got confused about something and jumped to the wrong conclusion, that's all." I try to sound completely casual to stop her from following it up and asking me why I needed to know, but it's too late, and she's looking at me, brows furrowed and interest piqued.

"Mmm, but why did you want to check that right now, specifically, in the middle of clearing up?" she asks with a determined glint in her eye. She's fully stopped what she's doing and is giving me a look that says she knows I'm hiding something, and she's not going to let me go until I've spilt the beans. I'm feeling totally backed into a corner now, and there's nothing really for it but to start answering her with the truth, or maybe just partly honestly for now.

"Erm, it was just something Ross said earlier that got me thinking about Kissgate again, and well, you know…my memory's still a bit hazy from that night, so I wanted to double check with you that's all really, no biggy. Anyway, thanks for clearing it up, I'll leave you to tidy up now."

Hoping that's enough to stop her from wanting to know more, I turn around to start to make my way back out, but she's clearly too involved now and grabs my arm, stopping me from leaving, and then asks me another question.

"Wait, I'm confused, what exactly did you need to check with me — that you both left the party? I would have thought that was obvious with or without a hazy memory, you loon. You woke up at home, didn't you?"

"Ha, ha, yes, you're right, erm, but no, just more that we left *together,* specifically, and that he drove me home and all that, but you've confirmed that, which is just what I wanted to hear so, yeah, that's great, thanks."

I can't seem to help it, and I'm trying my best not to show it, but my overwhelming feeling right now is one of bitter disappointment. In those few short minutes of smelling Adam's aftershave on his fleece, and added to what Ross said about there being only one kiss between him and me, I was thinking, and hoping quite a bit, really, that maybe it was Adam who drove me home that night, not Ross, and therefore that maybe it was in fact also Adam who I shared the kiss with before falling asleep. But what am I doing? It was only this very afternoon that my feelings for Ross changed when I saw his true colours, so I really shouldn't be thinking romantic thoughts about someone else already, should I? Even if it is just Adam. But, well, I do already know him so well and have known him practically all my life and well, love him like a best friend already. But no! Get a grip, Samantha, I tell myself sharply, putting a stop to any possible mind-wandering or daydreaming as I am rather prone to do. Today has been an emotional roller coaster of a day, and I'm in no shape to embark upon a rebound romance. I'm just not thinking straight, that's all, like an overtired toddler way past her bedtime.

"Oh right, I see," Emma says slowly, letting go of my arm but maintaining her stare, scrutinising me, her eyes narrowed and full of amused suspicion. I'm feeling extremely uncomfortable and on show, and more to the point, completely rumbled, knowing full well that she can see right through my fake blasé cover to my true feelings underneath.

"Only, although it's true what I said about both you and Ross leaving the party around the same time, I never actually said that you left *together*, as in *with* each other. In fact, you both left separately, and it wasn't Ross who took you home, Sam... it was Adam."

Chapter Seventeen

I don't know where I'm going, but I just know I need to get out of there. I can hear Emma calling my name as I hurry away, pleading with me to stay, but I don't stop. I can't stop. I need to get away. I need some space to think.

Today has been one hell of a crazy day, a truly bizarre, bats-in-the-belfry kind of day. Learning of both Ross' betrayal and his evident lack of feelings for me, and then everything to do with Adam and that kiss, on top of an already busy fundraiser, has left me overwrought and on the verge of losing my shizzle. I need a moment on my own to sort through the jumble of thoughts rolling around my head. If I don't get some space soon, I'm either going to do that terrifying thing we all sometimes secretly worry about late at night and just spontaneously combust right here on the spot, or I'm simply going to shut down completely and go into some sort of vegetative state. Obviously, the latter would be more preferable, given it would involve a great deal less mess, but to be honest, I'd rather avoid both if I can. I want to try and calm my emotions that are building up inside, and for that, I need some time alone.

I shout back some sort of garbled apology to Emma and tell her I'll be back when I can and then, for the second time today, although this time on foot rather than in my car, I charge towards the community centre exit as fast as my legs will carry me and high tail it out of there.

I realise I'm being a baby by running away, but I can't face

Emma right now. She's too close to both Adam and me, and she'll soon see from my face that there's more to the story than I'm letting on, and I know that if I stay there, she won't let it go, not until she's got all the juicy details out of me. And as much as I love and trust her, I'd rather speak to Adam first, once I've worked through it all myself, of course.

I leave the premises, turn left onto the pavement, and run without so much as a single thought to where I should go, and frankly, not caring one jot either. It doesn't matter where I go, though; I just need some time to figure things out. However, my fitness levels being what they are, I quickly tire and develop a painful stitch, so I slow down to a walk instead. I haven't gone far, obviously, but I'm alone, which is the important thing. The pain in my side isn't easing fast enough, though, so I look around for somewhere to rest. I spot a waist-high brick wall on the edge of a small grassy area a few metres up ahead, which I decide will be perfect for me to sit on for a few minutes and allow the stitch to fade.

Most ungainly, I push, wriggle, and hoist myself up onto the wall, praying no one's watching, and then sit and replay the events of the day in my head. An unpleasant task, but I do it in the hope that I might be able to formulate some sort of order to my agitated emotions.

So, it wasn't Ross who looked after me in my embarrassing drunken stupor, took me home and made sure I was safely tucked up in bed. And it also wasn't him who kissed me, giving in to my shameful demands as I lay there sozzled, puckering up and demanding a goodnight smooch before drifting off to sleep. It was Adam, not Ross. Not the man I've been dreaming of and obsessing over all these months. Not the man whose face I've pictured countless times in all my make-believe daydreams, picturing him as my lover, my husband, the father of my unborn children. Not the man, more importantly, I considered to be a real genuine sort, a good egg, going out of his way to help the hospice. Nope, in fact, he's not the perfect man I thought he was at all, not anything close to it. Yes, he might be handsome and sexy and have the ability to reduce me to jelly whenever I'm near him, but he has some seriously questionable morals if he can put together a secret, wicked plan to persuade the trustees to close down the hospice. The fact that he could so easily turf out all the patients, destroy the building, and use the land for new properties, simply to make himself a bag load of money, makes me feel physically sick. That's not the type of person I want to be with, no thank you very much. Sure, he's ambitious and successful, and well, I suppose he's not total pure evil. I'm pretty sure he doesn't go badger baiting or seal pup clubbing at the weekend or run around knocking toddlers over just for fun — although, I'd probably forgive him for that one as, I'll admit, it's always rather funny watching small kids faceplant — but if he's prepared to put himself before the residents of Green Meadow, then he's definitely not the man for me. I just wish I'd seen it sooner.

And I wish I'd seen that it was Adam who was there for me that night when Ross deserted me on the dance floor. That it was Adam that was a true gentleman, taking me home and ensuring I was safe, who didn't take advantage of me and who had to put up with my shameful boozy behaviour. I cringe as I remember it all, from being carted off the dance floor and manhandled into the car to the nausea-inducing journey home, and I'm mortified that he saw me in that state, intoxicated and so needy. Oh my God, how embarrassing! I feel shame wash over me and cover my mouth with my hands, shaking my head violently as if to erase the memory. This incites rather odd looks from the occasional passers-by, noticing me appearing to overreact to nothing at all whilst sitting all by myself.

On the other hand, well… it's only Adam, my mate, my childhood friend, and therefore someone I shouldn't really mind seeing me that way. We shared so much of our youth with each other, hell…we practically grew up together. Still now, as adults, we spend a lot of time in each other's company, often going through the same ups and downs at work together. He's always there for me, supportive and kind, and we've had endless laughs over the years. It never seems to matter whether we're alone or as a bunch, we always click. I've lost count over the years of all the times we've spent hour after hour messing about, being silly and laughing till the early hours.

Images of Adam's lovely smiling face suddenly start to flash in and out of my head rapidly. Lovely happy memories of us together. I see him laughing and his sparkling eyes lighting up his whole face. I see him looking at me, his kind, understanding face showing genuine interest when I talk to him about whatever's on my mind, or about my day, hospice woes, the latest book I'm reading, or juicy celebrity gossip I've heard about. I love his company, and I love his face, I think to myself. I know it so well after all these years, and picturing him smiling makes me smile too, and I want to see it right now. It's a pining feeling, sort of like it's not right that he's not here, and it makes me feel incomplete almost. Oh God! I realise, suddenly, with a rush of emotion, that I'm not in love with Ross. I'm in love with Adam!

Suddenly, everything around me is very quiet and very still, except for a high-pitched ringing in my ears, and it's almost as if someone has pressed the pause button on the world, and time has stopped all around me as my realisation dawns. It only lasts a few seconds and then passes as if it never happened, and I figure it's my body's natural response to such a strong feeling. I guess it must be true what they say about stress and emotions causing physical symptoms.

So, I'm in love with Adam… wowzer!

I guess it shouldn't come as a massive shock if I think about it. At times, he really has been my closest friend, a kindred spirit, a soulmate. Someone I go to when feeling down or needing advice, like earlier in the loos after my encounter with Ross. Damn! I kind of need him here right now so I can talk this through with him. Although I assume if he were sat beside me right now, it wouldn't quite work that way, would it? Me asking him what he thinks I should do about my newly discovered feelings I have specifically for him? Mmm, maybe not.

I really do wish he was here with me, though, even just to tell him all about all that horrible business with Ross' plans for the hospice — a problem shared is a problem halved and all that. Instead, I'm sitting here, sad and all alone, feeling wretched and worn out, overwhelmed by a myriad of emotions. Guilt, for one, knowing Emma has no idea where I've gone and is probably really worried about me. Hurt and anger still over Ross and that whole debacle and then, probably the most important of them all, these new simmering sensations of excitement, hope and fear as I acknowledge my true feelings for Adam. I know I love him. There's no denying it now; I really bloody love him! Holy moly…this is big! What am I doing? I have to speak to him. I have to stop sitting here like a saddo Humpty Dumpty and tell him how I feel.

I take my phone from my pocket and dial his number, but it only rings a couple of times before I realise what an idiot I'm being and quickly end it before he can answer. Hang on… I can't tell him something like this over the phone. I need to speak to him face to face. I'll have to wait until he's back. I switch my phone to silent, pop it into my pocket, jump down off the wall and start heading back to the community centre, this time in somewhat more of a steady walk than a frantic run. The stitch has thankfully gone now, and I'm feeling much more composed. It's amazing what a few minutes of 'me time' can achieve. I check my watch, however, and realise I've been gone a good three-quarters of an hour. Yikes!

Once back at the centre, I go straight inside to find Emma to explain my irrational behaviour. I see her straight away on her own at the back of the hall, packing away the last few remaining boxes. It looks as if all the volunteers have finished and gone home now, which makes me feel a right dick for having left her to manage all this without me. She hears me enter, and just like an anxious mother, at first, she looks extremely relieved to see me, before very quickly switching to one of those typical parental expressions of ever-so-cross-and-disappointed, so I start apologising straight away for running out on her.

"I'm so sorry for bolting, Em, it just all got too much, and I had to clear my head. And I'm really sorry for leaving all this to you as well. I've really been quite shit today workwise, but in my defence, before you hate me forever, it's been a right headcase of a day."

To be fair to her, my lovely, caring friend forgives me in an instant, and we sit down on the floor next to the leftover packing as I try my best to explain. I change my mind from earlier and decide I simply have to fill her in on the lot; I figure I owe her that much, seeing as I scarpered and left her to all the work. I start with Ross' shady hospice closure idea, my subsequent shock awakening to his true character, and his all too evident lack of feelings for me. Then I move on to the slightly harder job of telling her of mine and Adam's kiss and my recent awakening of my true feelings for him.

"Ugh, yuck! You and Adam? Pass the bucket," she teases, nudging me and smiling, then reaching over and giving me a great big hug,

"I'm only joking. This is ace, Sam! You two are easily made for each other now that you come to mention it. I don't know why I haven't thought of it myself before now. So much for that so called brother-sister psychic connection thingmajig. I can't believe you didn't know it was him who took you home either. I'd have mentioned it earlier, only I assumed you already knew."

"No, it's my fault for being so embarrassed about it all and never wanting to talk about it."

"Eek, this is so great, though, Sam. You and Adam... an item... I love it!" she declares cheerfully.

"Okay, hang on a minute there, Em," I warn her, trying to calm her excitement. "These are only *my* feelings I'm telling you about, remember? There is no me and Adam currently. I haven't told him how I feel, and I have no idea how he feels about me yet either. And don't forget there's that small yet crucial matter of that potential new girlfriend of his you pointed out, remember?"

"Oh pish! She'll be a distant memory once you tell him how you feel. It's clear to see that Adam adores you. I honestly don't know why this hasn't dawned on us before! Classic case of not seeing what's right in front of us. What's the phrase? Not seeing the wood for the trees or something or other?"

"Careful, Em, you're sounding a little bit too much like Dotty, spouting out old fangled sayings like that, you know," I say to her with a wink. "On a more serious note, though, I do realise, by the way, that this does make me appear a little shallow, and well, as if I'm happy to flit from one guy to another without much time in between."

"Well, yeah, sort of, but with good reason, Sam, and it's not like you've just ditched Ross and decided to give the very first person you see a go is it. You've already got a relationship with Adam, a long-standing, firm friendship, so you're already halfway there, and well, it seems as if Ross is a bit of a cock, so you're well within reason to kick him to the kerb if you ask me."

"I guess, and well, the thing is Em, I've realised now that I never really loved Ross, as in the actual man himself, did I? Because I never really *knew* him properly. I just fell in love with the idea of him, what I thought he was. And today's revelation showed me that he's not the man for me after all, and that I've been in love with a fabrication, a fictitious version of him that doesn't exist. So, it's actually very easy to let him go."

Emma nods in agreement, and I carry on. "I won't deny it hurt at the time when he told me he wasn't interested in me. I can't lie, it did smart a bit, but the more time I've had to get used to it, the more I've realised that it doesn't bother me, not now I know who he really is, and not now I'm no longer interested in him either. It's simple… I don't want to be with him, so I don't care that he doesn't want to be with me. It's really quite refreshing and like a big old weight's been lifted."

"Well, I for one am pleased to hear that," she says emphatically, and then, a little more softly, as if to be careful not to hurt my feelings. "You were a little bit obsessed with him."

"I know, I know," I say, cringing. "I was pathetic! I don't know how you all put up with me."

"Because we all love you, of course, and well, what would you have done if we'd have told you to snap out of it, hey?"

"I'm pretty sure Vicky tried to a few times, but I wouldn't listen, would I? Ever since you introduced him to me this time last year, I've been infatuated. I should have known it would never work simply from the way we first met. I'm pretty sure he's never quite been able to shake that image of me spread out on the floor covered in straw and donkey spit. I mean, the universe was sending me a pretty big sign that perhaps things were not meant to be between us. I just refused to see it."

"That was definitely an unforgettable moment, that's for sure!" Emma agrees, the two of us giggling as we both remember the ridiculous scene.

"What are you going to do about him then?" she asks once she's stopped laughing.

"Well, I may be fine on the heartbreak front but it's his betrayal of the hospice that I just can't forgive, Emma, and for that alone I can't see any way that we can be friends moving forward. Obviously, I'll remain professional and civil for Charles' sake, but Ross is not welcome at Green Meadow from now on, as far as I'm concerned, that's for sure."

"Mmm, I agree, and *I'm* sorry I ever introduced you to him."

"Oh, you weren't to know, none of us were, and I'd have met him eventually, what with him being a Carrington. Who'd have thought that lovely, kind old Charles would have such a git for a son, hey?"

"So, what are you going to do about my brother then?"

"Well, I was hoping to speak to him sometime soon, but I guess it all depends on when he gets back. I really missed him today, Emma, and I really wanted him here when I found out about the whole Ross thing, to confide in him, and well, cry on his shoulder, so to speak. I was holed up in the toilets stressed out and feeling sorry for myself and longing for him to come back, wrap me up in his strong arms and make the whole shitty situation go away with a great big comforting hug."

Emma puts two fingers up to her mouth and pulls a face like she's being sick. "Steady on, will you," she pleads. "This is my brother you're talking about, remember. He may be all attractive and manly to you now, but I still see him as a pigtail tugging, bogey flicking, prank pulling, pain in the arse sibling."

Laughing at her, I apologise and then, feeling much better for having talked it all through with her, I suggest we carry on with the last few bits of packing up so we can finally finish up and go home. It doesn't take long at all, and soon enough, we're in the car and making our way out of the community centre. I drop Emma back at hers and then loop back round to the hospice so I can put all of the fete's takings and donations into the safe. The unpacking of boxes can be done another day, but I always feel more comfortable knowing the money is safely deposited in the fundraising office. I have a small pack of muffins and pastries on my back seat, leftovers from the fete that I was hoping to use as an excuse to sit and chat with Adam once he was back. It's not going to be an easy conversation to start, but everything's better with cake... fact! I guess I'll have to save them for another day now, though, seeing as he hasn't made it back yet or, knowing me, I'll just end up eating them all myself once I get home.

As I drive along, I feel really disappointed Adam didn't show up at the community centre this evening. Although, I suppose trying to talk to him about gooey stuff like feelings and relationships while Emma was still there would have been a little awkward, to say the least, mainly for her, of course. It's getting quite late, though, now, and I'm starting to worry about him. Where is he, for God's sake? Shouldn't he be back by now? I'm sure he said he was going to be heading home soon when he texted earlier. I hope he's okay and hasn't had an accident on the way back. I suppose he could have just been delayed talking to some old fuddy-duddies about antique vases and the like. I'm not being funny, but if Emma's right and he does like me the way I like him, and we're going to have any kind of future together, then he's going to have to think seriously about this naff new hobby he's messing around with.

My fears are thankfully proved unfounded, however, when I pull into Green Meadow car park a few minutes later and see Adam's truck parked up in one of the spaces and Adam himself leaning up against the hospice doors, looking rather hot, I note, in a brooding Mr Rochester kind of way. I don't know why I was panicking, I think to myself. Of course he's made it back okay. I really do worry far too much. Whatever happened to my care-free upbeat outlook from January? I wonder. And then I remember today and realise, yes, *today* is what happened. That bloody bastard joke of today! Anyway, that's all over with now. Come on, Sam, I think as I park up in the next space along. Deep breaths. You got this! I grab the cakes from the back seat, step out of the car and walk towards him, abuzz with nervous excitement.

Chapter Eighteen

"Where the hell have you been?" he barks at me before I have the chance to begin. "You really worried me! I thought something had happened to you!" He looks so cross, and I'm instantly transported back to my teens, being reprimanded by my dad for staying out too late on a school night.

That was going to be one of *my* first questions to him, albeit not quite so angrily, and the sharpness of his tone and the grumpy look on his face, so unusual for Adam, throws me off-kilter. It's so strange to hear him speak this way, though, and I can't help but find it rather amusing. All the emotion from earlier added to the nerves I feel at seeing him again, and the shock of his unexpected mood bubble over and I let out a giggle.

On seeing this, his features instantly soften, and his mouth twitches a little too as if he wants to laugh along with me but he's trying hard to stay mad. God knows what he's so blooming cross about, though. Surely, he knows where I've been all day.

"Erm, I was just finishing up at the fete and then dropping Emma back," I explain, meekly at first but then, remembering *he's* the one who's been away all day, I bristle, reattach my backbone, straighten up, and give him a taste of his own medicine.

"Where have *you* been, more to the point? It's been a bloody awful day and you haven't been here to help. I could have really done with your support."

We stare at each other in silence for a few seconds, and then he takes a deep breath as if struggling to maintain his patience.

"Samantha…" he begins rather masterfully, the use of my full first name taking me by surprise. "You text me earlier, evidently extremely upset over that… dickhead Carrington and then, rather than wait for me to get back home, you tell me you're going to speak to him on your own. That's fair enough, you're a strong woman and more than capable of dealing with that spineless idiot, but then I hear nothing back from you except for a short, missed call and then when I try and call you back, thinking anything could have happened, my calls constantly divert to voicemail. I've been worried about you all the way back up, so I drove straight to the community centre to check that you were okay just to find it all locked up. So, then I tried your house, and you weren't there either. This was the last place I could think of you might be, other than Butterford cake shop, but seeing as that's closed now, I figured you wouldn't be there, so I was just about to call my sister to see if she had any idea where you might be."

Bugger! He makes a good point. I'd completely forgotten that I'd turned my ringer off on my mobile while I was sitting on the wall. Whoops! I reach into my pocket and pull out my phone to see the LED flashing at me like mad and several missed call alerts from him on my lock screen.

"Ah I see, right. Sorry Adam, I switched it to silent after I called you. My bad." I admit sheepishly, wiggling the phone at him. "But, I'm here now though and well, no harm done hey? Forgive me?" I ask hesitantly with a smile, trying to look as innocent as I can.

He's still looking rather annoyed with me, and it wouldn't at all surprise me to see him snort from his nostrils like an angry cartoon bull, so I resort to the age-old, tried and tested, sneaky tactic of apology food and hold up the little box of treats — my edible olive branch — for him to see.

"Please don't be cross with me. I meant what I said, it's been a real pig of a day and look... I have cakes."

"Oh, Sam, you and bloody cake! You'd fix the world's problems with a great big wedge of cake if you could, wouldn't you?"

"Course I would," I say with a shrug of my shoulders. "It's magical! And even if it can't *fix* a problem, it certainly makes it more bearable."

I gently jiggle the box and gesture for him to help himself. He lets out a loud sigh, letting go of all his pent-up anger and concern, and shakes his head at me. Then he takes a look inside the box and picks out a blueberry muffin. I choose a muffin too — a luscious little white chocolate and strawberry jam one — and we sit down next to each other on the cold concrete, our backs leaning up against the hospice doors, and tuck into our goodies.

"So," he begins a minute later, after swallowing his last morsel and wiping the crumbs from his mouth. "What happened earlier then with Ross? Did you confront him about what he did?"

"Uh-huh, sure did, and sadly, he didn't deny it. Turns out he thinks it's okay to treat the hospice like his own personal route to megabucks, not giving two hoots about the patients. He even tried to get me to see the potential in his plan and agree with him that it was the only way forward. 'Not on your Nelly mate', I told him, more or less."

"What a douche!"

"I know, and then, after that, he very kindly explained that, well, let's just say he's not that into me, and I've basically been making a big fat tit of myself all this time by trying to pursue a relationship with him. Cringeworthy, hey?"

"His loss if you ask me. Never could work out why you were so besotted with him, anyway, Sam."

"Yeah, I know. Don't worry, that thought's been plaguing me all afternoon too. I feel like a right dummy now, though, of course, but that's the wonderful benefit of hindsight and all that for you, isn't it?" I pause briefly and then add, "He wasn't all bad though, you know."

Adam raises his eyebrows at me as if finding that statement rather hard to believe.

"You, unlike me, never liked him from day one though, did you? Why was that? What exactly did you have against him?"

"I suppose I just always struggled to understand what you saw in him for one. Always thought he was a bit pompous and up-himself. You're way too good for the likes of him, you know, Sam, and to tell you the truth, I didn't like the way he tended to swan in and out like some gorgeous, dark-haired Thor-type dude with all the women, well, *you,* mainly, swooning over him all puppy-eyed and bewitched."

"Yeah, I guess it must have looked like that at times, but he was rather nice to me as well, you know. He wasn't a total jerk, when he wasn't plotting to buy the hospice, of course, but do give me some credit, won't you? He was actually very thoughtful at times, often leaving me little gifts, like cake, for instance, muffins like these actually," I say, waving what's left of mine at him before shoving it in my mouth. "Left one for me on my desk one day with a cute little note. In fact, I think I remember telling you, and you weren't exactly very nice about it if I remember correctly."

"Ah, well, seeing as you've brought it up and while we're having this little girly, heart-to-heart session right now, or whatever this is," he says, nudging me in the ribs playfully, "I guess I ought to be honest and tell you that it wasn't Ross who left you that muffin on your desk that day... it was me."

"Wait, what? But... I saw his jacket as he left the room. Are you sure?"

"Yes, I'm sure," he answers, chuckling. "Course I am, numskull."

I ignore his name-calling and think back to that day, trying to remember as much as I can and anything that might be important. The cogs whirr, and it doesn't take long for me to realise what must have happened. My clearly crappy powers of deduction at the time have let me down badly once again.

"Oh, hang on... of course! He was in my room to take the file, wasn't he? Not to leave me a muffin. Oh my God! I'm so dense sometimes. Sorry, Adam, I just assumed it was him."

"Yeah, I know you did, and you seemed so happy about that I didn't have the heart to correct you. I thought it would be best if I said nothing, but obviously you could see something was up with me, so I guess my poker face needs some practice."

"But why did you leave it for me?" I ask, still a little surprised after thinking it was Ross all this time.

"No big deal, really, you just looked rather sore when you turned up to work that day, hobbling in like an OAP and I thought you could do with cheering up a bit. Don't go all goo-goo eyed on me," he teases, nudging me playfully. "It was only a muffin."

I blush a little at his use of the term 'goo-goo eyed' but turn away slightly so he can't see.

"So, come on, what else did Romeo do for you that was so amaaaaaazing?" he asks in a mock high-pitched voice, putting his hands on either side of his cheeks, imitating a love-struck teenage girl. "Seeing as he's just so dreamy and all."

"Okay, okay, you've made your point," I chastise him, nudging him back. "Well, let me see. He organised a lovely thoughtful care package for me from him and the other volunteers when I was dying from that hideous flu type virus thing."

"Oh, did he? And what was inside this package, pray tell? No let me guess," he says and then goes on to list practically the entire contents of the parcel, item by item.

"Oh, come on! Are you having me on? Was that you too?" I ask, completely dumbfounded. "But Dotty said it was the handsome man at the volunteer meeting who arranged it, and well, I just assumed she meant Ross."

"Charming!" he says, throwing his head back, laughing heartily. "Offence *is* taken, by the way, before you say it."

"Oh God, I'm so sorry, Adam. I really have made a complete mess of everything, haven't I? I put Ross up on that pedestal and I've been so wrong this whole time. What an idiot!"

I cover my face in my hands and shake my head as he continues to laugh. There's a small pause, and I figure, seeing as all the truth's coming out now, this is as good a time as any to broach the subject of the Christmas party to finally thank him for looking after me and to tell him that I now know it was him who took me home.

"Erm, while we're on the subject of mistaken identity, I have a similar confession to make to you," I say timidly.

"Go on."

"Well, you know the night of the hospice party when I was a teensy bit tipsy?"

"When you were pissed as a fart you mean?"

"Yes, okay, fair enough, I was rat-arsed. Well, I never did thank you for taking me home and looking after me, and the main reason for that was well... I kinda didn't realise it was you, not until today, that is." I scrunch up my face again, highly embarrassed and bracing myself for his reply.

"Don't tell me you thought it was him again, Mr Happy-to-kiss-you-and-leave-you-stranded-on-the-dance-floor-knobhead… standing there waiting for him to come back like a total loser!"

I cringe at the description and feel myself reddening again. I've blushed so much over the course of the day I'm going to end up permanently bright red like a big fat tomato soon.

"Sorry, Adam," I say, shrugging and once again giving him my best 'forgive me' face.

"To be honest, it doesn't really matter in the grand scheme of things does it. It's not like I did it for credit or brownie points. I did it because I care for you, Sam, a lot, and I couldn't just stand there and watch him make a fool of you. There you were, off your face, swaying back and forth to some soppy love song, waiting for him to return while he happily chatted away to some waitress half his age. I could have decked him. But someone had to get your drunken arse back home or you'd have been standing on that dance floor until the cleaners came in the next morning no doubt."

"Aaarrgh, stop! It's so embarrassing!" I plead, and he thankfully does as I request and says no more. Neither of us goes on to mention the kiss we shared later on that night, and I sit there wondering why and what that could mean. I'm trying to decide how I should bring it up when Adam takes a deep breath, as if preparing to say something difficult, shifts his position and turns to face me, looking very serious all of a sudden.

"I have to say, that, although it must have been pretty horrible for you at the time, I'm actually really pleased that it all happened today, personally."

I look at him aghast, and he holds up his hands as if to say he hasn't finished.

"Hold on, let me explain. I hate the *way* it happened, obviously, with him upsetting you, and for that I want to smash the bastard's face in, and I'm not even talking about all the evil plotting-to-buy-the-hospice madness either, but basically, my point is, that I'm pleased you've finally seen him for what he really is. I can't tell you how frustrating it's been for me hearing you laud over him all this time. 'Oh, my gawd, I love him so much. He's so gorgeous, blah blah blah," he says in that whiny voice again, pretending to be me. "You've been like a lovesick teenager, and well, it's been getting on my wick a bit, if I'm brutally honest."

He continues to look at me, all serious and full of emotion, a little hurt almost, by my infatuation with Ross possibly and my ignorance of his feelings, and I know that this is it. This is my moment to tell him how I feel. I've never done anything like this before, and I'm absolutely bricking it. I'm romantic in many ways, always have been, and all my life, I've dreamt of being swept off my feet like a fairy-tale, the guy doing the sweeping and me being swept. However, today's crazy happenings have shown me that true life just isn't always like that, and I need to get with the times. I'm going to do it… I'm going to grab the bull by the horns and tell him how I feel. Oh God! This is not going to be easy, I think, picking nervously at my fingernails.

"Erm, seeing as we're admitting things, there's something else I want to say to you, Adam," I begin shyly, digging deep to find the courage. "I realised something today with everything that happened… I realised that I haven't been seeing things very clearly for a while and… I've been duping myself into believing things that just aren't true, and I think what I'm trying to say is…

I really did have it all wrong about Ross and I think, in doing so, it was stopping me from seeing you clearly, too."

My cheeks are burning, and I'm pretty sure I'm resembling that fat tomato now, but I've started to tell him how I feel, so I can't stop now. My heart's pounding hard in my chest, and I'm feeling giddy with nerves and excitement, but also with possibility and hope. After spending my whole life waiting for the romance to come to me, it's rather refreshing to be taking charge myself. It's a big risk, one I've never taken before, and I could end up with egg on my face, but taking the lead makes me feel emboldened and powerful. I picture how proud and impressed Vicky will be to hear about my newfound girl power, and it gives me the strength to push on.

"I thought that kiss… *our* kiss… after you put me to bed, was with Ross, or even that I'd imagined it somehow, but I know now that it was you, Adam, and well, it was lovely and… perfect. What I'm trying to say in a rather waffly way, is that I like you, Adam, you know like, *like* you like you, as in more than friends if you know what I mean. And erm… well, that's it, I guess. I probably shouldn't have said anything what with you having a new girlfriend and all, but after the day I've had, with all the deception and the misunderstandings, I'm trying to make a change and not go down that same path again. I want to be honest with you even if it means another rejection and making a wally of myself again. So anyway, yep, that's it really. Just wanted to tell you how I feel."

He says nothing, and I can't look at him, so I turn away and stare at the ground. He's been sitting looking at me the whole time, listening without interruption, letting me say what I needed to say and he's still watching me now, still saying nothing. I can feel his eyes burning into the back of my head, and I'm starting to feel uncomfortable, wondering whether I've just made a massive mistake and totally bollocksed up a perfectly good friendship.

"Sam," he says, but I don't respond. I can't. I'm so embarrassed. I remain looking away, my hands twiddling nervously on my lap. "Samantha, look at me," he says softly but firmly, taking hold of my hands with one of his and stopping me fiddling with them. He lifts my chin gently with his other hand, turning my face towards his, making me look at him. I have tears in my eyes as I try to be brave, but I'm not feeling strong any more. I'm panicking, thinking I've made a total mess of things. He lets go of my chin and takes hold of both my hands in both of his.

"Sam, are you on drugs?" he asks with a serious face before easing into a soft, slow smile.

This is not what I was expecting at all, and I snigger unexpectedly.

"No, why do you ask? Is what I said just so absurd that I must be high or something?"

"Well, not the having-feelings-for-me bit, that's completely understandable and to be expected, of course, given my incredible personality and rugged good looks."

I shake my head at him, but his joke takes the edge off, relaxing me a little.

"It was more the bit about me having a girlfriend. What *are* you on about? I'm sure I'm not always the most observant, only being a lowly male mortal — you women are always keen to tell us men how crap we are at not seeing objects that are right in front of us — but I think I would have noticed if I had a *girlfriend*. It's not the kind of thing you can easily miss."

"Well, it's just that Emma said she thought you must have

someone special in your life or some sort of beginnings of a romance going on, seeing as you've been acting so weird all the time, especially whenever she mentioned anything to do with relationships or the latest episode in my and Ross' tragic love story, for example. To be fair, I saw it for myself the other day in this very spot when she asked you what you thought about me contacting Ross."

"Honestly, you two... what are you like?" he says with a little chortle and an exasperated sigh. "You'd be dangerous if you had half a brain cell between you. Don't ever think about changing careers and becoming a detective, will you? We'll all be screwed. Good Lord! Give me strength!" he adds, shaking his head. "I don't have a girlfriend, Sam, or any other kind of romantic liaison type thing happening at the moment. If I seemed moody, it was because I didn't much like hearing about you and Ross all the time. It was bad enough watching it unfold in front of my eyes here at work without being drawn into lengthy discussions about it too. In case you haven't noticed, Sam, I'm in love with you. I have been for years."

I stare at him open-mouthed, utterly astonished by what he's saying.

"You're my best friend Sam, my buddy, my soulmate. It's been torture watching you pine after someone else for the past year, someone who in my eyes doesn't come anywhere close to deserving you. I'm not saying *I* do, of course, but I'm pretty sure I'd do a better job of loving you than that cock, if you were to let me try, that is."

"Wait, hang on. Are you telling me that the only reason you were grumpy all those times is because you were jealous? Jealous of Ross and me?"

Now it's his turn to look bashful, and he grins boyishly as his cheeks turn a light shade of pink.

"Suppose so," he says quietly. "I'll admit, I was rather jealous, yes. Who wouldn't be in my shoes, though, Sam? As I keep saying, you're way too good for that schmuck, and here I am, little old me, someone who knows you like I know myself, who's loved you for an embarrassingly long time, and I'm basically invisible to you. All you could see was him. Bloody infuriating, let me tell you! I was beginning to think you'd never see me as anything more than just Emma's irritating older brother, who used to tease you and chase you and do all those typical things brothers do to their younger sister's friends. It isn't easy hiding my feelings for you, working in the same place day after day, and I'm amazed you haven't worked it out before now. Even mad old Dotty could see it. Actually, I felt sure you'd rumbled me the day of Jim's funeral when you came over right in the middle of mine and Dotty's conversation. She was asking if I'd plucked up the courage to ask you out yet, and I was saying I didn't think there was much point while you were so infatuated by someone else."

"Oh, so that's why you and her seemed so shifty. I did feel as if I'd stumbled in on something private, but I never guessed it would be that."

"I don't suppose you would really, although, at the time, it felt painfully obvious to me."

Wow, I think, taking it all in and realising just how blind I've been. That must have been what Dotty was on about at the fete earlier also, the fact that I couldn't see how Adam was right there in front of me all this time because I was so flaming infatuated by Ross.

"So, shall we start again?" Adam asks, squeezing my hands and looking at me with a little cheeky grin.

"I think that would be a very good idea," I agree, looking back at him and feeling immensely relieved, happy, and amazed all at the same time.

Chapter Nineteen

We continue to look at each other for a moment, neither of us speaking. Oh my God! He's going to kiss me, I think, with seconds to spare before he leans towards me and very gently places his lips on mine. I close my eyes and kiss him back. He lets go of my hands and then brings both of his up to my face and cups my cheeks. He presses his mouth on mine a little more firmly, and I open up to him, moving my lips with his, tentatively at first and then more keenly.

The kiss deepens, and I go with it, exploring him, tasting him, rising up to him and pressing myself against his firm chest, my arms lifting up and curling around his neck, my fingers stroking the back of his head, playing with his hair. I hear him moan softly, and he drops his hands from my face and wraps them around my upper body, his hands on my back, holding me tightly. I relax into his embrace, feeling small and delicate — not words I would normally use to describe myself — and he smells divine, that lovely familiar vanilla aftershave wafting over me again.

His hands start to move around, stroking and caressing me. It's thrilling and sensual, and I respond without question or hesitation. We continue like this for a while, thoroughly enjoying each other and relishing in this new version of each other, kissing passionately like a pair of sixteen-year-olds behind the bike shed. It feels naughty and daring, like we're misbehaving, doing something we shouldn't, but it's glorious, and I'm acting purely on impulse, without thinking or planning. Without me telling them, my wicked hands find their way inside his jumper, stroking his strong, toned back and shoulders. I'm not usually one for public displays of affection and would normally shy away from such unbridled passion unless safely behind closed doors. There's no one around, as far as I know, but to be honest, I'm so lost in the moment I don't think I'd know if the entire town turned up to watch.

One of his hands makes its way slowly around from my back to rest gently on my waist, and I want more than anything for him to unzip my fleece, lift up my top and touch my breasts. This brazen thought jerks me back to reality, and all of a sudden, I'm conscious that it's Adam who I'm doing this with. Adam, who I'm kissing like a sex-crazed teenager. I have a mini moment of panic that it'll start to feel weird, but it doesn't. It feels wonderful... perfect, even. And I banish the worry from my mind, mentally tearing it up and picturing tiny shreds of paper floating off up into the sky, being carried away in the breeze, never to be seen again.

His hand stays where it is — more's the pity — and we carry on kissing a good while longer, neither one of us showing any desire for this blissful encounter to end. After several minutes, however, we break away, both breathless and flushed, and both of us clearly wanting more. Adam smiles at me slowly and sexily, and I'm complete mush.

"Wow!" I say when I can speak again. "That was intense!"

"Uh-huh," he agrees, breathing heavily. "It's all down to you looking so fucking sexy in my dirty old work fleece."

I throw my head back, laughing, and playfully push him in the chest, breaking the sexual tension for a moment and allowing us to have a breather. I reflect on what's just happened and try to get my head around the fact that, somehow, in the blink of an eye, we've moved from being best buddies to a couple of horny young lovers who can't keep our hands off each other. I'm suddenly shy again after such a disgraceful display of X-rated behaviour and worried I might have got far too carried away, enjoying it way more than he was, but one look at him sitting there, gazing at me, grinning from ear to ear, and looking like the cat that got the cream, reassures me that he feels the same way.

I look across the car park and suddenly notice how late it is. The sun has almost set, and I can just about see it fading away in the distance, peeking out between a couple of clouds in a dark blue sky. While we were talking, and kissing, time has raced on with evening all but turning into night, and I sadly acknowledge that it's time to rein in my passion and take the fete money into the hospice.

"As much as I could stay here like this with you all night, I think we ought to make a move. It's getting really late now, and I'm shattered after an absolute bonkers day. Plus, I've also got a bit of a numb bum situation going on after sitting on this cold hard floor for so long!"

"Ooh, let's have a feel. I reckon I could warm you up a bit more if you like," he says, reaching around and trying to give my bottom a squeeze.

"Easy tiger. We've got some boxes to pack away, and I need to get the fete takings into the safe."

"Spoil sport!" he says, jumping up then reaching down, grabbing my hands, and pulling me effortlessly up to my feet. "Come on then, I'll help you get everything locked away and then I'll tell you about my day."

"Oh yeah, sorry, I forgot we haven't talked about your day yet. Let's put all this away and you can tell me everything."

We lug the essential items, buckets, and money bags up to

the offices, store them away securely and then head back downstairs.

"So, how did the fete do by the way? Was it a good day, takings-wise?" he asks as we walk towards the doors.

"Well, I haven't counted it all yet, but from what I've seen so far it looks promising. It's not going to solve the general lack of funds issue we have unfortunately, so I'll have to keep plodding on and searching for a solution with regards to that little problem. It's frustrating to have lost time on lots of the local trusts and foundations that I thought Ross was working on, but it is what it is. I'm trying to stay positive and hope that something will turn up eventually." I lock up and turn to face him. "Right, so, now... your day. Where is it exactly that you went? Emma said something about an antiques fair, I think."

"Yeah, sort of, and I'm sorry I couldn't be here with you today, although it's probably a good job given what happened with Ross the tosser. I may have ended up with assault charges. But, yeah, the reason I wasn't around today was because I went to an antiques roadshow type of exhibition, with some unusual pieces I happened to find in the hospice grounds a short while back."

"Oh, okay," I say, wondering where he's going with this.

"I often come across a load of junk and scraps when I'm digging and landscaping in the gardens, but these particular pieces seemed different, more peculiar so to speak, so I did a bit of research into it and discovered that sometimes stuff like this can be considered valuable. I couldn't quite find out enough on my own, not being an expert myself, and realised I needed to speak to someone knowledgeable in that area of expertise who could check them officially and give me their opinion on what they might be worth. To cut a long story short, that's where I went today and the good news is, it does seem as if the objects I found are, in fact, worth quite a bit of money."

I'm almost too scared to speak and far too scared to hope, especially after what happened with Dotty and the disappointment of the legacy cheque earlier today.

"What do you mean by 'quite a bit of money'?" I ask, then hold my breath and wait for him to put me out of my misery.

"Well, it seems as if the hospice could be sitting on a bit of a gold mine. So far, solely going by the items I took with me today: some coins, buttons, brooches, fragments of a shield, a couple of helmets, and a few pieces of pottery, I was quoted £1.6 million."

I'm dumbstruck. Totally and utterly stupefied!

"Fuck off! Are you serious? And you're only just telling me this now?" I say, grabbing him by his jumper and shaking him in disbelief.

"I know, sorry," he says, laughing. "Although, in my defence, I was a little distracted earlier, firstly thinking something bad had happened to you and then by your wanton womanly seduction."

"£1.6 million," I repeat dreamily, still not able to fully take it in.

"And, apparently, anything found buried in the earth belongs to whoever now owns that piece of ground, which, in this case, is Green Meadow, so we'd be free to sell anything we find to museums or collectors. From what you told me about the hospice's outgoings, I'm thinking that if we can sell the pieces I've had valued so far, we'll have a good amount to play with, initially to maybe cover this year's fundraising target, and possibly tackle any other financial problems or debts there may be, am I right?"

"Well, yes, bloody hell! That kind of money is more than enough for this year's target and then some. And yet you say there could be even more pieces buried in the garden too?"

"Yes, most probably. I've dug some others up already, but haven't managed to sort through those yet and I'm guessing we'll unearth more at some point too. Fancy getting down and dirty in the soil with me and searching for some more?"

"You bet!" I say, squealing and jumping into his arms. "I don't bloody believe it! We can save the hospice Adam... we won't have to close. Thank you, thank you, thank you!" I say, squeezing him and showering him with kisses. "You're a lifesaver!"

He holds on to me tightly, laughing as I kiss him all over. "Listen, I just dug it up. This stuff was always here, just lying about waiting to be found, and it was what you said on the night of our unplanned sleepover here that got me thinking about this possibly being the site of an Old English community. I take it you're pleased then?"

"Adam! 'Pleased' is an understatement. I'm bloody effing over the moon! Whoopee!" I scream loudly, pulling out of his hold and bouncing up and down. "I can't wait to tell everyone! Emma, the patients, the medical staff, Charles, and the trustees, they'll all be so happy and relieved. All except Ross, of course. Ha! In your face Ross Carrington!" I shout rather childishly.

I think back over today's crazy events. Revelation after revelation; some bad, some good, some *really* good, fantastic, in fact! I'm not sure dealing with this many reveals in one day can be all that safe for my heart. I've been on a wild ride of highs and lows, and frankly, I'm now starting to doubt if any of this is actually real. There's a large part of me that's convinced none of this is at all true, that I'm actually fast asleep and simply having the longest, nuttiest dream, and in a minute, I'm going to wake up and find that none of it has happened, that the day hasn't even begun. Oh, please don't let that be the case, I think desperately. I'd take the heartbreak with Ross a thousand times over if it meant that getting together with Adam and hearing the good news about the hospice would remain true.

I'm so happy I reckon I could even manage to run a few laps of the car park, but I resist the urge and throw myself back into Adam's arms, opting for a good long therapeutic smooching session instead.

A little while later, accepting that it really is time to go home, we walk to my car holding hands and say good night. What started off as a real pisser of a day turned into one of the best evenings of my life. I don't want it to end, but it's completely dark now, and in a few hours' time, it'll be morning, and I know I'll be leaping out of bed, eager to start spreading the good news of the hospice's windfall.

As I go to open my door, Adam stops me, spins me round, then places both hands on the door frame, his arms on either side of me, trapping me in between him and the car. It's an extremely dominating and manly move, and I find it incredibly sexy. Then, nuzzling into my ear, he rests a hand on my hip whilst the fingers of his other hand softly stroke my skin down from the bottom of my other ear along an invisible line on my neck to the top of my collar bone. He does it so slowly and with such a light touch it's tantalisingly erotic but also a little bit ticklish at the same time, and it makes me shudder involuntarily. Spurred on by my reaction, he pulls me to him and kisses me with such passion I think I'm going to melt into a puddle of goo on the floor. It's so tormentingly good I have to fight hard to tear myself away.

"Enough, Mister, I need my beauty sleep," I say to him,

pulling away and easing out of his grasp. I nudge him aside and quickly slip into my car, lowering the window but closing the door before he can engage me in any further debauchery. I'm running out of resolve, and I don't trust myself to stay here much longer without serious repercussions of a very naughty nature.

"Beauty sleep is something you absolutely do not need, that's for sure. You're bloody gorgeous, Miss Samantha James, and you know it!" he says, smiling handsomely with a cheeky glint in his eye.

"You're not so bad yourself," I reply, smiling, then wondering briefly what all this newfound sexual attraction will mean for us. I know I shouldn't risk spoiling the mood by asking, but I feel so relaxed with him that I hear the words escaping out of my mouth before I can stop them.

"So, what's going on with us then Adam, what exactly *are* we to each other now? Boyfriend and girlfriend, or just friends with benefits?" I ask, hating sounding so serious and cringing as I say the words. After the constant flow of misunderstandings today, though, I need to know we're on the same page right from the get-go. I don't want to just be mates who get together every now and then for a quick roll in the hay; I want to be his, to belong to him properly and for him to belong to me, and I have to know he wants the same; otherwise, it's not going to work.

"Boyfriend and girlfriend sounds pretty damn cool to me, seeing as I'm not especially keen on sharing you with anyone else," he replies, bending down and giving me another quick kiss on the lips. "That is, of course, if you'd be happy with that."

"Sounds good to me," I tell him, relieved and happy.

"So, seeing as we're an item now, and you're a teensy bit sentimental at times, I reckon I'd best take you out on a first date sometime next week. Don't want you thinking I'm a rubbish boyfriend this early on, do I?"

I quickly start thinking what might be the easiest way to tell him that, although a 'bit sentimental' I may be, fancy complicated dates and over the top gestures are really not my thing at all. It's totally unnecessary, however, and I'm pleasantly surprised to find he's already one step ahead, proving just how well he knows me.

"The thing is though, Sam, we've been best friends for a very long time now and I happen to know you're not one for lots of fuss and palaver when it comes to dating. So how about we just keep it simple, yeah?" he says, taking my hands in his and giving me the loveliest of smiles. "Tell you what, Sam… let's go for coffee."

Epilogue

Four months later

"Woohoo! The view is fantastic up here!" Emma squeals, looking down at me and Leo from the top of the thirty-foot climbing wall she's currently standing on. "You really should come up here and see for yourselves," she bellows down to us.

"Not on your nelly!" I shout back to her, my hands cupped on either side of my mouth to make my voice as loud as possible.

"Your girlfriend's a nutter, you know that, don't you?" I say to Leo as we stand together, half-watching, half-looking away as she boldly steps off the top of the platform and starts to abseil her way down to the bottom. It's a temporary structure that Emma has hired from an outdoor pursuit company — her own madcap idea, of course — specially for Green Meadow's highly anticipated Summer Fete, due to take place tomorrow. At her request, the construction team arrived about an hour ago to assemble the wall smack bang in the middle of the hospice car park, and Emma has gallantly volunteered to be the first guinea pig climber. Or *not* gallantly, rather, seeing as she loves this sort of thrill-seeking activity and is actually having a whale of a time testing it out before the hordes arrive tomorrow, and she probably won't get another look in. Suffering from vertigo and being terrified of heights, Leo is choosing to stay firmly rooted to *terra firma*, and also somewhat height averse myself, I've chosen to do likewise. We're currently standing side by side, the two of us clinging on to each other in mutual solidarity, marvelling at

Emma's fearlessness.

It's early evening on the last Saturday in August, and the weather is glorious! We're experiencing an extremely pleasant mini heatwave this week with clear blue skies and sun-drenched days, making for the most brilliant of circumstances for tomorrow's fundraiser. Even now, towards the end of the day, it's still soul-pleasingly warm, and the hospice grounds look so attractive in the bright sunshine. The gardens are lush with fresh, green grass, speckled with rampant clusters of daisies and the odd vivid yellow dandelion weed, and there's an abundance of different bushes and shrubs bursting with rich, healthy leaves of all different variegations bunched together in the borders, with small colourful bundles of pretty flowers mingled in between. It's due to the hospice's stunning environment in the summertime that we always choose to hold the fete here rather than the community centre like with the Easter one, and with this gorgeous weather, we have the most idyllic setting. It's the epitome of a perfect summer's day scene ready for what I hope to be a very enjoyable, fun, and carefree fundraiser for everyone involved.

As it's a big event, the whole gang and several volunteers are here helping with the set-up in some way or another. Vicky and Will are marking out part of the lawn for the dog show, which they have so kindly offered to run, and Dotty and her crafty crew are tying their homemade bunting to the fences along the full length of the hospice boundary. Adam and my parents are also in the garden but further down, out of sight, busily pitching various gazebos and marquees and securing them to the ground with pegs and ropes and whatnot. I've spent the last hour arranging umpteen mini fairground-type activities and games such as hook-a-duck, foam darts, beat the goalie and hoopla.

Everything's going great guns so far, and there's not much more to put up. One of the benefits of this event is that, due to it being held during the summer months, the days are longer, and the evenings are much lighter and warmer, so a great deal of the preparations can be carried out the day before without us freezing our bits off or struggling to see in the dark. Much like the Easter Fete, the tables and stalls and all the other smaller stuff will be put together and arranged in the morning, but the bigger stuff can be taken care of in advance like we're doing this afternoon.

Emma bounces nimbly down the wall like some sort of expert abseiler, detaches herself from the safety harness, and sprints over to us like an excited child running to her waiting parents.

"That was amazing!" she declares, fizzing with adrenalin and grinning from ear to ear. "Are you sure you don't want to give it a go, you two? You're tied on the whole time so it's perfectly safe, honestly! And the view is spectacular! It's such a rush as you step off the edge onto nothing but air!"

"Nope, we're fine where we are, aren't we, Sam? We've got absolutely no desire to leave the security of the ground and step off the precipice into the abyss, thank you very much," Leo replies, looking a bit pale at the mere thought of it and even wincing slightly at his own description. "I'm super proud of you, though, babe, even though I could hardly watch at the time," he says, shaking his head vigorously as if to erase the memory of it and giving her a quick kiss on the forehead.

"And before you look at me... I'm with him," I say, jumping in and jabbing my thumb in Leo's direction. "There's absolutely no way you're getting me up there, not in a million years! Harness or no harness, and view or no view."

"Well, it's your loss," Emma replies, shaking her head with

a smile. "You're missing out on a wicked experience! Don't you agree, Adam?" she shouts, suddenly looking to the right of my shoulder behind me.

I follow her look and turn to see Adam strolling over with what looks like a box of cakes in his arms. I watch him approach, and I like what I see. He's wearing a stripey blue t-shirt, denim shorts, dark grey trainers and a cream baseball cap, and he looks young, fit and totally gorgeous. Who needs a stunning view from the top of a climbing wall when the sight down here is as scrummy as this? I think, feeling all warm and fuzzy inside. Plus, he's carrying cakes, for goodness' sake. It's really no contest.

"If you're trying to get my girlfriend to risk her beautiful neck up on that thing, you'll have to go through me first," he says, walking up to me and slipping his free arm around my waist, pulling me in close for a kiss.

"Fat lot of good you are, bro." Emma sighs dramatically. "I'm trying to encourage these two wimps out of their comfort zones and you're just pandering to their so-called phobias!" This last thing she says with a cheeky grin and then squeals, trying to dodge Leo as he tickles her in punishment.

"What have you done with my folks?" I ask Adam, looking around but not seeing them anywhere.

"Well, we've finished putting up all the tents so they're heading off home now to have dinner, but they asked me to say bye to you and that they'll see you back here sometime in the morning once the fetes open. Oh, and these are from them as a little pre-event treat for everyone," he says, gesturing to the box.

"Mmm, I noticed you came bearing gifts," I say, taking the box from him and peeking inside. "Ooh, scones, lovely!"

I pass them round to the others and then take one for myself before reaching up to give him a peck on the side of his face. I inadvertently leave a smudge of flour on his cheek, so I gently wipe it off with my fingers and then softly run them down to his mouth and over his lips. He kisses them, which shoots a little electric buzz right through me, making me shudder.

"Haven't you two finished your gooey honeymoon phase yet?" Emma asks with mock disgust, having witnessed our little display of affection. "Not sure I can take much more of seeing my brother and my bestie being all slushy with each other."

"Get used to it, sis. This 'honeymoon phase', as you put it, isn't going anywhere for a while, I'm afraid. Your *bestie* is just too bloody sexy!" replies Adam, winking at me and giving my bottom a sneaky little squeeze.

"Ugh, get a room," Emma says jokingly, covering her eyes with her hands while we chuckle at her discomfort.

"Left any for us?" asks Vicky as she and Will walk up to join us, having finished with their dog show preparations.

I hand them the box and then check my job list on my phone for any outstanding tasks. There isn't anything left to do, and I'm pleased to see Dotty and the other volunteers are also heading over, having completed their lovely garland display.

"Well team, it looks like we're all done here for today," I say happily to the group. "Thanks again everyone for all your help. As always, Emma and I couldn't do any of this without you guys. Let's head off lickety split and get some rest before the big day tomorrow."

With several nods and murmurs of agreement, we all start making our way to our cars, satisfied with our efforts and feeling optimistic about tomorrow. Adam and I walk hand in hand to his truck and start discussing our meal plans for tonight. We agreed earlier in the day that if the set-up didn't drag on too late this evening, we'd grab a takeaway on the way home and have an early night together at my place. Happy at the prospect of a lazy snuggly night in with my man, I jump into the passenger seat and sigh contentedly.

As Adam reverses out of the parking space, I take a good look at the hospice and note how impressive it looks, always naturally pretty with its plentiful flora and greenery at this time of year, but now resplendent in all its lovingly created fete decorations. The multi-coloured garlands hang proudly on the railings, cheerful and vibrant — a perfect reflection of the people here: the true heart of the hospice. Their ever-present optimism shows through no matter what the troubles. This time last year, the trustees and other members of staff and I were so worried and anxious about the future of this place, yet the majority of the patients and volunteers never seemed to waver in their belief that all would be all right in the end. And they were right.

Today, the hospice is safe, flourishing in fact. Just as Adam predicted, the discovery of the buried artefacts rescued the hospice from potential financial ruin, removing the threat of having to close its doors. Several of the items he found sold for crazy sums of money, and with numerous other newly exposed relics awaiting sale but already valued to a high amount, the finances are well and truly out of the danger zone and in the best state they've been in for years. With such an influx of funds, any notion of having to give up and close its doors has been dismissed, and the trustees are even making grand expansion plans to extend the residential section of the hospice and create extra bedrooms, increasing its overall capacity and offering care to more patients.

Needless to say, Green Meadow's newfound financial security means that Ross' attempts to buy the hospice and turn it into new housing have been thwarted thankfully, and his selfish scheming has come to an end. He's also found himself in a spot of bother with the Board of Trustees, when, frustrated that his plans were being hampered, he foolishly tried broaching his intentions with his father, hoping to persuade both him and the other board members to sell up. Naturally, Charles was quick to reject the idea and was suitably disgusted at his son's secretive and underhand dealings. He was so ashamed of him, in fact, that he pretty much frogmarched him into the hospice one day and made him publicly apologise to all of us: staff, patients, volunteers, the lot! As much as it pained me to see Charles' sadness and disappointment at his own son's deceitful exploits, I won't lie, it was a satisfying sight.

After all the anxiety of the last year, I couldn't be happier with how things have turned out for Green Meadow, and I'm so pleased the weight of that particular worry has been lifted from all our shoulders. I'm also incredibly relieved that Ross didn't have the chance to get his devious little hands on the land, especially now we know about all the hidden artefacts. That would have been far too tragic to bear.

As for my own personal circumstances… well, life could not be better! Great friends, loving parents, and the cherry on top… the most caring, thoughtful boyfriend a girl could ever wish for… and a sexy beast to boot! I think, gazing at him as he swings the truck around and starts heading for the gates.

"Why are you looking all doe-eyed and gushy all of a sudden, missy?" he asks, noticing my expression and smiling back at me.

"Oh no reason," I say happily. "Just thinking how lucky I am to be part of such a wonderful place like Green Meadow, and to have such a little hotty like you in my life too," I say, blowing him a kiss.

He winks sexily in return, places his left hand on my right, and then drives us out of the car park to head home towards Butterford. That special little place where our friendship first began when we were just kids all those years ago. I never knew back then, of course, that we would still be here so many years later, the best of friends but now also very much in love.

As a young girl, I often used to imagine what type of man I might fall in love with, wondering what he might look like or where we might meet. I'd feel a tingle of excitement knowing that there was possibly someone special out there already, growing up at the same time as me, as yet a stranger still to meet. The romantic side of me loved the idea of soulmates moving through life, unaware of each other's existence, but both happy in the belief that they would meet each other one day when the time was right. Little did I know back then, of course, that I had already met mine, that he was already in my life, securing himself a solid place in my heart. As we weave down the narrow winding lanes towards home, I glance at our hands clasped together lovingly in my lap, and I chuckle at the fact that, just like the hospice's hidden salvation, my perfect love was right there all along.

THE END